Red Handed Dawn

Red-Handed Dawn

Papyngay Press, Brightwood, OR

ISBN 978-0975574959

chapter **1**

The radish resembled a Milesian oar master Skaphis
had once rowed under. He sliced it from chin to ear and
gnawed on the torso while dividing the last of the bread
into two equal portions. The bread was yesterday's. Lusilla
claimed that nobody was selling bread today at a price that
her conscience permitted her to pay. She contended that it
was the citizens' collective moral responsibility to control
inflation in the agora by keeping a death-grip on their small
change in the face of rising prices.

Skaphis suspected this was merely an excuse to serve
him short rations of old bread. He passed the remainder
of the loaf towards his partner Barysthenes, who was
ladling water from a pitcher into a mixing bowl. The rising
tide of wine threatened to engulf a squadron of painted
ships that rowed off to war around the inner edge of the
bowl. A woman stood on the shore behind them holding a
single branch in her left hand. She stared with porcelain
impassivity at the departing fleet, and the corner of her
mouth betrayed the slightest curl of a smile. Skaphis
thought she looked glad to see them go.

He refilled his cup and drank, "At least the wine is not
in short supply."

Barysthenes looked up at him, but didn't speak.

3

Skaphis carved another slice of radish, and laid his knife on the table next to the wine bowl. A woman edged through the door, then stopped to let her eyes adjust from the glare of the street. While she blinked in the interior darkness of the tavern, Skaphis stared. She was not the sort of woman you'd expect to see walking into a Piraeus tavern in the middle of the afternoon. Her dress was finely-spun, and hung in folds from a belt of black leather that was fastened with a bronze clasp. Skaphis was reminded of the way that a sculptor can, while depicting only the outer layer of his subject's clothing, suggest the figure beneath. Her hair was cut short and held back by tortoiseshell combs. Her features were strong, like the dancing-girls you'd see painted on vases where you suspected the artist had more of an eye for male than for female beauty. The very strength of her features spoke of intelligence and wit. Or perhaps Skaphis, like a vase artist, was projecting his own desires onto otherwise unremarkable clay.

The woman, eyes settled to the gloom, walked over to the bar and muttered something inaudible to Lusilla, who pointed to Skaphis' table. She approached Barysthenes who stood and, almost imperceptibly, bowed his head.

"Barysthenes?" she said, "You have been recommended to me as someone who can perform certain kinds of tasks discreetly and efficiently."

He acknowledged this with the raise of an eyebrow and offered her a seat and a cup of wine from the mixing bowl.

"I wasn't aware our fame had reached Athens."

"I have friends both in the town and in the Piraeus. By Dionysus, this wine is rough: you should mix it with more water to dilute the taste."

"Maybe from the shipyard latrines."

4

"I need to find an old friend. He has disappeared from town, but has been seen in the Piraeus."

"I doubt you'd have any trouble finding new friends."

"Perhaps, but this one owes me quite a large sum of money."

"My name is Psamathe," she said, turning to Skaphis for the first time, "Aristophon has been generous to me in the past. I lent him 20 minas at a drachma per mina some months ago, for a trading venture. The principal came due at the start of last month and he has not repaid me.

"He has an apartment in Athens which he shares with a certain Stephanos. I have called round there several times since the money came due - each time there was some reason why Aristophon was not available: 'He's exercising at the gymnasium', 'He's at the assembly', 'He's shopping in the market place'. Eventually Stephanos admitted he had not seen him for over a month. Aristophon had been spending a lot of time in the Piraeus on business, and Stephanos said that he had moved in temporarily with friends there. He would not say who they were or when he expected Aristophon to return.

"Then yesterday a friend from the Piraeus told me he had seen Aristophon in the free trading zone by the docks. My friend overheard him setting up a meeting for tonight at moonrise by Ktesiphon's barber's shop on the north side of the corn market."

She looked down, "I can't afford to lose that money. I need you to find Aristophon."

"And when we find him?" Skaphis asked.

"When you have found him I need you to help me serve him with a summons to repay his debt."

"Do you have documentation or witnesses to the loan?"

"Oh, I can produce witnesses when we get to that point."

Skaphis had been absorbed in studying her face. Close inspection revealed her nose to be somewhat large, her chin square, and on her upper lip the faintest of down of the sort that, in a boy, would be the subject of much teasing. His gaze washed over her features but was sucked into her eyes, as inevitably as bilge water finds sunlight through the opened cocks of a beached craft. Helen's face, they said, had launched a fleet; these eyes could lure a ship into whatever shoals they chose to flash across.

A disturbance wrested Skaphis' attention to the back of the tavern. An argument had been smoldering and now erupted in shouting. A heavily bearded man sat at the table. By his side, one of Lusilla's girls shrank into the corner. A younger man stood opposite, gesticulating wildly and directing a stream of words through clenched teeth at the older man. A wine cup had been knocked over, its contents dripping unheeded from the table into a spreading dark stain on the flagstone beneath.

Skaphis did not recognize either of the men. Lusilla's tavern was situated on the landward side of the Piraeus, close to the spot where the long walls connecting Athens with its port had joined the outer walls of the Piraeus. It was frequently used as a meeting place by Athenian businessmen and their Piraeus counterparts. Athenian wholesalers would meet with Piraeus importers, traders with money-men, ship owners with insurers. Sometimes these meetings would become acrimonious, occasionally, but rarely, coming to blows.

As part of Skaphis' rent deal with his landlady, he would lend a hand on the occasions where trouble might be looming. Lusilla believed that a wet blanket smothering a blaze before it got started was preferable to buckets of water once it caught hold. Skaphis was one of her wettest blankets.

He looked up at his landlady, who shook her head slightly. The younger man had sat down and refilled his wine glass. He was talking now with a pleading tone. Skaphis glanced round at the rest of the tables. A couple of mid-afternoon regulars sat playing dice at a table in the corner with a third man Skaphis did not recognize. Three of Lusilla's girls were at work carding wool. Lusilla liked to keep them productively employed in the day as well as at night. Between Skaphis and the dice players sat another stranger. He had his cloak drawn up over his head and was holding a wine cup to his lips with both hands.

"How long have you known this Aristophon?" Barysthenes asked.

"I met him three years ago. His family was rich - from the cavalry class, but had invested heavily off shore. In fact most of the family wealth had been coming from estates in the islands. They still had money at home, of course, and were rich enough to be obligated for special financial services to the state. In fact, Aristophon's father was unfortunate enough to be called on to maintain a trireme the year that the Athenians lost their ships to the Spartans. He was on active duty with the fleet and killed at Aegospotamoi when his ship was captured.

"Aristophon inherited the estate, but its value was greatly reduced, because all the island property was seized by Lysander and redistributed to Spartan-leaning locals.

"I met Aristophon after this. He was very generous. He was, I must say, a pleasant companion. Born an aristocrat, he was no longer able to follow the old style. He had turned his property into liquid assets and was trying his hand at commerce. His education and urbanity, I think, were no substitute for the low cunning needed in that occupation. Besides, he had expensive tastes."

Skaphis wondered if Psamathe herself was one of those expensive tastes.

"Five months ago he came to me with a business proposition."

A crash from the rear of the tavern. The younger man was on his feet and the mixing bowl was on the floor. Lusilla inclined her head towards him; Skaphis was up and, in a couple of strides, standing beside their table.

"Who in Hades are you?", shouted the young man, he was tall, but still had to look up at Skaphis.

"I'm a messenger from the god," Skaphis said, "I have an oracle for you: 'put your feet on a long wall or your head under a short one', I'd interpret it to advise in favor of a healthy stroll back up to Athens over an afternoon spent drinking in Piraeus dives."

The Athenian's answer was a grunt. He made as if to leave the tavern quietly. However his hand came out from under his cloak holding a dagger. He lunged at Skaphis in the style of a heavy infantryman pressing an advantage with a spear. This was not how you fought with a knife in the Piraeus. Skaphis dodged the thrust easily, tripping the Athenian with his leg as his momentum carried him past, helping him on his way down with a two handed blow to his back.

Skaphis stood on the Athenian's arm, and kicked the dagger over to Lusilla. He lifted the young man up and marched him out into the street.

"Beware," he said, "the gods don't take kindly to their messengers getting roughed up."

When Skaphis returned into the tavern, the older man was by the bar with Lusilla.

"It's a problem with business these days, some of these younger chaps seem to think that they have a god-given right to earn high interest on their investment, but do not realize that they are being paid interest because they are assuming risk."

He spoke with an island accent, but with a hint of the Dorian. Skaphis placed him in one of the Corinthian colonies in Sicily.

"I once asked a trading friend of mine what the difference was between gambling and investing," Skaphis replied, "he told me the only difference was that in gambling, you could not load the dice too much because it would be obvious and nobody would play with you."

The foreigner laughed, "But either, it seems, can end in knife-play."

Skaphis returned to his table. The hooded stranger was still absorbed in two-handed contemplation of his wine cup.

Barysthenes spoke, "While you were providing moral guidance to our young friend over there, Psamathe and I came up with a plan of action. I will attend this moonlight rendezvous by the corn market. If Aristophon shows up I'll follow him home from there, and we can do the summonsing tomorrow. Meanwhile you can go up to Athens and talk to Stephanos, see if you can get more information out of him to give us a lead if he doesn't appear tonight, or if I lose him in the dark."

Skaphis was about to object, but Barysthenes interjected, "You looked slow to me just there, you need some exercise - a jog up to Athens should be just the thing for you. And besides, I have another meeting here this afternoon."

"Psamathe, can my partner escort you up to Athens? He may be a slow knife-fighter and his repartee too influenced by old comedies, but he should be able to see you back safely to the city by nightfall."

"Thank you, I'm spending the night in the Piraeus." She reached inside her tunic and pulled something out which she placed on the table, covered by her hand. She removed her hand to reveal two silver coins. "Some payment on account," she said.

The coins were four drachma pieces. On one coin, the curious large eyed Athenian owl stood, its body in profile, but its head staring straight up at Skaphis from the table. "My favorite bird," he said, palming the coin. "Do you know that owls can turn their heads right round and look behind them, while their bodies point forward?" He half-clenched his fist, then opened it again and the coin appeared on the back of his middle finger, the owl looking at Psamathe. He curled and uncurled his fingers again and the bird disappeared. Twice more he made the coin appear then disappear, each time the bird was looking at Psamathe.

She smiled. "A useful skill for a small Athenian bird in the Piraeus."

chapter **2**

Skaphis was half way to Athens when he realized that he had left his dagger on the table in Lusilla's tavern.

The road between the Piraeus and Athens was five miles long and at this time in the afternoon, most of the traffic seemed to be going in the opposite direction. Mule teams returned unloaded from the city, to sway back the next morning loaded with produce stored in the Piraeus warehouses. Fishmongers' carts trundled back empty, having sold out early in the Athenian market. A Piraeus householder strolled homewards accompanied by an elderly slave who was carrying an ornately carved three-legged table. A group of young Athenian men chattered as they trotted seawards for a taste of adventure in the exotic nightlife of the port.

Alongside the road, the foundation of the northern long wall was still visible. The walls, which had connected Athens with its port, were destroyed under the supervision of the Spartans as part of the deal under which they lifted their siege of the starving city. The foundations now formed a knee-high dike. The bulk of the masonry from the wall had been hauled away for use in other urban building projects. Here and there, however, a stone block too large for economical salvage lay where it had been levered out of the wall by the victorious Spartans. Stonework thought too fragmented for re-use had been left strewn alongside the road. At intervals, this loose rock had been gathered up to form rough lean-to shelters, sometimes incorporating the remnant of the wall itself.

The waste-land between the long walls had traditionally been used as a sanctuary for country folk when danger threatened their farms. During the war years, when the Spartans would wander almost at will through the outlying Athenian countryside, an entire makeshift shanty-city had grown up here inside the defensive wall system of the paired cities, but part of neither city. Now, with peace, the region supplied a sanctuary to the financially dispossessed.

11

Fleet rowers, unable to find work in one of the five Spartan-sanctioned warships, slaves whose owners were no longer able to provide accommodation, prostitutes not young or pretty enough for a room in one of the brothels in Athens or the Piraeus, adventurers, mercenaries, colonists from all over the Athenian diaspora: all patched together a livelihood among the cast-off rubble of a crumbled empire.

At the entrance to one of the hovels, an older Thracian woman sat on a folding stool, offering for sale three figs and a half dozen olives laid out on a broken shard of pottery. Her arms were tattooed in a zigzag geometric pattern and her head was covered with a black shawl. Skaphis wondered where the produce had come from. He imagined that a certain loss from panniers would be inevitable as mule trains stumbled up the trail in the pre-market dawn.

He bought one of the figs and sat down on a large wall-block to eat it. Reaching for his dagger to peel the fig, he realized the dagger was not there. Athens was safe enough if you stayed in the busier parts of town - but it would be dark by the time he got back, and the Piraeus after dark was never entirely safe - even for a 200 pound ex-fleet top tier rower and amateur night-club bouncer.

"What can there be at Athens to draw you away from the pleasures of Lusilla's?" It was the third dice player. He bought a handful of olives and sat down beside Skaphis.

"Most of Athens passes through Lusilla's eventually," Skaphis replied, "but sometimes you get tired of waiting."

The dice player nibbled the flesh from the outside of the olive, gradually exposing the pit. He worked at this like a sculptor exposing the figure concealed in a block of marble. On completion, he examined his creation from front and back. Seeming satisfied with the aesthetic qualities of his work, he threw the pit away and popped a second olive straight into his mouth.

"That's what makes Athens great," he mumbled, nodding to a mule team that was jostling up the road. Each mule was attached to the previous one by a rope. A muleteer held the first mule's rope. A second muleteer provided encouragement with a stick at the rear of the column. Each animal carried a pair of wicker panniers slung over its back. Each pannier carried an earthen amphora.

"Chian wine," he said.

Skaphis wondered how he could tell.

"Without this road, Athens would be the center of a modestly sized, not particularly productive cluster of farming counties. It'd be the aristocratic ideal - morning going over the estate business with the overseer, a brisk walk into town, afternoon listening to debates in the assembly, evening drinking and whoring with companions from the old regiment. It'd be Sparta without the Spartans. With this road, Athens is the center of Greece.

"Medicinal plants and shield-leather from Cyrene, mackerel and assorted kippers from the Hellespont, black pudding and beef ribs from Thessaly."

Skaphis completed the quotation.

"Scabies for the Spartans from Sitalces, and boatloads of lies from Perdiccas."

The stranger smiled,

"You know your comedies. Anyway, the Spartans had no objections to Athens as a power on the Spartan model. So they didn't demolish the city wall. But they did object to Athens as a world power and they removed the long walls. This is the air that Athens breathes," he nodded at the road, "and this is Athens' windpipe, cut it and the city suffocates. Compress it and the city gasps for breath."

"My name is Euboulos," he said, spitting out his second olive pit, "In the tavern I'd have listed you as a light infantryman - a peltast, but you have the arms of a rower."

"I had some experience of both," Skaphis admitted, "The war seems a long time ago."

"You are Barysthenes' partner and live upstairs at Lusilla's?" he asked. Skaphis grunted assent.

"I'm a trader," Euboulos continued, "I trade bulk commodities: wine, wheat, olives. I'll buy a cargo of wine at the docks from a Rhodian merchantman and warehouse it in the Piraeus. I'll sell to an Athenian wholesaler, who will load up his mules with my wine, haul it up to the city, and supply the retailers in the market place. Or I'll sell to a Piraeus distributor, who will buy a wagonload of wine at a time and deliver direct to the local taverns.

"The key to making money trading is timing. If three cargoes of Rhodian wine have landed in the last week, the market will be flooded in the stuff, and you will not be able to sell for a decent price. So you are better to warehouse your goods while the extra supply is washed down the gullets of the Athenian populace. But every week you hold your wine in store, you do not have space for another cargo - perhaps you have been introduced to a Sicilian captain with a cargo of wheat which he is anxious to unload - you don't have anywhere to put the wheat until you get rid of your wine nor, until you sell your wine, do you have the silver to invest."

Skaphis had finished his fig, "I won't have silver to invest or wine to wash down my gullet if I don't get on up to Athens."

"Timing is everything," Euboulos repeated, "One way to insure yourself against price fluctuations at the dock is to buy the cargo before the ship sails to get it. Here's how it works. You buy the merchant's outbound cargo - perhaps a shipload of Athenian olives. He contracts to sail to Rhodes, sell the olives and with the proceeds acquire a cargo of wine. On his return to the Piraeus, the wine is yours - no haggling.

"Of course," Euboulos smiled ruefully, "if the ship disappears at sea, the loss is yours - no haggling."

Skaphis rose to go. Euboulos put a hand on his arm.

"Information is also a commodity," he said, "With the right timing it can be extremely valuable. And Lusilla's is a market place of information - some common knowledge and cheap - other information quite distinctive, rare and precious."

"Are you a buyer or a seller?" Skaphis asked

Euboulos didn't answer but drew a map in the dirt at his feet. The plan was of the quarter of Athens between the assembly hill - the Pnyx - and the market place - the agora. Skaphis could recognize the Peiriac Gate and the road in from the Piraeus. Euboulos marked a side street and an individual house.

"In trade I am always both," Euboulos replied. He indicated his mark in the dirt, "This is my house. At the moment I have space in a warehouse and money to invest. The price of wheat is starting to climb, and the storm season in the Black Sea will begin in a month's time. I am particularly interested in finding a cargo of grain to buy," he smiled, "Such information would be very well timed and quite valuable."

He released Skaphis' arm, "However, all information has its price."

Skaphis told him he'd keep his ears open and ambled off in the direction of Athens, leaving his companion nibbling thoughtfully at his third olive.

Stephanos' house was at the end of a courtyard that reached through a network of narrow alleys in the Scambonidae district. An elegantly dressed young man answered Skaphis' knock.

"Stephanos is not at home," he announced in response to Skaphis' request.

"When do you expect him back?"

"I am his slave, I expect him back at all times."

"Perhaps I can wait for him to return."

"No problem," said the slave, making to shut the door.

Skaphis moved his stance so that he was blocking the door from closing, "Perhaps I can wait inside for him to return."

The slave scowled through the half open door. He had fine features of an eastern cast and spoke Greek well but with a foreign accent.

"Listen," he said, "One look at you tells me you are not one of Stephanos' companions from his old cavalry regiment, and you don't look his type - I doubt he picked you up at a party. So my guess is that you are a sycophant: a free-lance prosecutor, chancing your arm with some trumped up charge against my master. Oh, you'll be prepared to be reasonable - you'll entertain a plea bargain and let him settle for a fine of 200 drachmas, paid to you personally of course."

He made to close the door again.

"You've got it bang on," Skaphis said, "But if we can't get a plea bargain, we'll have to go to trial. I suspect Stephanos will claim he was at home when the fracas occurred. In which case I'll be forced to offer a challenge to torture his slaves to discover the truth of the matter."

"Stephanos would never accept such a challenge," the slave retorted, but he opened the door and showed Skaphis into a sitting room. In the center of the room was a long table. At either end of the table a bronze torch holder balanced on three slender feet fashioned in the shape of goats' legs. In each holder a torch of vine twigs coated in wax resembled the finger of a long dead corpse accusing an inconstant adversary. On the longer sides of the room sat pairs of low couches. Skaphis chose the nearest one.

"Just don't make off with any of the candles," the slave muttered as he retired through the far door.

"There's only one thing I'm inclined to do with one of those candles," Skaphis replied, "You wouldn't be in any doubt about where to find it."

Skaphis examined the room. The couches had old mattresses with covers of the best quality linen, decorated with floral stitch work. The dye was faded, and the covers had seen years of use. Skaphis noticed, however that the couch he was sitting on had a new cover of coarser material. Some attempt had been made to match the color and pattern of the other couches, but the material and workmanship were clearly inferior. He found himself wondering if this replacement was symptomatic of a decline in the fortunes of the household, or whether it indicated a rush job.

Skaphis was beginning to regret forcing his way into the house, and was visualizing the conviviality that a four drachma piece would entitle him to, with change, in one of the taverns along the Panathenaic Way when the slave scurried back through the sitting room and out of the house. He returned in a few minutes with his master.

Despite his thick beard and a hairline that was beginning to recede, Stephanos had a boyish look, as if surprised on the way back from school, he'd suddenly found himself grown up. But his eyes had a hardness, and his mouth a curl of contempt which belied his youthful appearance. Skaphis put him a year or two older than himself.

"What is it this time?" Stephanos snarled, "Did I bump into your ailing father on my way back from the dinner party last night, causing him to break a rib, which stopped him from working and put him on public assistance? Or are you my long lost step-brother come to pardon me for my father's indiscretion, and to sue me for half the estate... but you'll settle for a hundred drachmas. Or did you catch me insulting your garlic plants by pissing in your vegetable patch? Come on, I'm sure you have a plausible story, and of course you can produce witnesses..."

Unclipping a key from his belt, he thrust it at his slave, "I need some wine."

"It's not you I'm interested in," said Skaphis, "although it sounds like it might be a profitable pastime at that. I'm trying to locate Aristophon."

"Aristophon doesn't live here. I have no idea of his whereabouts. He and I are old comrades, which you and I are not."

"I need to find Aristophon as a witness in a lawsuit against a certain woman. She has been harassing my client for money, which she claims he owes her. According to my client, Aristophon used to be an associate of this woman and might be prepared to testify as to her character, or lack of it."

The slave returned with a pitcher of pre-mixed wine and a single two-handed cup. He gave both to his master, who filled his cup and drank greedily, before refilling the cup. Neither master nor servant offered any to Skaphis. Stephanos looked up from his wine.

"Who is this client?" he inquired.

"A young gentleman from a well-known family who is a little too free with his affections," Skaphis replied, "but who pays me to be discreet."

Stephanos nodded, "The woman, though, I can guess, is that whore Psamathe. She was over here pestering me every day for the last couple of weeks - tried to convince me that he owed her money. Eventually, I got tired of giving her excuses, and told her that Stephanos had gone to live at the Piraeus."

"And has he?"

"Well, for the time being, yes. But I expect him to return here to Athens once he tires of his commercial adventures."

"Have you known Aristophon for long?" Skaphis asked.

"We were in the same year-group and did our military training together. When we came of age, we served in the same cavalry unit, and when the democracy was restored after the war, we both found ourselves in somewhat reduced circumstances. Aristophon decided to sell off his house to finance his business ventures and moved in here with me.

"Several months ago, a big deal in the Piraeus came up, Aristophon was spending most of his time down there. He decided to lodge with a trading partner, Alexis by name. I can show you where he lives."

He pulled a wax tablet from a hook on the wall and with his finger nail scratched a map of the Piraeus.

"But he's not there any more," Stephanos continued, "I went down there last week to ask about my friend, and they told me he had left a week or so before that and had not been back since. Maybe he had to go on a voyage to secure a cargo, or something like that."

"Was that typical?" asked Skaphis.

"No, he never traveled, he bought and sold here on the mainland. But this was a special deal." Stephanos sounded as if he was trying to convince himself.

"Thank you," said Skaphis, getting up to leave, "If he has left the country, he will not be much use to my client, but it is probably worth my while to do a little nosing around in the Piraeus to see if I can find him. From what you tell me he might be quite an effective witness against Psamathe."

Stephanos rose from his couch and reached out to Skaphis. His hand held a small silver drachma coin. "If you find him, would you let me know, you see he borrowed some money from me for this venture, and he might be trying to avoid me.

"Or would it be unethical for you to serve two masters," his tone was sarcastic.

Skaphis palmed the coin.

"I serve a small Athenian bird with large round eyes," he said, "there is no conflict."

The sun was setting by the time Skaphis reached the Panathenaic Way. The last few market-goers were sauntering home with their purchases. Most of the stalls had already sold out, or their owners had given up on making that one last sale and headed for the consolation of the local taverns. With dusk, the remaining stall holders were packing up their wares, to repeat tomorrow the endless cycle of commerce.

Two days after full moon in the month of Eleutheraion, moonrise would be in a couple of hours. The road back to Piraeus was easy enough to follow by starlight, but he'd make faster progress with the moon. He headed for the consolation of a local tavern.

Skaphis vaguely recognized the barman, "A pint of your house bilge-water, if you please."

"Dog mix, for a sea-dog?" asked the barman.

"No, mix it two and five, this Athenian dust gets in your throat."

The tavern was busy with the post-market crowd; nobody Skaphis knew. Skaphis took a free stool in the corner of the room, sipped his wine and wondered what he was doing here.

Why come to Athens today, when Barysthenes might track down Aristophon on his own tonight? Couldn't they have waited till tomorrow to start a second line of investigation? Skaphis himself did not have much faith in the overheard assignation, but why not wait till tomorrow to trail off to Athens. Presumably Barysthenes thought it was best to get both of them on the client's payroll as soon as possible, as the job might turn out to be simple. A thought crossed Skaphis' mind - did Barysthenes have any intention of staking out the barber's shop in the moonlight? - the old rascal, maybe he was heading for home and a good night's sleep.

With that thought, Skaphis finished his wine, bought a torch from the barman, launched onto the street, pointed his bow for home, and settled into a distance cadence.

Skaphis entered Lusilla's by the back door. From the bar came the sound of loud male talking and female laughter. It was early in the night, and the revelry would build to a higher pitch before subsiding in the hours before dawn. Skaphis turned away and climbed the back stairs. He felt his way into the darkened room and probed for his couch with his foot. This was not difficult, as the couch was the only piece of furniture, and the room was barely big enough to contain it. A dozen identical rooms subdivided the upper floor of the tavern.

Muffled sounds from some of those rooms and the attenuated clatter from the tavern below lulled him to sleep.

From deep sleep, he awoke instantly, adrenaline pumping through his body. The hairs on the back of his neck were standing on end and every nerve screamed danger. He rolled out from under his cloak and off the bed onto the floor. He kept moving and in an instant was on his feet with his back to his room's tiny window. By the light of the faint pre-dawn refracting through the aperture, Skaphis could see that the presence in his room was female. He relaxed slightly, although his heart was still pounding at ramming speed.

Lusilla turned from facing the couch to facing him. "By the two goddesses, you move fast Skaphis. Listen, I was just closing up the tavern and a message came from Barysthenes. He needs you down by the corn market. He'll wait for you in the street by the barber's shop."

"Who was the messenger?"

"I didn't recognize him, but he's downstairs waiting for you. He says Barysthenes promised you'd give him an obol when he delivered the message."

"Fat chance! Lusilla, I left my dagger downstairs yesterday, the one with the Phoenician writing on the handle, did you pick it up?"

"No, lover, but you look like you have a decent weapon there," her gaze drifted downwards over his naked body.

Lusilla had a strict rule about her girls not being over friendly with the lodgers. Skaphis wondered if she felt that the rule applied to herself.

"Oh this is an unreliable weapon at best, it's always to hand when its not needed, but it seems to shrink from real work." He draped his short travel cloak over his shoulders. "As do we all, dearie."

chapter **3**

Dawn's red fingers stroked the eastern sky as Skaphis reached the corn market. He found Barysthenes in the doorway of the barber's shop. He sat hunched in the shadows with his back to the door. One hand was clutched to his chest and the other was raised as if stretching for the door handle. Dried blood reached like spilled wine in long black tentacles through the dust.

Skaphis rolled the body into a horizontal position. In the corner of the doorway, behind where Barysthenes had been sitting, was a broken pitcher. The shards were spread in the dirt, but the base of the pitcher was intact and contained a trace of liquid. Skaphis smelt the pottery - wine. He smeared his finger over the liquid and tasted. Skaphis was not an expert in expensive imported wine, but he would have said Rhodian, if pressed. He pocketed one of the largest pieces of the broken pot.

He attempted to open the corpse's mouth. It was too stiff. Two traders were talking earnestly as they strolled down the morning street to the market. Skaphis called them over.

"Witness this," he said, "this is my partner, Barysthenes - I found him here dead."

"The body is cold and stiff," he continued. One of the traders hesitantly touched Barysthenes' arm to confirm his claim.

Skaphis inspected the dirt around the doorway. There was a confusion of scuff-marks and indentations, but no clearly defined footprints. There was a drag mark coming from the street, as if Barysthenes had been pulled into the door, or perhaps, he had crawled there from the street. Skaphis backtracked the drag mark. He could see the dark stain of blood congealed in drops in the dust. In the middle of the street, the early morning mule traffic had obliterated the track, but he could follow the blood trail. It led across the street into a narrow alleyway.

The alley led back from the street to a courtyard rimmed by windowless buildings. There were plenty of clear footprints: large male prints, sandaled and bare, smaller narrower feet, female or boys, and animal prints: small donkey prints and larger mule prints. There was, however no blood.

Skaphis returned into the alleyway. In the early morning shadows, he was unable to determine where the blood trail started. He knelt and peered at the ground in the alley entrance. The ground was heavily trampled. Skaphis imagined standing here stamping out a long evening's surveillance. From this position, you could see the barber's door, but it was shadowed from the light of the glowing dawn. Likewise it would be in the shadow of the newly rising moon.

He felt around on the ground, and picked up a tiny object. He rolled it through his fingers and examined it. It was an olive pit. He dropped the pit and stood up. A small cluster of men had gathered across the street around the body. One was crossing the street towards him. Out of the corner of his eye, something metal on the ground across the alleyway glinted in the light of the new day's red sun.

The man approached, and introduced himself, "I'm Bion, for my sins I'm a Piraeus Street Commissioner this year. Hell of a job - makes me regret putting my name into the lottery. The goddamned dung collectors - if you don't keep your eye on them, they'll be building whole shit cities just outside the walls. And regulating the bloody women, I tell you it's worse than being a grain commissioner."

Skaphis angled out into the sunlit street. The commissioner's back was to the metal object. "Just last night I was dragged away from my dinner to arbitrate over one. Couple of fellows both wanted to pay her the maximum. I had to leave a pitcher of wine I was beginning to get on friendly terms with, and stumble about in the dark, just to toss a coin. Can't see how a few curls were worth two drachmas myself, she didn't even play the kitharos. And the damnable thing is, by the time we'd settled the price, she'd vanished."

Skaphis kept his eyes on the commissioner. His round face, smooth and shaved, reminded Skaphis of the unformed clay on a potter's wheel; the whites of his eyes, filigreed with red, suggested that last night's break-up of his relationship with the pitcher had been temporary. The commissioner rambled on: Skaphis' attention was not on his words but on the dull metal object, which he had the sick feeling he recognized.

"Shame they don't regulate the fish market that way - can you imagine - 'I'm sorry sir, I can't charge more than a drachma for this tuna steak. No madam I'd lose my place in the market if I were to take three hemi-drachmas for those sprats, but, here take a number, and we'll draw lots for them.'"

Skaphis glanced across the street. The majority of the passersby had moved on. A death on the streets was a cause for concern, and worth the attention of a citizen, but nothing to lose business over. A couple of men remained, but seemed to ignore the body and were engaged in an animated conversation.

"My slaves," the commissioner said, "Well, not mine, but the city's. We'll watch him until the family is told - he was your partner?"

Skaphis nodded assent, "He lives on Munichia hill in the slingers' section. His wife's name is Astra, but I don't know about any male relatives."

"Strange you should discover the body."

"Not really, said Skaphis, we had arranged to meet down here this morning, Barysthenes had a deal of some sort going on at the corn market." Skaphis felt that a message from a dead man might be too sophisticated a concept for a city commissioner this early in the morning.

"Well, it doesn't look like a case for the Prytanies," the commissioner said, "the body's cold, apart from the fact you found it, there's nothing here that connects you with the death, and there's no other suspects I can see."

Skaphis walked the commissioner across the street back to the doorway through which his partner would never pass, and away from the long bladed seaman's dagger lying in the alleyway.

"It'll be up to the family to deal with the body. Can you tell the wife, and arrange for her to pick it up? The slaves were still talking - discussing the relative merits of different island wines. "I hate to interrupt this scholarly debate," the commissioner said, "I want you to watch the body till the family comes to get it," he turned to Skaphis, "do you think they can manage that by noon?".

Skaphis nodded.

"If there's any problem come get me, you'll find me surveying shit."

The slaves resumed their discussion, ignoring Skaphis. Barysthenes, curled in the dust, ignored him profoundly. Skaphis turned and sidled across the street and back through the alleyway. The courtyard was still in shadow. Three doors led off into different buildings, one on each side of the court. None of the buildings had any windows. Skaphis tried each door in turn. None would open. There were tracks that indicated a substantial amount of mule traffic to and from one of the doors. He crouched down and picked up a handful of dust. As he stood up, he shook his hand gently, letting the dust sift out through his fingers. Strained from the dust, his hand contained four small grains of wheat.

Emerging from the alley onto the street, Skaphis knelt down on one knee to adjust his sandal strap. When he stood up, his left hand was curled around the handle of a dagger, its long blade splinted along the inside of his forearm: a dangerous object conjured into invisibility.

He walked up the street in the direction of the Munichia hill, against a steady stream of people and animals welling into the morning market. He could feel on the handle of the knife familiar ridges and indentations of writing in a script not quite Greek but not entirely Oriental.

Barysthenes' house was on the side of Munichia Hill, which had seen fierce fighting in the insurrection. The town army had launched an attack from the base of the hill: cavalry fighting on foot, heavy infantry stiffened with Spartans from the garrison in the Acropolis. They had been repulsed by the Piraeus-based democrats. Heavy infantry fought shoulder to shoulder in the streets, their huge round shields interlocked in an egalitarian wall. Each house was turned into a fortress, rubble from its walls arsenals for the slingers who pelted the town army from their roofs. They were the margin of the improbable victory. Munichia Hill happened to be the section of town where all the slingers lived, and they were democrats to a man.

Barysthenes' wife was carrying water into the house. She turned and saw Skaphis.

"You shouldn't be here." Her shawl fell back from her profligate curls as she straightened from resting her pitcher on the ground. Her eyes held a mixture of surprise and fear.

"It's daylight, anyone could see you."

Skaphis lifted her pitcher and carried it inside. She followed, curling a strand of hair repeatedly round her finger in a childlike way.

"Barysthenes is not home. You should not be here."

"Barysthenes is dead, Astra, down by the corn market."

Her eyes stared up at him with the frozen look of fright they'd had since he arrived. She still curled her hair with her right hand. The hair didn't need it. It fell in luscious ringlets over her shoulder.

"My god, you didn't need to kill him, what's going to happen to me?"

"I didn't kill him, Astra, I found him dead an hour ago. And nothing is going to happen to you."

"Hold me." She buried her curls into Skaphis' chest, her body nestling under the crook of his arm. Her shoulder fit snugly into his armpit and his arm dropped limply over her back. Under the weight of his arm, he could feel her small body tremble. Typical of Athenian wives, Astra was many years younger than her husband. They were childless. Skaphis wondered if her sobs were for her husband, or for herself.

"Astra," he asked, "did Barysthenes come home last night?"

She pulled back from his arms and looked up at him. "Yes, he came home before dark, but did not have any dinner. He had a visitor for a half an hour, but I did not see who it was: he stayed in the andrikon, and I did not interrupt. He went back out before moonrise, taking a torch with him. He said he had a business meeting down by the docks."

"I was with him in the afternoon at Lusilla's, did he bring anything back from there?"

"No, well, maybe. He did go up to our chest in the attic. I assumed he was taking money out for his meeting. But he could have been putting something in there."

She sat down on a couch and buried her face in her hands.

"Oh god, what am I going to live on, we don't have much cash up there."

"Did Barysthenes have any money out on loan or any investments that you know about?"

"I don't know, he didn't talk to me about his business dealing. He did use Pheron as a banker, though, he would likely know if he had any money on deposit."

She had lifted her head out of her hands, and her eyes seemed to have brightened a little at the prospect of further financial resources.

"Can you talk to him for me?"

"Sure," said Skaphis, "I know where he sets up his table. I'll go down and have a chat with him for you."

"Astra, you need to deal with the body, shall I arrange for a cart to bring it back here?"

She nodded, reaching down for the water jar. As Skaphis left, she was edging this carefully through the narrow door to the secluded, female, interior of the house.

It was afternoon by the time Skaphis made it back to the tavern after delivering his partner home from his last all night surveillance. When he had arrived with the body in a hired donkey cart, news of the death had filtered through the neighborhood and a small group of women had gathered to provide a chorus to Astra's personal drama. The ritualized responses to loss would wear off the hard edges of whatever her real emotion was. Skaphis, male and unneeded, had been left to his raw unritualized feelings. The strongest of which was a need for undiluted wine, and answers to some questions. At least the first could be had at Lusilla's.

The tavern was quiet. The daily pulse of commerce had not yet pumped its stream, oxygenated from its trip through the agora to this capillary of the Athenian civic body. Unbid, Lusilla brought Skaphis a krater of neat wine and some new bread with a small piece of smoked mackerel. She sat opposite him.

Skaphis broke off a flake of the mackerel and a large chunk of bread. The salty smoked flavor and smooth oily texture of the fish offset the hard grainy consistency and bland taste of the bread. He washed them down with a long draught of wine and looked across at Lusilla.

"Left over from a party last night," she explained. Skaphis' rental agreement did not stretch to fish. The bread, he noticed, was new.

"I heard about Barysthenes," she said, "I guess his message was too late."

"Too late by three or four hours," Skaphis broke off another piece of bread and chewed it thoughtfully. "I'd be interested to talk to that messenger."

A knot of girls was clustered round a loom in the back of the tavern. One was spinning, the others were chatting. A bubble of laughter rose from the group. Lusilla turned, "How many of you does it take to operate a loom?" she snapped, "Thrassia, come here a moment, please."

The group bustled in several directions with a show of industry. A small girl shuffled over to Skaphis' table, her head downcast, her eyes fixed on the floor just ahead of her feet.

"I'm sorry mistress, but Xenia was telling us about..."

"It's all right Thrassia, I wanted to ask you something about last night, here have a seat."

The girl sat down beside Skaphis, her face still downcast, but her eyes glimpsed up at him from below a fringe cut in an exotic boyish fashion. It was the girl who had been with the Syracusan merchant the previous afternoon.

"Thrassia, you brought me a message for Skaphis from Barysthenes, what do you remember about the messenger?"

"I was busy sweeping the floor. The last of the customers had left, and the door was already barred when I heard a loud knocking on the door. You were in the back in the wine cellar, mistress."

She stretched her hand towards the bread and looked up at Lusilla, who nodded almost imperceptibly. The top of her arms bore a faint zigzag tattoo, which enhanced the exotic effect. She tore off a piece of bread and reached for the fish. Lusilla frowned, and the girl's arm snatched back like the head of a startled tortoise.

"I thought it was a customer so I told him to get lost, we were shut for the night. However he kept shouting something about Skaphis, so I opened the door and let him in. He told me he had a message from Barysthenes, so I came back to get you, mistress."

Skaphis landed the remainder of the mackerel with the last of the bread. He divided his catch in two and handed half to the girl. "Can you remember seeing him before?"

"I'm not sure. I may have seen him in the tavern."

"What did he look like?"

"He looked pretty rough to me. Smaller than you, but quite powerful, bearded, tanned, your age or a little older."

"Had he been drinking?"

"At that time of night everybody has been drinking." Lusilla answered, draining the remainder of the unmixed wine into her cup, "But he didn't act drunk. I'll tell you what is funny, though - he didn't wait around for payment, when I went back downstairs from your room, he was already gone."

Thrassia rose to go, but Skaphis held her arm, "Yesterday afternoon, after I left, what did Barysthenes do?"

Thrassia sat down again. "After the lady went away, the place became quiet. The dice game broke up. My merchant went over and sat with Barysthenes. I couldn't hear what they were talking about, but I took wine over to them twice before they were finished. The merchant left, then Barysthenes a minute or so later."

Skaphis turned to Lusilla, "Do you know this merchant?"

"His name is Kotos. He is an important man amongst the Sicilian traders in the Piraeus. He is rich, but that's not all. He is powerful and, I think, dangerous. He seldom comes here. And when he does, it is not for pleasure," she looked at Thrassia, "despite the many pleasures we have available."

"One more thing, Thrassia, when did the man sitting there leave?" Skaphis indicated the table where the hooded man had nursed his wine and watched.

"I didn't notice anyone there."

Thrassia got up again to return to the cluster of girls, all of whom were apparently working industriously at the various stages of textile production. Textile production, however which involved a significant number of sideways glances and muffled sniggering.

"He was still there when Barysthenes walked out," said Lusilla, "And still drinking the same bowl of weak-mixed wine. We got busy shortly after that with a cluster of rich kids from the city who wanted food, drink and entertainment all at once. I didn't see when he went."

"This Kotos, where can I find him?"

"I don't know where he lives, but he is well known in the trading zone."

She got up from her stool. "Skaphis?"

"Yes."

"Be careful, dearie."

She gave him a lascivious wink, "These Sicilians don't shrink from using their weapons."

chapter *4*

The afternoon tide of business had risen and fallen at Lusilla's, isolating pools of serious long term drinkers until the late evening revelers flowed in from their dinner parties and washed the place full again. Like so many pieces of driftwood, three empty wine kraters lay beached on Skaphis' table. He was starting on a fourth when Psamathe swept into the tavern.

"I was hoping you might have some information for me," she said, sitting down opposite him, "but it looks like you are hard at work on another commission."

"This is a libation to the Gods. Only problem is, whenever I start pouring the wine onto the ground, I find my mouth has got in the way."

"Don't you find that is typical, our appetites get between us and the Gods?"

"I saw Stephanos yesterday, he seems to share your concern about Aristophon."

"Did he tell you where he is?"

"No, but he told me where he has been. I'll check it out tomorrow, if you'd like."

"Where is Barysthenes? Did Aristophon not show up at the meeting last night?"

"Barysthenes is at his house. I don't know if Aristophon showed up at the meeting, but I'd like to find out if he did."

Her eyes sparkled with an icy anger and she stood up, "Listen, you were recommended to me as competent. I paid you good money in advance to do a simple job. Now I come to our meeting to find you drunk and Barysthenes not even here, and no obvious progress made. My friend must have sent me to the wrong tavern."

"Barysthenes is at home out of necessity, not out of discourtesy. He's dead. Someone stabbed him last night while he was watching the barber's shop."

She sat down again in silence for a few moments. Skaphis fancied he saw a small tear condense in the corner of her eye as she looked blankly at him. If so, it froze before it left the eye.

"Have you been partners for long?"

"I met him in the revolution. We were manning the same barricade. It turned out the barricade was adjacent to his house. I was a rower for a fleet that no longer existed. He told me to look him up when things settled down, that there were bound to be openings in his trade, and he could find work for me."

"So you became a private investigator?"

"Yes, of course, the reason that there were openings in the field was that the aristocrats had killed off all the private investigators. It was their first move on grabbing power, and a popular one at that. It wasn't till they started killing off upstanding citizens that their support began to wane."

She stiffened slightly. Skaphis picked up his wine krater.

"He was a morose, twisted, secretive bastard, but he gave me a job, and he was my partner. So in his honor, I pour this libation."

He held the Krater high and poured a stream of wine into the back of his throat as a shepherd would drink from a skin.

She reached across the table and touched his hand, "Will you keep looking for Aristophon for me? I am afraid he is mixed up in something very dangerous, and I'd hate for anything to happen to him."

"At least until you get your money back."

She withdrew her hand and straightened, "Aristophon was a friend, and more than a partner to me. I am concerned primarily for his welfare. He is apparently involved in dealings whose secrecy is excuse for murder."

The faintest reflection of a smile rippled across her face as she got up to leave, "And he owes me money. Report to me in a couple of days, whether you find him or not. I live close to the nine-mouth fountain. Ask anyone for directions."

The ship walked stiff-legged out into the bay, the oars stepping rhythmically on the glassy surface. Beyond the protection of the headland, a light morning breeze was beginning to darken the sea. From this height, the boat resembled an insect on the surface of a pond. Skaphis' head throbbed in time with the oars. He was hot from his climb and a knot of unease spliced his stomach: either a reaction to Barysthenes' death or to the wine of the previous night. Skaphis suspected the wine.

"Double-manned by the look of it. She's moving smartly."

A broad brimmed hat shielded the man's eyes from the morning sun. He sat on a stool under an olive tree, which would afford shade later in the day. Behind the grove of trees was a house. In the man's hand was a knife, with which he whittled on a piece of wood. He was making a miniature warship, shaping with his knife the sweep of the bow, just above the ram.

"I'm looking for Alexis, I was told he lives here."

The man looked up from his work; he had a gray beard, cropped short.

"I'm Alexis, but I think you've had a long climb for nothing. I don't hire oarsmen directly any more, you have to talk to one of my captains. And they're out of port just now."

He resumed his carving, "I do have a boat due back in about a week, though, I can tell you where to find the captain. He may need a strong fellow for his next trip."

"You've got the bow shape very well," Skaphis said, "but it looks out of proportion, shouldn't the beam be narrower?"

"For a modern Athenian trireme, you're right. But this is an old Spartan boat. They built their ships solid. They thought of their fleet the same way as they think of their army - an unflinching line of shields impenetrable to an opponent and awesome in its solidity.

"But in the sea nothing is unflinching. The tide, the wind, the waves will break up the firmest line of battle. In the end your strength is not defined by your size, but by your speed."

The ship in the bay had rowed out into the wind-textured channel. It had turned into the wind, and every second oar had been shipped. The faint sound of shouted orders echoed across the bay. Alexis stopped his carving and watched. The boat in the bay looked no bigger than his carving. The remaining oars plied the water gently, keeping the ship on station. Meanwhile the mast appeared to bifurcate, as a boom was hauled into place, making briefly an oblique angle, then a right angle before a sail was unfurled and flapped chaotically in the strengthening breeze.

More barked commands and the oars on the starboard side of the ship backed water, while those on the port side rowed forward, turning the ship to the right. The sail stopped flapping and began to fill as the ship pointed more and more downwind, picking up speed under the combined effect of wind and oars.

"That was smart; in the war you couldn't get good hands for gold. Nowadays, with the navy decommissioned, you can man a ship properly, and still turn a profit."

"I didn't come up here looking for a rowing job. I'm trying to find Aristophon. His friend Stephanos hired me to look for him; he's worried that something may have happened to him."

"I'm not sure what business that is of yours, or Stephanos' for that matter."

Alexis resumed his carving, "This bow line is still not right, the real boat was squarer, uglier, slower."

Skaphis squatted beside the older man, with his back rested against the olive tree.

"She was called the Lysimachia, I was put in charge of a prize crew when we captured her off Pylos, she was my first command. She leaked badly from damage she'd sustained in battle, and I had a skeleton crew of rowers. We'd have been defenseless if we'd encountered any Spartan patrols. But we made it back to the base at Naupaktos.

"My reward was a post as helmsman for one of our older and leakier fleet triremes, but I was as proud of her as any aristocrat of a new chariot team. Her trierarch that year was a certain well-known political speaker. Fire and brimstone in the assembly with proposals for major state spending on war, but when it came to paying out of his own money to outfit a single ship, he scrimped and saved at every opportunity. Our tackle was old and half rotten. I'd hardly dare to hoist sail in anything over a light breeze for fear I'd lose the mast and kill half the crew in the process.

"The next year, Aristophon's father took over the trierarchy, and things were different from the start. He commissioned a complete new set of sails and running gear. He provided extra money for wages so we could hire the best crewmen available for our top deck rowers. He took great pride in the ship and sailed with us, not just on campaign, but also on training cruises. He spent more than his fair share in his year, and although he certainly had a legitimate cause for action against the previous trierarch for the sorry state of the ship after his tenure, he didn't take him to court, or even complain in public.

"When I left the navy, he lent me money to buy a share in my first ship, and advanced me my first cargo, from one of his island estates.

"A couple of years ago, I recognized his son Aristophon in the trading zone in the Piraeus, and invited him over for dinner. His father had died at Aegospotamoi, and he had been trying to establish himself as a trader. Not, I must say, very successfully."

Alexis put down his model ship and pocketed his whittling knife.

"An obvious rule of trading is that you have to buy goods at a cheaper price than you sell them. In order to be able to do this consistently, you have to add some value to the goods yourself. The merchant adds value by transporting the goods from one place where they are abundant and cheap to another place, where they are scarce and expensive. A wholesaler adds value by breaking up a large shipment of goods into small consignments. The sum of the prices paid for the small consignments can be larger than the price paid for the original shipment. But there are costs involved. The merchant must pay the costs of his ship and crew, and absorb the risk of losing the cargo at sea, the wholesaler has to pay for warehouse space and must ensure that he has an ample supply of customers for any cargo he takes on. If you can reasonably estimate your costs, and the price you can expect from sale of goods, then it is a simple matter of arithmetic to assess a fair purchase price. Without such information, it is impossible.

"Aristophon was engaged in a wholesale business, buying cargoes from ship owners in the Piraeus, storing them in his warehouses and shipping to retailers in the Athenian agora. He would buy whatever cargo took his fancy - either because some rumor suggested that supply of a particular commodity might soon be short, or because he was convinced the seller had some urgent reason for disposing of his goods below cost. He would then work in the agora in the Piraeus and also in Athens to find buyers. The problem was, that with each cargo being different, he had to find a new set of buyers for his goods, he was unable to create any stable long term customers. One month he would be selling wine, the next week wheat. In the end he was watching his resources dwindle, but could not understand why, as most of his trades looked like good ones.

"As I was grateful to his father for my start in business, I determined to do what I could to help along the son. I looked at his accounts and found that he was indeed paying a fair price for his wares and had been able to charge an appropriate mark-up. His transportation and warehousing costs were high. He also had a fair amount of wastage - portions of cargo for which he found no buyers. I persuaded him to buy his own warehouse facility rather than leasing. This way he controlled storage costs, and didn't have his rent inflated just when cargoes were plentiful and cheap, but storage space hard to come by.

"I also suggested he specialize in one commodity, and sold him my next cargo of wheat to get him started. He has since built up a network of customers for his wheat that he supplies regularly. He has a small number of merchants, such as myself from whom he buys only wheat, and he has a fixed cost storage facility, which he always keeps partially full. In short, his business started to prosper, not by the sort of get-rich-quick deals you hear in any Piraeus tavern, but by providing a stable well run service - if you want wheat at a fair price you can rely on getting it from Aristophon, if you have a cargo of wheat you want to sell for a fair price - Aristophon always has some extra room in his warehouse.

"Naturally, this business entailed him spending a lot of time in the Piraeus, and he would frequently spend the night as my guest, rather than walking back up to the city. Recently, he has been expanding his business in a direction which I feel is a little unwise, but this entailed him spending even more time down in the port. I suggested he could move in with me, as you can see I have a large house, and no family to share it with."

The shadow of the olive tree had shrunk back from the threshold of the house as the morning sun climbed in the eastern sky.

"Is he still living here?" Skaphis asked.

"A month ago he set sail for the Black Sea in a ship called the Nauplia, she's due back in Athens in a few days."

"Could Aristophon have returned early?"

"He could have transferred to a homebound ship in the islands, but I don't know why he would do that. If he was in port I'm sure he would have come up here, and he has not."

Another ship was working its way out into the bay. The sea breeze had picked up and Skaphis, no longer hot from his climb, pulled his traveling cloak closer to him. Below, the ship fought against the wind and waves to round the headland. The oars moved with a shorter stroke and a faster cadence.

"The tide has turned, that's the last of the outbound boats we'll see this morning. I am an old man who likes to carve and watch ships, and who talks too much about the past, but I still have business I need to attend to."

He picked up his model ship, turned his back to the wind and walked back towards the house with a surprisingly active gait. Skaphis found himself wondering if it was accidental that Alexis lived in a house from which he could observe every arrival and departure from the great port of the Piraeus.

"By the way," he said, "What was the business expansion you didn't approve of?"

The older man turned at the entrance to his house.

"He was getting into maritime insurance - buying outbound cargoes, to be paid back with the return cargo. In my opinion, that business is too risky, and I told him so. But sometimes, when you are a young man, you have to learn such things for yourself."

He opened the door and disappeared into the shaded interior of the building

Skaphis set off in the direction of Munichia Hill with the feeling he was in the process of learning a lesson the hard way, but damned if he knew what it was. The sea glistened in the freshening breeze and mocked, with its beauty and vastness, his petty concerns.

Perhaps it was cowardice that made him delay visiting Astra, but the Piraeus agora was almost on the way. The market place was bustling with midday shoppers. The smells of fresh baked bread mingled with those of fatty fish grilling on open braziers by the fishmongers' stands and conspired to pull the knot in Skaphis' stomach tighter. The stall holders' voices rose above the background chatter of the market goers.

A crowd had gathered by a stand that sold pottery. The salesman was in the middle of a joke:

"… so I was leaving her house by the back door so's nobody would see me, when who should I run into but her husband. He was asleep in the yard until I just about stepped on him. 'Just delivering some pots,' I said, thinking quickly. 'Aye, he said, you must be an agile potter, turning your own funeral urn with your prick.'"

The crowd laughed as the salesman segued into his closing pitch, "So here is the very urn, as you can see, it's a big one." The crowd laughed again, as the potter held up a 3 foot tall urn.

"Normally I'd sell this urn up in Athens for 4 drachmas, but I'm not going to ask you for 4 drachmas today. I only have 5 urns like this, and look what is inside this one."

He reached inside the urn and pulled out a smaller pot, this one painted with a black glaze and with small red figures.

"I have not just one storage jar,"

He pulled out another similar pot,

"Not just two storage jars," he pulled out a third pot, then a fourth pot, then a fifth.

"And on each storage jar, a scene from the classics. Match the content to the scene. Here is Zeus seducing

Leda as a swan - now there's an agile prick - put your pickles in that one." The crowd laughed again.

"Separately these are worth a drachma each, but these are included absolutely free." He deftly packed the painted jars back into the large urn.

"And in this first urn, I'll add this beautifully turned drinking cup," he lifted a large, gaudy looking cup from the display on his stall and added it to the urn.

"Now I'm going to sell all 5 of these urns, and I'm going to sell them at different prices, but the first one is special. I'm not going to ask you 4 drachmas for it, even though the urn is worth that alone and I've added a set of 5 storage jars and the exquisitely crafted drinking cup. No I'll not even ask 2 drachmas, but just to get you started, I'll take a loss on this first urn and give it away for 3 half drachmas."

Skaphis drifted away from the back of the crowd and jostled his way to the small colonnade where Pheron usually set up his bank. His table was in the shade between two columns. Guards stood like two human pillars on either side of the table, staring impassively over the crowd. They were as expressive as the stone columns, and it looked as if tangling with them would be equally ridiculous.

Pheron was sitting behind the table counting coins out of two money bags on the table. In front stood a trader, watching the process intently. Pheron was compact in stature, dressed in a cloak of the fine cloth typically associated with feminine attire. As he counted, gold rings flashed on the third and fourth fingers of each hand. On his left wrist was delicate golden bracelet, ornamental, but shaped like a manacle, with three links of golden chain dangling onto the table. Pheron was a slave, and reputed to be one of the wealthiest men in Athens. The irony of this situation was clearly not lost on the banker.

"Do you want it all in cash now, or would you like me to hold some of it on deposit for you?"

"I'll take it in cash, I suspect I'll have most of it spent before the day is out."

Pheron counted coins out from a chest underneath the table into one of the bags, and handed it back to the merchant along with the other, empty, bag.

"Never looks as much when you get it into Athenian money," the trader grumbled.

"Yes, but your bag's heavier. That's because we make our coins out of pure silver, not half scrap bronze or whatever unassayed alloy you can pass off on colonial farmers."

The trader turned away without further comment, secreting the moneybag in the folds of his cloak. Pheron's bank did not always have the best exchange rate, but it was reliably willing and able to convert between most of the major Mediterranean currencies, and had an excellent reputation for safeguarding any money left on deposit. Customers grumbled, but still they came back to Pheron.

"You look familiar," Pheron said, addressing himself to Skaphis, "do I know you?"

"I'm Barysthenes' partner, I've been by your table with him a couple of times in the past."

"Now I remember, but I think he won't be by my table any more?"

"Not unless you ferry it across the Styx and start working out of Hades."

"I'm not so dedicated a plutocrat. By the time I cross that river, I'll have retired from business and taken up scholarship. A study, perhaps, of the effects of long exposure to wine and idleness on the human body."

"His wife says he has some money on deposit with you."

"He did until a few weeks ago. I was holding a few minas for him, but got it all out in Cyzican staters."

"She will be disappointed. I don't suppose he said what he was going to do with the cash? If he invested it in some project, I ought to try and track it down so his widow can claim her share."

"No he didn't say, and I make it my practice not to ask."

Pheron stood up to greet another customer who was carving a wake of importance through the market crowd directly towards the table. Skaphis turned to leave.

"He did lodge a document with me for safe keeping at around that time. It may have some information which would help you. I could bring it to the table with me tomorrow, if you want."

"Aye, do that."

As Skaphis walked out of the shade of the stoa and into the harsh noontime glare of the market place, Pheron was already deep in negotiations with the newcomer, his right hand absent-mindedly turning the golden shackle-amulet as he talked.

The crowd had gone from the potter's booth, and the potter sat in front of his wares, drinking wine from a skin.

"I see you found some more urns," Skaphis said.

"Freshly delivered from Athens, the paint's not even dry on this one." He pulled a drinking bowl out of one of the urns, with the flourish of a conjurer. The scene on the side of the bowl was meant to be pornographic. A youth in an obvious state of arousal reclined on a couch, wine cup by his hand, his cloak draped beneath him. A girl was in the act of climbing up onto the couch. The scene intended was one of debauchery. Both faces were in profile, and were staring at each other. If striving for lust, the artist had failed. In its place he had created a mutual absorption that made the scene appear more like a young married couple in the first flushes of their enthusiasm with each other. Long suppressed memories surged, uninvited, into Skaphis' mind. Instead of erotic, he found the painting heartbreaking.

Skaphis reached into his cloak and pulled out the broken pottery fragment he had picked up from underneath Barysthenes' body.

"Do you have any idea where this was made?"

The potter took the fragment and examined it. First, he looked at it end on and scraped at the broken edge. Then he inspected the glaze on the inside and outside, and finally looked at the artwork painted on the outside of the fragment.

"This is good work," he said, "Athenian obviously, but of a much higher quality than you'll see down in this market. Look at the head on that young chap. I'm not sure I've seen anything quite like that."

The potsherd contained the face of a young soldier. Individual locks of hair were discernible in the unruly curls which cascaded from beneath his helmet and in his wispy goatee beard. Most startlingly of all, however, he was looking out from the fragment. Conventionally the figures on pots were depicted in profile, thus confining their gaze to the flat surface they themselves occupied. This soldier seemed to look out from his ceramic universe to regard the real world beyond.

"You could talk to my friend Ktesion in the Kerameikos. He makes my better stuff, like this one." He replaced the cup he had shown Skaphis carefully in the urn.

"His workshop is close to the Dipylon Gate. He might be able to point you to the artist. Now are you sure you aren't interested in a wine cup?"

"I'd have to become interested in wine again first."

chapter **5**

Nobody was home when Skaphis reached Barysthenes house. Nobody that is except Barysthenes himself, who lay on a low table in his own andrikon, as if sleeping off the effects of a long evening's drinking. The body had been washed and clothed in a clean white robe.

Skaphis had forced himself to eat some bread in the market place and finally worked off the effects of his own long evening's drinking. He was surprised that Astra had left the body unattended, and sat on a couch by the head of his former partner to await her return. He remained there in silence for a long while. The occasional murmur of voices outside only served to accentuate the dead still within the house.

"Well, old partner, I misjudged you. You did stake out the meeting after all. But what did you see there that made them kill you? And why did you take my knife? Why did you send for me? And what in the name of Apollo did you want with Cyzican staters?

"So many questions, it's almost worth the ferry fare to go down and ask you. Only problem is it's hard to get back once you buy that ticket.

"'Wretched to go living into Hades clime,

Twice-dying when others die only one time'"

Skaphis sat in silence again, drowsiness blurring the edges of his consciousness, as if by mimicking the stillness of death he could somehow will his dead partner to communicate answers to his questions.

At first Astra did not notice him. She was flushed and out of breath, and headed directly through the andrikon. Halfway across the room she glanced across at Barysthenes and spotted Skaphis.

"You startled me."

She altered course and sat on a stool at the foot of the body.

"I had to get out. I couldn't stay here with that any longer," she nodded at the corpse.

"I couldn't sleep a wink last night, so today, I sent away all the neighbors and walked. I don't know where: down by the docks, in the market place, everyone was going on with life as normal. Do you understand, I had to see for myself that life was going on? I know it's my duty to watch him, I think I can manage now."

"I went to see Pheron. Apparently Barysthenes did have some money on deposit, but he withdrew it all a few weeks ago."

Astra looked down. As she bowed her head, ringlets of hair spilled like spiraling tears from beneath her veil.

"He left a document with Pheron, though, it may tell us what he did with the money. That amount of cash he has to have invested somewhere. I'll get the document from Pheron tomorrow."

She peered up at him, her eyes seemed to hold a mixture of hope and fear.

"Astra, can I take a look at what is stored in your strong box?"

"It's upstairs, I'll show you."

She led him through the door in the back of the andrikon and up a narrow dark flight of stairs. At the top of the stairs were two rooms. In the smaller room, a large wooden hoplite shield rested against the wall, the emblem of a bull's head faintly discernable through the tarnished bronze finish. Propped in the corner of the room was the long heavy-infantry thrusting spear, and hanging from a dowel, a scabbard held a short wide sword. Incongruous among this panoply of war, a loom stood on the floor in the center of the room, across which a patterned blanket stretched, unfinished, like a lingering, unspoken thought.

Skaphis followed Astra into the other room. Most of the room was occupied by a pair of beds, at the foot of which a blanket, of a similar pattern to the one in the loom, covered the bare floor. She knelt down and pushed the blanket to one side. She prised up a floor board and pulled a wooden box out from within the cavity thus exposed. She unlocked the lid, and handed the open box to Skaphis.

Inside were two worn leather money bags. There were no documents. Skaphis carefully untied the drawstring in the first bag and spilled the coins out into the box. There was a mixture of small denomination silver coins, mostly 4 drachma pieces, all Athenian. The other bag was harder to open and contained fewer coins. They were not Athenian, nor did they come from the Black Sea. Skaphis recognized the head of the Syracusan despot Dionysus. These coins were from Sicily. In total, Skaphis estimated, they were worth less than 100 drachmas. If these were the proceeds of a deal which Barysthenes did with the cash he withdrew from Pheron's bank, the deal had not been a profitable one.

A bulging moon paled in the early sky. In the east an ice-blue glow spread like rumored death. Small clots of mourners congealed around the grave. Skaphis recognized some as Barysthenes' neighbors. An older woman stood apart. She was dressed in a fine black robe, which she held close to her body to ward off the pre-dawn chill that seeped down towards the tepid sea. Astra poured oil from a lechythos, the fluid mixing unnoticed with the dry hard baked ground.

The faint ululations of the mourning song accompanied by the throaty rasp of the low register of the aulos heightened Skaphis' sense of dislocation. Had all these shadowy figures, hunched between night and day, been in the thin cortege that stumbled in the moonlit darkness out through the city gates? or were some themselves shades, up from the underworld to observe the initiation of their new fellow citizen? The gray figures lurking at the back of the small cluster of neighbor men, for example: they had not been pall-bearers, nor did he remember them in the tight and silent cluster of men who had preceded the coffin through the empty streets. Would they linger here once everyone had departed for the funeral feast to escort Barysthenes through the half-light to his long home underground?

Skaphis shuddered. Having completed the libations, Astra crouched down and held the oil vessel over the grave. Her fingers uncurled, and the lechythos dropped casually in. She straightened slowly, then turned abruptly and started to walk back to the city. The mourners followed her example. The older woman paused first for a moment above the grave. She bent down to pick up a handful of dirt and sifted it through her fingers into the grave. Skaphis thought he saw a small golden object fall from her hand amongst the dirt. But perhaps it was a rock turned golden in the dazzle of the newly rising sun.

Skaphis stayed behind to complete the non-ritual task of filling in the grave. He picked up a spade and started to dig. The three gray-clad men remained. Two of them came forward to help Skaphis with his work, on instructions from the third. If these were ghosts, they were strong ones: heavily muscled forearms swung with the rhythmic ease of long-accustomed toil. They worked in silence with a nod to Skaphis. The third man seemed familiar, but his gray cloak concealed all but his beard, and he was standing in the direct glare of the new sun.

"Appropriate job for someone with your name."

Skaphis recognized Kotos, the Sicilian trader who had been at Lusilla's the day before Barysthenes' death.

"It can also mean 'skiff'. I always took my name to say I was destined for the sea, not for spadework."

"Spades and oars... one tills the ground, the other tills the waves, but which harvests the most wheat? You were Barysthenes' partner, and you were of some help to me in the tavern. Perhaps you are now in need of work? I can't offer you anything with a spade, but I could use someone who can handle an oar."

"Thank you, but I had intended to continue Barysthenes' business."

"As a private investigator? That's a thankless profession, and a risky one."

"Barysthenes met with you in the tavern after I left. Did you hire him to do a job?"

"You can't be in the private investigator business for long without making enemies, sea-spade man. Barysthenes had been an investigator for a long time and had enemies. But I was not one of them."

"You did hire him then?"

"We met in the tavern. We chatted about business issues of mutual interest. You were Barysthenes partner, but you are not mine. You should follow your calling to the sea - healthy lifestyle with only the occasional pirate to worry about."

Kotos' companions had stopped shoveling earth and had dragged into place the grave marker. Kotos turned to join them.

"One more thing," Skaphis said, "Do you know what Barysthenes would want with Cyzican staters?"

"I don't know, maybe he was planning a trip abroad."

The three left Skaphis by the graveside. He stood for a moment and looked at the grave marker. On Astra's instructions, he had ordered a plain unadorned marker. He had not paid for any engraving; however, there were letters carved into the stone. Skaphis crouched down to read the inscription.

"A good man died."

Astra must have changed her mind and decided on an inscription after all.

The funeral feast was subdued and, by the time Skaphis got there, almost over. The morbid early morning exercise had given him a voracious appetite, and the need to reaffirm life through eating. The other mourners must have had the same impulse, however, and the trenchers had been mainly picked clean. Skaphis was able to salvage a few scraps of meat from the carcass of a roast hare and the remainder of a blood pudding. This still left him hungry, but he had to be content with ladling himself a bowl of thick porridge.

"I used to eat like that, but now I find I don't have the appetite for food, or sometimes for life itself. But youth and hunger are oxen pulling the same cart."

It was the old lady who had stood apart with her attendants at the funeral. The attendants were now nowhere to be seen.

"Aye madam, fortunately gruel fills the belly just as well as roast hare."

"They tell me you were Barysthenes partner. Will you find out who killed him? An unresolved murder pollutes a family, unfortunately there are no male relatives left to pursue the matter. I am just an old woman, but I have some resources, and will use them to do my duty for the family."

"You are related to Barysthenes?"

"He was my brother's son. There were two boys: Barybromos and Barysthenes. Barybromos was the younger, and his mother died the day he was born. I saw a lot of both as boys, but less after they went off for military training."

"Barybromos is dead?"

"Of course the war was on, and Barysthenes was posted up in the garrisons in the north. He seemed to enjoy soldiering, and stayed on with the army when his age group was demobilized. Barybromos settled down and got married." She glanced over at Astra. "She was a sweet young thing and Barybromos was a gentle young man. They seemed to be very happy. Astra and I became good friends. She was like a daughter to me."

"Astra was Barybromos' wife?" Skaphis filled a goblet of wine for himself, and one for the old lady.

"Oh yes, then Barybromos was called up again, for the expedition to Sicily. She was proud to see him leave, we went down to the Piraeus together and watched the fleet depart. It was a splendid sight, ship after ship rowed out of the harbor, it seemed like there was no end to them. There was no way such a powerful force could fail, however grand its objective. But inside, we trembled."

She took a long drink from her wine cup.

"For a long time there was little news from Sicily, and then we heard that the army was besieging Syracuse, and that it was a somewhat bigger task than they had initially planned. All was going well, but we needed to send a second fleet to ensure a quick victory. Barysthenes was recalled from his garrison duty in the north to be part of this new force.

"He was in town only for a week before leaving, and most of his time was taken up with preparing for the expedition, although I'd have to say that a fair amount of the preparation seemed to take place in the taverns of the Kerameikos. He came to see me once before he left, and I told him to look after his brother. Barybromos was a delightful young man, urbane, well-mannered, moderate in his habits, but I had the impression that when it came to killing, Barysthenes would be the better of the two. Anyway, in a strange way, I felt better knowing that Barysthenes would be there too."

She paused from her story to finish her wine. Skaphis offered to refill her cup, but she refused.

"At first there were dispatch ships every so often, we heard there had been a night battle, that the Syracusans were attempting to wall in the besiegers. Then, we heard nothing but rumors. The fleet had been victorious, and was now coasting up and down Italy. They had captured Syracuse, and had now landed on the coast of Africa and were besieging Carthage. They had met a terrible storm on the way home and were dispersed over the Western sea. The most terrible rumor of all, though it was the truth: the whole expedition had been wiped out, and the pitiable few captives put to work as slaves in the stone quarries.

"We wept for Barybromos, and Barysthenes. But our grief was a small teardrop in the ocean which was the city's loss. We grieved not just for our dead, but for ourselves. What was to become of us without all our fighting men? It seemed only a matter of time before the Spartan regiments would be pillaging through our beautiful city. Eventually, a few men made it back. Some had been bought by wealthy Sicilians, and then released. Barysthenes was one of these.

"He told us that his brother had died when the army was surrounded by Syracusans. But he had survived to be captured, and eventually was one of the lucky ones to be released. He worked his way back to Athens on merchant ships. Barysthenes had never been the most convivial of boys, but Sicily changed him. He was morose and taciturn, barely seemed to recognize me. He even looked different, as if the experience there had taken the heart out of him and left him hollower, smaller.

"Of course, he inherited Barybromos' estate and married Astra. Soon after that, he moved down to the Piraeus, and I have seen him perhaps twice in the years since then. I have seen Astra more often, at the women's festivals."

"And now, I must say goodbye to her and get onto the road back to Athens. Please find the killer for me. A killing is not something a family should leave unanswered, even a family as weak as ours. Now where are those two slaves of mine?"

Skaphis went to seek out the attendants, while the old woman held Astra in a tear wracked embrace. Astra watched Skaphis over her aunt's shoulder.

Chapter **6**

Pheron was weighing coins in a balance. On the left side of his table, silver coins were arranged in neat piles, like columns on the temples of a miniature but affluent people. On the right side was a large heap of coins and another smaller cluster. One by one, Pheron took the coin piles from the left and put them in the balance, made a notation on his wax tablet, then transferred the coins into the heap on the right. A trader stood beside the table making notes on his own tablet.

Several piles were treated this way. The next pile must not have measured up on the balance. Pheron took each coin in turn and examined it closely. He held each coin in the palm of his hand, tossing it gently up and down and catching it. He then held the coin between his forefinger and thumb and rapped its edge on the table, releasing the coin just before it hit on the hard surface of the table, deftly catching it again as it bounced. Most of the coins he consigned to the large heap at this stage. Two of them he placed by themselves in neither of the heaps. A shiny black stone was sitting on a square of leather on the table by the balance. Pheron took the suspect coins and scratched them on the stone. He shook his head, and added them to the reject pile.

"Skaphis, is it not? I have your document; I'll get it for you once I've done this lot. I've been busy all day, the tide washed in shiploads of foreign money to be changed, it seems."

Skaphis nodded, "Pheron, do you know a man by the name of Aristophon?"

"The grain dealer? Sure, he used to change money with me all the time, but he has not used my services for about a year now. He must have found another bank that gives him a better rate of exchange. His eyes twinkled. My rate of exchange is not the best in town. But my money is."

As he talked, he continued to weigh, feel, taste and scratch his way through the pile of silver.

"Have you seen him recently, say in the last couple of days?"

"No, now that you ask, I haven't noticed him down in the emporium for some time now, a month or two."

"He sailed east on a vessel called the Nauplia, about a month ago."

"Then he should be back in a couple of days, the Nauplia is expected before the end of the week."

"Apparently, he was seen in the Piraeus last week."

"Then he must have come back in a different ship. If he did, he probably changed money at one of these tables."

Pheron finished weighing the last pile of coins. He stood and showed his wax tablet to the trader who compared it with his own tablet. After some discussion, Pheron filled a sack with the large pile of silver, and the trader dropped the coins from the other pile into a small money bag. Pheron unfastened another money sack and counted coins out of it. He grouped the coins into piles of ten and constructed another miniature temple of cash on his table. He then took some smaller coins from a box at his elbow. The trader counted the piles, referring to his tablet, then nodded and swept the temple into an empty sack.

Pheron opened the box, which was by his feet, and produced a scroll of papyrus, which he placed on the table. With some difficulty, he lifted the sack of silver coins and pried it into the box. He handed the papyrus scroll to Skaphis.

The scroll was made of coarse papyrus, and tied with cord. Skaphis thanked Pheron and carefully pocketed it inside his cloak.

"You might ask Thumion about Aristophon," Pheron nodded to the seaward end of the stoa, "He sets up his table down there."

Skaphis threaded his way through the bustling portico. In between the bankers' tables, clusters of men stood doing business: traders pooling resources to buy a cargo, ship owners looking to rent out their craft, investors, hucksters, swindlers. Thumion was counting coins from his table into a small bag. A sailor was scrutinizing the proceedings, and when Thumion had filled the bag, took it with a grunt and plunged eagerly into the market crowd.

"What can I do for you? I'll change your money into Athenian owls, and then all the pleasures of town can be yours. And this is a town with pleasures of all kinds for a man with the stamina."

Skaphis opened his hand, and seemingly from nowhere, an Athenian drachma appeared in the middle of his palm.

"I already have one or two of those birds, and I've had all the pleasure I can take today. I'm looking for a friend of mine - Aristophon - I've heard he is back in town, and I'm told he banks with you."

"I never talk about my clients. Their comings and goings are their own business."

"Taking a bit of a chance with that sailor weren't you." With a ripple of his fingers, Skaphis palmed the coin, it seemed to have disappeared into thin air.

"I suppose you reckon he'll be drunk and in the hands of some whore, before he notices that all the coins you counted out did not make it into the bag. Now, how difficult will it be for me to find him in the market and suggest he counts his silver?"

"Aristophon came to my table five days ago. He changed a small bag of Persian gold Darics. I haven't seen him since."

"Did he tell you where he had come from, or what ship he came in on?"

"No, he was in a hurry and did not stop to talk. Now, information has a value. I believe you are in my debt." He looked greedily at the coin that had re-appeared in Skaphis' hand.

Skaphis held his hand out to the banker, who grasped for the coin. The coin magically disappeared just before he grabbed it, and Skaphis turned to go.

"Five days ago, was the full moon, let's see, we had a dozen boats in that day. Here they are."

The customs official showed the ledger to Skaphis. They were seated at a table underneath a small stone shelter which crouched with its back to the wind at the end of one of the twin piers which projected into the bay like an insane attempt to extend the long walls beyond the Piraeus and across the Aegean.

"Ports of origin?"

The official read down the list, interpreting the shorthand for Skaphis.

"Here is a cargo of grain from Memphis in Egypt, another cargo of grain, from Sicily. This one is carrying wine from Cos..."

"Any from the north-east?"

The official scanned the list with his finger, and stopped at two names.

"This one: the Penelope transshipping Black Sea grain out of Cyzicus, and this one: the Lukokumia, from Lesbos carrying wine."

In the bay, a cargo ship was furling its single broad rectangular sail as it approached the pier, beginning to wallow in the light afternoon swell as it lost way.

"Are they still in harbor?"

The official skimmed through the remaining entries in the ledger.

"The Lukokumia left yesterday with a cargo of earthenware for Italy. The Penelope is still in port. Now, if you'll excuse me, it looks like I have more work to do."

As the official prepared to board the incoming freighter, Skaphis paced his long way back to the inner harbor.

The Penelope was the outside of three ships moored in parallel to the quay. The inner boat was actively unloading. Crew members manhandled earthenware amphoras out of the hold. Each pot was 3 feet tall with two handles. With contents it would weigh upwards of 100 pounds. When it was passed out of the hold, a crewman would hold the pot with one handle, its pointed base balanced on the deck. Designed for efficient stacking in the hold of a ship, an amphora on its own was an ungainly, unbalanced object. A longshoreman would board the ship, hoist the amphora onto his back, and grunt back up the gangplank, just as the next amphora was lifted into daylight and the next dock worker bounced unladen back to the ship.

Injecting himself into this stream of activity, Skaphis followed a stevedore on board but continued to the other side of the ship and clambered easily over the rail. The second ship was a scene of tranquility in contrast to the manic bustle on the first. A crew member was sleeping against the port-side rail. Another sat drinking from a wine flask. He waved casually acknowledging Skaphis as he balanced across onto the Penelope.

The deck of the Penelope was empty, but noise was coming from the hold. With the sound of Skaphis' footsteps on deck, a head appeared out of the hatch.

"The captain is ashore with the ship owner, but he will be back before dark."

"I'm looking for a friend of mine who just came back from the east, Aristophon by name."

"Aristophon sailed with us from Cyzicus. We had two passengers, Aristophon and a young Cyzican called Protonikos. The ship owner was also traveling with us, so the passengers had to sleep on deck."

"Do you know where Aristophon went after he landed?"

"No, but you could talk to the ship owner. His name is Asclepiades. You should be able to find him in the trading zone. He is looking for a new cargo. He is intent on one more run to the Black Sea, before the weather closes in. For myself, I'd call it good for the year."

The sailor ducked his head back under the deck, while Skaphis clambered back across the other two ships to the dock.

He eventually found Asclepiades in a waterfront tavern. The place teemed with seamen in various stages of sobriety. The ship owner sat alone at a table in the corner of the room. He was drinking wine from a large goblet. A mixing bowl sat on the table in front.

Skaphis sat opposite him at the table, "I'm looking for Aristophon and was hoping you might be able to tell me where I can find him."

"Aye, I'd like to find that bastard myself. I'd carve a fair price for wheat into his backside with the point of this." A dagger blade glistened in Asclepiades' hand. "Your friend is he?"

"I buried my partner this morning. He was at a meeting with Aristophon a couple of nights ago. My partner never returned. I'd like to ask Aristophon a few questions about the meeting. I'm not sure I'll go as far as tattooing commodity prices, though."

The ship owner laughed and ordered another goblet to be brought from the bar and ladled some wine for Skaphis out of the bowl. "You'll join me."

Skaphis drank. The first taste of the wine awoke a slumbering thirst in Skaphis' throat. The second draught brought back the memory of this morning's funeral. The third draught quenched both.

"I'd dealt with Aristophon before, and he usually gave me a fair deal for my wheat. So when he showed up in Cyzicus offering to buy my load in advance for cash, and give me over the odds at that, I took the deal. Even gave him free passage back to Athens into the bargain. Now, when I get here I find that, far from dropping as Aristophon told me, the price of grain in Athens has been climbing steadily. I could have sold my cargo for twice what Aristophon paid me.

"He supervised the unloading of the cargo. It was done smartly, I can tell you, like a cavalry operation. Then he made himself scarce. Meanwhile, I have to find an outbound cargo. You wouldn't be interested in going in with me on a commercial venture, you look like a young man of means. It's better to have your money working for you than sitting idly at home."

Skaphis wondered how much wine it took to mistake him for a member of the moneyed classes.

"My money works hard enough just staying in my purse. You don't have any idea where Aristophon went to?"

"No, but he was very friendly with the other passenger, a Cyzican youth by the name of Protonikos: a rich boy of an aristocratic family. It was his first visit to Athens and Aristophon promised to show him around. The youth spent his first couple of nights down at the Piraeus. I let him sleep it off on the ship. But then he headed up to the city. Aristophon had apparently told him he could stay with a friend of his up there."

The ship owner rose from the table.

"I should go now, but feel free to finish the wine." He nodded at the mixing bowl, which had not been entirely drained of its shallow red contents. "I wish you luck in finding your partner's killer."

He threaded his way through the bustling tavern. Skaphis remained in the gloom for a long time in silence, sipping his wine thoughtfully. Eventually he signaled over to the bar and had a terra cotta lamp brought to the table. He filled his cup with the remains of the wine, and untied the scroll he had been given by Pheron.

He unrolled the scroll and read it carefully in the sputtering light of the lamp. Once or twice, he angled the papyrus toward the lamp to squint the meaning from a word. When he had finished, he rolled up the papyrus and carefully replaced it in his cloak. He gave a low whistle, and sat, deep in thought, while the dimming oil timed the wine's slow titration of his thoughts.

chapter 7

There was no longer a pitcher of water outside Barysthenes' house. Death was not in residence any more and the ritual purification was now unnecessary. The men's room, which had held the body, was now rearranged for the use of the living. Skaphis used it. He sat on a couch and produced the document again from within his cloak. He was weighing it absent-mindedly with his right hand when Astra eddied through the door from upstairs.

She was unveiled, and she had cut her hair for the funeral. The luscious exuberance of ringlets had been replaced by a startled garland of short tufts, like the flightless feathers on a nest bound fledgling. The effect was to stress the youth and vulnerability of her tear dewed face. She sat beside him and settled her head against his upper arm. He had a surprising urge to run his fingers through the stumps of her mutilated hair, as if by touching, he could accelerate a cure that only time could properly effect. The papyrus scroll, though, seemed to hold his hand with a gravity beyond its weight.

"Do you want to stay with me?"

Skaphis looked into Astra's eyes as if by staring he could pry some confirmation of her unspoken and true desire. But her eyes held nothing but a dark reflection of his own accreting lust.

"I can't."

She pulled away from him.

"Oh, I suppose you need to get back to the little whores at Lusilla's. A few hours away and you are pulled back to them."

"I can't, Astra, because you are my mother."

A wave of laughter washed the petulance from her face. "Skaphis, you have been watching too many plays. And ridiculous ones at that. How can I possibly be your mother? I have never had a child! and even if I had, you are too old to be my son."

"It's in this document," Skaphis opened up the scroll: "Barysthenes adopted me in the event of his death, which makes you my adopted mother. Did you not know about this?"

Astra stared blankly at the opposite wall. Skaphis could see the muscles of her cheeks tighten as her jaw clenched.

"I didn't ask for this, Astra, and he didn't tell me about it either."

"So there's no contract, only this?"

"No, which means the money he withdrew is unaccounted for. But I'll do my best to track it down."

"Yes, I'm sure you will, it's your money now."

Skaphis didn't know how to answer.

Eventually Astra broke the silence.

"I'm sorry, it was an unexpected turn of events. I had hoped the document would tell me what happened to the money. Instead it was this. I let my disappointment show.

"It's also hard to adjust to having you as a son, although a finer strapping lad, no mother could wish for."

The rumor of a smile spread across her face.

"I was talking to Barysthenes' aunt at the funeral. She told me there is no near male relative in the family."

"Barysthenes was not a big one for keeping up with his relatives. He did have a cousin who lived abroad – Italy, I believe."

"He will be disappointed. She also told me you had been married to Barysthenes brother."

She looked at him, and her lower lip quivered before she spoke.

"I was just a girl when I was married to Barybromos, and I was terrified of him. He seemed huge and heroic, back from the wars: tall, athletic and handsome as a god. How could I be a wife for such a man? But he was gentle and considerate, and taught me patiently what was expected of me and how to run the household. He taught me also how to love a man, and love him I did. Until that terrible expedition took him away from me."

She ran her fingers through her mutilated hair, as if evoking the tactile memory of a prior grief.

"I had never met my husband's brother. He was always away on active duty up north, and then in Sicily. When the news of the disaster came, I told myself that Barybromos had survived the slaughter and was being held prisoner, and that one day he would escape and return to me. But my heart told me he was dead. And then, a year or so later, a member of my husband's regiment did make it back to Athens, and came to me to tell me that both Barybromos and his brother were alive and being held as prisoners. Conditions, apparently were dreadful, but my husband was strong, and I began to hope that he would return to me some day.

"Every so often someone would make it back to town from Syracuse. Either they had escaped from the quarries, or more frequently, some local had bought them as a slave and given, or sold them their freedom. I would always try to seek them out to ask for news of my husband. Eventually, I learned that both brothers had been bought as household slaves by a Syracusan family. My hope grew, and I knew it was only a matter of time before Barybromos made it back to Athens. He was such a strong man."

She looked down, holding her forehead in her hands. Then she straightened up and continued.

"Well, Barysthenes did make it back, and being the surviving brother, inherited Barybromos' estate and, of course … me. He told us that Barybromos had been weakened by sickness in the quarries. Conditions there were terrible, and soldiers were dying off like flies. They were both purchased to work as slaves in the grain fields of a Syracusan farmer. The work was not as hard as in the quarries, but Barybromos never regained his health and died of a sickness in the winter. Barysthenes escaped the next spring and made it over to a friendly city in the north of Sicily. From there, he worked his way back to Athens.

"It was a shock to be married again to someone I did not know. And the two brothers were like night and day. Where Barybromos was open and generous, Barysthenes was secretive and mean."

She looked up at Skaphis.

"But he provided for me, and I got used to him. In the end he was not such a bad husband, I suppose."

Skaphis sat silently for a few minutes, with Astra's arm touching against his like the fender between two boats docked together in a careless evening swell. He rose to leave.

"He was my partner, and taught me his trade. Astra, I'll make sure you are taken care of."

"Yes, I'm sure you will." Her voice sounded hollow and unconvinced.

Skaphis lay in his bed above the late night clatter of Lusilla's tavern, but could not sleep. The weariness of his body was counterbalanced by an alertness of his mind. In the three days since his partner had been killed, Skaphis had not had much time to consider his own future. He had assumed that he would be able to continue in the private investigation business on his own, and that he should be able to acquire some of his partner's former clients. The law courts were getting into their stride again after the restoration of the democracy, and information, mined or manufactured, was the raw material of the law courts. There would be no shortage of private investigation work.

Inheriting Barysthenes estate would make it much easier to continue in his business, without any conflict. But it carried diverse complications. He now owned a house, and could move out of his digs at Lusilla's - but he was comfortable here, he enjoyed the easy rhythms of the tavern, liked it's muffled silence in the morning, the noisy evening clamor which resonated with his night thoughts and drowned out his darker broodings. There was some money, but there was also Astra. He would be responsible for finding a husband for her. He was not sure what sort of dowry would be needed, but he suspected the money would barely be enough.

And then, as the adopted son, it was his responsibility to find and prosecute his new father's murderer.

A knocking at his door was faint enough to be imagined, but loud enough to interrupt his thoughts. The tapping repeated, a little louder and more insistent. Skaphis sat up and grunted an acknowledgment of the knock. A small figure tentatively entered his room. The dancing shadows from the terra cotta lantern in her hand played illusionary games with the alien tattoos on her arms.

"Thrassia, what is it?"

"It's all right, the mistress sent me."

"Come, sit down." He could only offer her a seat next to him on his couch.

She sat demurely, apart from Skaphis, placing her fluttering lantern on the floor beside her feet.

"I was busy earlier tonight," she looked down at her hands, clasped primly in her lap, "but mistress told me that I should talk with you now, as you are sometimes out early in the day."

Skaphis waited for her to continue.

"I was at the market today, mistress sent me to buy some wool. I saw the man who came here that night with Barysthenes' message. I knew you wanted to find him, so I started to follow him. I followed him for a few blocks. He was heading in the direction of Munichia. But I was afraid that mistress would be angry if I was late."

"So you let him go?" Disappointment was displacing the initial wave of interest, which her story had piqued.

"No, I caught up with him and told him you were looking to pay him for the message. I told him to come to the tavern tomorrow at dusk, and you'd give him a couple of obols for his trouble."

Skaphis looked at her in surprise. "Good girl Thrassia, that's brilliant. Thank you." He wanted to kiss her, but felt the gesture might be misinterpreted.

She smiled up at him, her smile a mirage in the flickering shafts of darkness cast by the sputtering lantern.

"I also asked him what delayed him on his way to deliver the message. He swore he had delivered the message promptly. He had a little trouble finding Lusilla's in the dark, but that was all."

She picked up her lantern and rose to leave. "However, he may have been telling me that, just to safeguard his two obols."

chapter 8

"Wait there and I'll get my master."

The five-mile early morning hike to Athens was yielding as warm a reception as yesterday's pre-dawn march to the graveyard.

Eventually, Stephanos came to the door and gestured Skaphis into the house.

"That boy seems to have taken a strong dislike to you. Can I have him bring you something? That would really annoy him."

Skaphis demurred and sat down on a couch opposite Stephanos. If the slave's welcome had been cold, at least it had been consistent. The master's tone was distinctly more pleasant than on their previous encounter. Perhaps having Skaphis on his payroll made him more comfortable: he could deal with the lower classes, so long as it was clear who was boss.

"Have you located my friend yet?"

"No, but I'm getting closer. I talked with Alexis: apparently Aristophon shipped out east on one of his boats last month. The ship is due back in a couple of days."

From the back of the house came the sound of raised voices.

Skaphis continued. "However, Aristophon will not be on board. He left Alexis' ship in Cyzicus and returned from there a week ago. But then you knew all that."

The voices in the back had fallen silent. A tall youth surged into the room. His fine features had an androgynous quality that the whisper of beard on his delicate skin only served to accentuate.

"That slave of yours is the absolute limit, he needs a good beating if you ask me. I'm sorry, you have company." The boy noticed Skaphis and turned to go back into the interior of the house.

"No, stay with us. Skaphis, this is Protonikos, who is on his first visit to Athens. I have been showing him some of the sights of the city."

The youth sat on the couch beside Stephanos, who regarded him with the tolerant smile of a patient teacher for a bright, but willful student.

"We don't treat our slaves so high-handedly here in Athens. They're too damned expensive. Still, I suppose you are right."

"So you sailed from Cyzicus with Aristophon?" Skaphis asked the young man.

"Yes. I was asking round the docks to find a ship bound for Athens. I met Aristophon, who set me up with passage on the Penelope. A damned uncomfortable barge that was. The slightest swell would have her wallowing around like a drunken hag."

The boy's features seemed to Skaphis to take on a green remembered seasick hue. He guessed this had been his first sea trip.

"Anyway, Aristophon was very friendly to me, and when we arrived, he suggested I come up and stay at his place in Athens. I had arranged to stay with a guest-friend of my father's, but I guessed that I'd have more fun here." He glanced at Stephanos.

"When we arrived in the Piraeus, Aristophon was suddenly all business. I hung about on the boat for a couple of days waiting for him to take me up to the city. Eventually, he told me that something had come up and I should go on ahead: Stephanos would take care of me. He would make it up when he could. He hasn't made it up yet, but Stephanos has been kind."

"He did tell you where he was staying?" Stephanos prompted.

"He said that if I needed to find him, he should ask at Psuchion's tavern by the emporium."

Stephanos spoke. "If you find Aristophon, please tell him to come back up to Athens. I'm sure he's embarrassed

72

about the money he owes me, but that is not so important."

Skaphis rose from his couch. "That's an attitude I should try to teach my landlady next new moon, when my rent is due. She's likely to respond with the moral value of the toughening to be acquired by sleeping rough out of doors."

The sarcasm in his tone seemed to go unnoticed. But Stephanos stood to accompany him to the door. On his way out, he slipped Skaphis a coin and spoke in a low tone, "Find Aristophon for me, I'm worried about what he is mixed up in. He may have got out of his depth."

The Kerameikos was named for the red clay that was dug in the promontory of Kolias and shaped here into pottery for the whole of the Greek, and much of the non-Greek world. The quarter had a noontime bustle. If every third building seemed to contain a pottery, the other two were a tavern and a brothel. As well as being the hub of Athens' pottery trade, the Kerameikos was the center of the seamier side of its nightlife. The daytime shoppers, visiting potteries to look for that special piece of bespoke earthenware would, as night fell, give way to visitors seeking customized pleasure of a less aesthetic nature. The lives of artist and prostitute overlapped in the narrow streets of this quarter, whose bustle was built upon the malleability of a certain clay. Outside the walls, the Kerameikos was also the site of the city cemetery. Earth again, Skaphis thought.

Skaphis found the workshop he was looking for close under the city walls.

"Can I help you? I'm a bit backed up at the moment, but I do custom jobs, and could get a piece for you in a couple of weeks. There are some samples of my work in the back. Take a look around, I'll be with you in a few minutes."

The potter did not look up. He sat crouched on a short three-legged stool in front of a squat oven; one hand supported a substantial vase, whose base was propped on the top of the oven. He was shaping the pot with a piece of leather in the other hand.

In the center of the shop, a large pitcher stood beside a clay-splattered wheel. Behind the wheel was a table with an assortment of tools and brushes. Skaphis guessed this was where the painting was done. Along the back wall, finished vases stood like a phalanx of perpetually still and disciplined Spartans. A shelf above contained a set of plates propped on their edge, with the painted scene on their surface displayed to the viewer.

Skaphis looked at the plates. In the first, a woman sat in front of a tall loom. Hanging over her head was a roll of completed tapestry. She sat cross-legged, with her right forearm propped between her thigh and her chin, as if without its support, her head would droop from sheer sorrow to the ground. Behind her ankles, the weights dangled on the long threads of the loom, like a reserve of unshed tears. The woman's dress was modern; her palpable sorrow could be for the loss of a husband or brother in battle. The scene in the next plate showed a man fitting an arrow to a bow. In front, banqueters looked on with shocked expressions. The wine cup was in the process of falling from the hands of one of the revelers. The liquid was depicted in the act of spilling out of the cup.

The return of Odysseus, Skaphis guessed, which would make the woman by the loom his wife Penelope. Her sadness at the loss of her husband, Skaphis thought, was a little ironic, considering he was probably at the time cavorting with the sea nymph Calypso. Nine years it took him to escape from that island. He supposed you'd tire even of a sea nymph in nine years. He thought Odysseus looked a little bored loosing the first shaft at the suitors, as if he was just going through the motions. Was Penelope really glad to see her husband return, or would his actual presence prove irritating after all those years of contemplative loom work? Would his stories grow repetitive in the telling, his scheming and constant restlessness prove annoying in contrast to her prior autonomy? In some ways, her position had been an ideal one for a woman. With her husband gone, but not actually dead, she was the head of the household.

The potter looked up from his work.

"I have some less expensive items in the corner."

"I saw some of your stuff down in the Piraeus. I like it, but I'm not buying at the moment. I was wondering if you could help me find where this came from."

He handed the potter the fragment with the young man's head. The potter balanced his pitcher on top of the oven and stood up. He walked over to his painting station and examined the potsherd in the shaft of light, which angled over the table from a high window.

"This is unusual, look at the fine work on his hair. The shoulders are just suggested, but it looks like you can see every individual strand of hair. And the face is three quarters front, not profile. It's not easy to get the nose just right from that angle - and you can see he hasn't been entirely successful. Yes, this is unusual, but I've seen something quite like it before - there's a young painter that Antandros has hired, I'd wager this is his work. His studio is round the corner from here. You can't miss it."

In the chaos of back alleys and studios manufacturing, it seemed, identical ranges of earthenware, Skaphis was sure he could miss it, but thanked the potter anyway and left him to his silent contemplation of the symmetry of another half formed storage jar.

As it turned out, he had no problem finding the workshop. A narrow alleyway led into a tiny central courtyard. At the shaded side of the courtyard, a potter worked at his wheel, elbow deep in the messy delivery of an urn. A boy crouched beside him, turning the wheel. Bright sunlight shafted down the other side of the courtyard, but was only able to penetrate halfway down the high wall. A painter sat on a stool with his back to this wall. He was curled over a mixing bowl balanced in his lap, scratching at its surface with a knife-like tool. At one side of his stool a table contained a number of bowls and a variety of brushes. At the other side was an oven.

He looked up from his work when Skaphis approached. He was beardless, and working naked in the heat from the kiln. His body had an almost effeminate paleness. Even now, at noontime, the direct sunlight did not penetrate to the floor of the courtyard.

"I was told this might be your work." Skaphis handed him the pottery fragment.

The artist propped the bowl he was working on against the wall by his feet and held the piece up to the light.

"The funny thing about vase painting is that you draw the picture in reverse. You fill in the black background, and leave the figures the natural clay color. So by painting what isn't, you define what is."

"So if the figure is white--or really—reddish, because of the color of the clay, and the background is black, how do you draw the figure's hair? It will be black against a black background."

He looked up at Skaphis, his mouth holding the beginnings of a smile, his lips making Skaphis think of a girl's lips.

"Of course, you have to make a white line round the hair so its blackness can be distinguished from the background. This line is typically thin, so it gives the hair a matted look."

"See what I've done here." He handed the potsherd back to Skaphis. "I've made a much broader band of white round the head, so that I can make the hair more realistic. I wasn't sure if I would achieve the right effect. Too big a swathe of light round the head might give the impression of some sort of supernatural aura..."

"Oedipus at the crossroad." he continued, "I made it only a month or so ago, it's a shame it was broken, I was quite pleased with the result."

"Who did you sell it to?" Skaphis asked.

"I don't know, ask him." He nodded in the direction of the potter. "He handles the business, I'm just a hired hand."

He picked up the bowl again and started applying a substance to its surface. To Skaphis' eye the substance looked to be the same gray color as the pot itself. Only by angling himself to the light was he able to distinguish nuances of shade that defined the outline of a group of figures.

The painter glanced up from his work. "Looks like the same clay doesn't it? Yet this one is inherently dark. The blackness comes out in the firing."

The potter had stepped back from his urn, which still rotated slowly on his wheel.

"Oedipus at the crossroads, it was one of a matched set: Oedipus with the Sphinx, Oedipus as king and Oedipus the blind beggar. I sold them to Mnesicles a month ago. He has a booth at the agora and carries only top quality merchandise. But we can make you another pitcher, every bit as fine. We can even put the same scene on it for you."

Skaphis shook his head, "I prefer my heroes to be more straightforward. I can't see Heracles blinding himself because he'd inadvertently killed his father and married his mother."

"Difficult, though, in his case." The potter nodded to his assistant who resumed turning the wheel. "His father being immortal."

Skaphis had not found Mnesicles at the market place. According to one of the stallholders he was at the agora on alternate days. He had been there yesterday, and so could be expected tomorrow. He had, however, found his client at home. A maid showed him into an upper room, and announced that her mistress would join him in due course.

The room was tastefully and expensively furnished. On a table in the corner were a bowl and a pair of goblets. The goblets were made from metal, silver probably, and of a Persian design. The bowl was Athenian pottery. On the bowl a girl argued with a tall bare-headed man. A round hoplite shield rested on the ground, its upper edge balanced against the man's thigh. A broad brimmed hat dangled on the man's back from a cord around his neck. Around his head was a thick white aura against which Skaphis could pick out the fine detail of each curl of his hair, as if the figure was back-lit by an early sun. Skaphis thought he knew who had painted the scene.

"Oedipus' daughter Antigone, arguing with her uncle Creon."

Psamathe moved with poise and assurance in a Piraeus tavern. In her own house she had the grace of a royal princess. She sat down on an elegant chair and gestured for Skaphis to occupy its twin. The chairs faced each

78

other, and both were within arm-reach of the table containing the goblets.

"She's begging him to let her bury her brother, despite Creon's law that rebels should not be buried. Don't you find it an interesting dilemma: is it more important for her to obey the law of her country, or to fulfill her duty to her family?"

Her hair was tied by a broad leather sling. It was decorated with geometric patterns and at the front bore a metal plate with an inscription written on it. Skaphis tried to read the inscription, but found his gaze drifted down and was captured by her eyes, which were smiling.

"Of course the situation is not that simple, because Creon is the king and the law, but he is also her uncle and family. And her brother and she herself are the product of the incestuous marriage between Oedipus and his mother Jocasta; so they are doomed from the start."

"Where did you get the pot?"

"What do you think, Skaphis?" She leaned closer to him. "Should she go ahead and bury her brother, flouting the law, but doing her duty to her family, flawed though it is? Or should she stay within the law and bide her time?"

"I don't usually pay too much attention to the tragedies, but you have to sit through them to make sure you have a seat for the comedy."

"A metaphor for life, Skaphis. You sit through three tragedies, just for one comedy."

She leaned back and smiled.

"And when the moment of fun comes, it's just disgusting slapstick and grossly enlarged phalluses."

"Mind you," she continued, "I always thought Oedipus as good comic material as tragic. Look at the story - the god has made a ridiculous prophecy, that Laius' son will kill his father and marry his mother. To try and dodge this fate, Laius does the very thing that makes the prophecy come true - exposes his son at birth. Thus he enables Oedipus to grow up unaware of the identity of his true parents, and capable of justifiable homicide when he meets an arrogant stranger at the crossroads.

"Skaphis, you look dry, and my talk is parching you more. Let me offer you a little wine." She leaned over from her seat and poured wine from the bowl into one of the metal goblets. "I think you'll find this a little more drinkable than the swill you get around the Piraeus. Although it springs to mind you were not having any trouble drinking that last time I talked to you."

"The trouble came the next morning."

He sipped the wine, which was indeed good. "But I got over it."

Psamathe leaned back in her chair, crossing one leg over the other. The picture of Penelope at her loom flitted briefly across Skaphis' mind. He wondered what returning Psamathe longed for as she entertained her suitors in this upstairs room. He wondered if it too would prove a disappointment.

"I'm getting closer to finding Aristophon. He shipped out to the Black Sea in a cargo boat called the Nauplia a month ago. But he transferred at Cyzicus, and arrived back in the Piraeus last week. He has been dabbling in marine insurance, I believe, buying cargoes before they are shipped. It's a high risk game, but he has just brought in a shipload of grain, which he bought cheap in Cyzicus. He ought to have made a handsome profit if he has sold it on."

"So now would be a good time to tap him for the return of my loan."

"Yes, so long as we can find him. He has put up a friend of his with Stephanos. He has told them he can be contacted at a certain waterfront tavern in the Piraeus. I'd like to keep my eye on this friend of his, in case they have not been totally straightforward with me. He might lead us to Aristophon. But I'm inclined to think that it'd be more productive for me to check out the tavern first. And I can't be in two places at once."

Psamathe replaced her wine cup on the table. "It sounds like you have been very busy."

Her eyes narrowed. "Did you make any progress on your partner's murder?"

"No, but it turns out Barysthenes left a paper adopting me. So, as his son I suppose it is my job to find out who killed him."

"And to look after his pretty young wife. You should pay more attention to the tragedies, Skaphis they have lessons for us. A stranger appears from nowhere and saves Thebes by his cleverness. As a reward they wed him to the widowed queen. But he is not what he seems.

"What part are you playing, Skaphis?"

"Me, I'm just a member of the Chorus. Tell me Psamathe, when I left you at the table with Barysthenes that afternoon, did you see what happened to my knife?"

She looked at him blankly. "No, I didn't notice a knife on the table. Have you lost it?"

"Temporarily, but I'd like to know where it went."

"Sorry, I can't help you there."

The sound of voices came from downstairs. Psamathe leaned forward and gently brushed her hand against Skaphis' knee. "I have guests I must attend to. But, please come again any time. And if you can find someone to help you be in two places at one time, I can afford to pay for a little extra work. If Aristophon is in the money now, then the sooner I find him the better."

"I'll let you know." Skaphis got up to leave.

"You didn't tell me where you got that bowl."

"No I didn't," she smiled, "an admirer gave it to me."

"A secret admirer?"

"They all are, Skaphis my love."

Skaphis noticed that her visitors had been ushered into a downstairs room, and he did not catch a glimpse of them as he departed.

Skaphis was on his way out of the city for the long walk back to the Piraeus when he realized he was close to the house of Euboulos, the third dice player in Lusilla's. On a whim, he threaded into the side streets under the Pnyx hill, following a mental image of the map the trader had scratched in the dirt. His mental image was not clear enough, and it took a couple of false tries before he found himself at the correct door.

He was greeted by an elderly slave who immediately showed him in to a sparsely furnished front room before going to fetch his master.

"Skaphis, you're lucky to have caught me at home, I was on my way out, but come, sit, you have information for me?"

Euboulos gestured for Skaphis to sit in a high backed hard wooden chair. He himself squatted on the edge of a low stool, his hands on his thighs, leaning forward expectantly.

"So, have you found me a cargo of grain to buy?"

"I know someone who has just brought in a cargo from the Black Sea. I only need to locate him, and that is proving a little hard." Skaphis leaned back in his seat and studied Euboulos face.

"Did you know Barysthenes was killed the night you talked to me?"

He could detect no change in the merchant's demeanor.

"I had heard something, yes."

"What happened in the tavern after I left?"

"My dice game broke up a few minutes later. I can't say much of anything happened. Psamathe went shortly after you, Barysthenes stayed and more wine was brought for him."

"You know Psamathe?"

"Psamathe is quite well known."

He stood up with a sudden movement, and called for his slave, who must have been lurking close to the door, having divined the nature of his master's forthcoming request, for he appeared immediately with two cups of wine. Euboulos handed one cup to Skaphis, and reclined on a couch with the second cup. Skaphis drank. It was good wine, mixed with equal quantity water.

"Rhodian," Euboulos said, "You know, the Spartans and us, we make opposite mistakes with our women. In Sparta, citizen women have enormous freedom and are very independent. They even exercise in public: races, athletic contests and so on. Unthinkable here in Athens. But the boys lead such a regimented life, separated from their families and any female influence, that by the time they reach marriageable age they are uninterested in girls. In fact, they say that on their wedding day, a Spartan bride is dressed up as a boy, in order to make her attractive to her husband. And they meet only in the dark and in secret, presumably to get over his squeamishness at actually consorting with a woman. But he does his duty for the fatherland and begets the next generation of warrior.

"Here in Athens, on the other hand, our citizen women are kept under lock and key, and given little chance to learn anything about the topics which interest Athenian men:

war, politics, trade, law. We marry mature men, in their late 20's or early 30's to maidens in their teens. Ideal for the man, you might think. But the very inexperience that guarantees an unsullied succession soon bores him. He thirsts for an intellectual companionship, which his wife's youth and cloistered upbringing make almost impossible. And so we are famous for women like Psamathe, professional 'companions' who fill this gap."

A conversation with Euboulos, Skaphis thought, seemed to continually teeter on the verge of becoming a lecture.

"Did you notice the individual seated at the table between yours and ours?" Skaphis asked.

"Yes, he came in shortly after Kotos. At first I thought he might be a bodyguard."

Skaphis raised an eyebrow at the mention of Kotos' name.

"He didn't make a move when that scuffle broke out, so I came to the conclusion that he was not a bodyguard. I've seen him before, somewhere. Hanging around the docks, I think. He was perfectly positioned to watch Kotos' table, but come to think of it he was also well placed to overhear the conversation at your table."

Euboulos sat upright in his couch and lowered his voice.

"If Barysthenes was involved with Kotos, you may never find out who killed him. Kotos is the center of a web of enterprises down at the Piraeus. None of them entirely on the up and up, and some decidedly crooked. But nobody has ever dared to take him to court. People have been bold, or desperate enough to consider prosecuting him in the past. They have a tendency to find themselves in a mesh of legal difficulties of their own, fending off prosecutions from different quarters on a slew of charges ranging from reasonable to completely trumped up. Or sometimes they simply disappear. In either case, Kotos is no longer troubled."

"Anyway, if you find the owner of that cargo of grain, I am still in the market."

The slave shuffled into the room, silent and unbidden. Apparently anticipating his master's next need, he took away Euboulos' wine cup. Skaphis finished his wine and handed the empty cup to the servant.

"The other day you were telling me about marine insurance," Skaphis said, "is it usual for the underwriter to travel with the cargo?"

"Typically, no, although sometimes he will send an agent to observe the voyage. You'd be amazed at the sorts of scams ship owners will try and pull. I've heard of a case where the same cargo was "sold" two or three times to different insurers. Then a shipwreck was engineered to lose the cargo and pocket the insurance money."

"How about a local grain dealer, like yourself perhaps, would he sail off to the Black Sea to buy wheat there?"

"That's a new one on me, although perhaps that is what things are coming to. No, a local dealer will buy grain at auction in the long colonnade on the Piraeus waterfront. He'll then warehouse it locally and sell it on to retailers, bakers and so on. I can't imagine him having the leisure to go traipsing around the Aegean looking for grain. Unless he knew that there was none to be had in Athens, and his granaries locally were empty or spoken for."

"Or," he continued thoughtfully, "his granaries were full and he had no intention of selling any for the time being."

Euboulos rose from his couch.

"I have to go now, but keep in touch with me. I would be interested to talk to your itinerant grain dealer."

"So would I," said Skaphis.

On the road back to the Piraeus, Skaphis found himself pondering the observation that if the hooded stranger had been perfectly positioned to watch Kotos and listen to Barysthenes, Euboulos had been ideally stationed to observe Barysthenes and overhear Kotos.

chapter **9**

A scuffle was taking place in the back of the tavern when Skaphis returned to Lusilla's. A gangling, well-dressed man had hold of one of the girls by the hair and was pulling her over to his table. The girl's arms were flailing wildly, but the man stayed out of range and she made contact with nothing but air. Two stouter men looked on. One of them, Skaphis noticed, held Thrassia, who was shouting and straining to get into the fight. Lusilla, behind the bar, was looking around the establishment for aid. She spotted Skaphis, blinking through the door, and inclined her head in the direction of the troublemakers.

Skaphis took the thin man from behind, kicking his feet out from under him. Man and girl fell in a heap on the floor. The girl, on top, recovered her composure first and wriggled free, scurrying over to Lusilla, who held her and hugged her like the lost child that in some perverted sense, she was.

One of the thin man's burly companions launched himself horizontally at Skaphis, attempting to grab him round the waist and drag him to the ground. He was built like a wrestler, and if the fight were reduced to a wrestling match, Skaphis wouldn't lay an obol on his own chances. As he came in low and hard, Skaphis kneed him in the face, while stepping aside to deflect the main energy of his charge. The wrestler ended up sprawling across the floor. The third man would have been on top of Skaphis by now if Thrassia hadn't kept a grip on the arm with which he had been restraining her. He was trying to shake himself free and make a grab at Skaphis' back at the same time. She held onto his arm and was yelling a warning to Skaphis. At the same time, Skaphis turned round, and the man finally threw off Thrassia. The sudden release of her restraint made him stumble forward, directly into a two fisted blow which Skaphis unwound at him with all the coiled energy of a discus thrower at the Pan Hellenic Games.

Skaphis stepped back to assess the situation. The victim of his discus punch was out cold at the foot of the table, his head resting sleepily against the leg. The thin man sat on the floor, his face turning purple with rage. He looked about to speak. Skaphis was sure the speech would be strong and full of fighting words. But words were the only fight left in him. Which left the wrestler. He was on one knee, wiping blood from his mouth with the back of one hand. With the other hand, he was reaching for something inside his cloak. Skaphis was faster. Seemingly from nowhere, he conjured a long slender blade into his fist. The wrestler pulled his hand empty from his cloak and stood up, stepping back acquiescent, his unarmed palms facing Skaphis.

The thin man was apoplectic.

"Hubris," he spluttered, "treating a free man as a slave, I'll have you up on a capital charge. You'll regret this day's work."

Lusilla was by Skaphis' side.

"Listen, sir," the 'sir' with all the layers of sarcasm accrued in twenty years of her trade. "These girls belong to me, and you were abusing them. I just asked Skaphis to help me protect my people."

To Skaphis, she said in a stage whisper,

"I see you found your weapon again, sweetie."

The thin man was smiling, his anger seemed to have gone, to be replaced by a self-satisfied smirk.

"So this is Skaphis, ah well, in that case we can forget about this little disagreement." He nodded at his fallen companion. "Wake him up will you."

The wrestler hefted a water jar from the corner of the tavern and poured its contents over his slumbering comrade, gargling him back to life.

The thin man's smirk splayed into a lop-sided grin.

"One capital charge is as good as another." He straightened himself officiously. "Skaphis of the deme Piraeus, I charge you with the murder of Barysthenes, son of Serambos of the deme Aithalidai."

He continued, naming the date on which he should appear before the Archon for preliminary hearings, and then made the pro-forma warnings that Skaphis must not, under pain of death, defile any of the city's sacred places with his presence. As an unacquitted homicide, he would bring pollution to the city. These sacred places included the agora. In Athens, commerce was a religion.

"And now," he concluded, "I have done my duty and must leave. I will not share a roof with a murderer."

His exit was theatrical, flanked by his two companions, self importance reinflated by the very air his words seemed to have sucked out of the tavern. Thrassia threw a drinking horn after them, but her aim did not match her anger, and the horn clattered against the wall beside the door and stuttered to the floor.

"Who the hell was that," Skaphis asked the tavern in general.

Lusilla answered. "His name is Orthagoras. He is a small time legal hack. Prosecutes for hire. He does business mostly with the resident alien community: he'll take their cases to court for them. Or he can be hired for a tactical prosecution. Barysthenes used to do some business with him. Before your time. I wonder who he is working for now."

She continued, "Meanwhile, lover, take the ban seriously. If they catch you in the agora, they can hand you over to the Eleven, for summary execution. No niceties like trials or anything. Someone is behind Orthagoras and wants you out of the way. They'll have eyes and ears in the market."

Her eyes twinkled, "And it's hard to find a lodger who has such a way with the customers."

"Aren't you afraid your roof will be polluted by harboring an unjustified killer?"

"Oh, my roof's been polluted by worse than that in its time, and anyway, if you killed Barysthenes, I'm sure you were justified."

Thrassia was trying to attract Skaphis' attention, pointing at the door of the tavern. He spun round, legs spaced, half crouched ready to lunge or sidestep as the situation might demand. His hand still held the dagger which he had retrieved from the street where Barysthenes body lay. A figure disappeared out of the tavern door.

"It's him," screamed Thrassia, "The messenger - I told you he'd come."

Skaphis slipped the dagger back inside his cloak and plunged out into the road.

Up the street a cluster of men argued as they surged towards the tavern. In the other direction a dull glow from the setting sun lit a despondent mule's measured homeward plod. A mule man held a rope attached to the animal's neck. In the shadows on the far side of the street, a hooded man matched the animal's deliberate pace. There was something contrived about his casual saunter. Skaphis strode after him. The man glanced back and quickened his pace. Skaphis broke into a run and caught up with him as he was about to dart into an alleyway.

"Were you looking for me?"

"I'm sorry, I was told you might have an obol for me."

He cast a hungry look at Skaphis. He had the appearance of a sailor, but one who had spent a little too much time in port.

"I could have two for some information. Why did you run away?"

"I don't know, I saw you there with that big knife, and I said to myself, 'Tertios, is it worth dying for an obol?', 'No,' I answered, 'You'd only spend it on wine anyway, and have nothing left tomorrow. Do yourself a favor and forget the obol, you'll feel better in the morning and be just as broke.'"

Skaphis held out an obol, "You brought a message to Lusilla's for me a few nights ago?"

The sailor nodded and snatched the coin. Another appeared in Skaphis' hand.

"Tell me who gave you the message."

"I was down by the docks late. My ship was wrecked in the spring coasting down from the north. I survived along with the captain, but my master has not been able to replace the ship yet, and hasn't been able to rent us out.

With the navy out of action, there are plenty of seamen to be had. Without us earning our keep, he doesn't let us have any extra coins for pleasures." His eyes were fixed on the small coin in Skaphis' hand.

"I was by the long colonnade and this man came up to me and asked me if I knew where Lusilla's tavern was. He gave me an obol and said there'd be another one for me if I delivered the message that Skaphis should join him. He said his name was Barysthenes."

"And did you come straight here?"

"He said it was urgent, so I hurried. In the dark, I may have lost my way just a little, but I ran to make up for it." He was clutching the obol in one hand, and clasping the hand with his other hand, as if afraid the coin might be talked out of his grasp.

"You didn't stop to spend the obol you had earned?"

He shook his head in vehement denial. Skaphis grabbed a handful of the sailor's cloak and lifted him straight pushing him against the wall. He was surprisingly light. "Are you sure?"

Tertios stammered. "I'd been thirsty for days and I passed an open tavern. But an obol's worth of wine wouldn't delay me for ten minutes."

"It was more than that." Skaphis released his grip on the cloak and the sailor slid to his haunches. "Barysthenes had been dead three hours by the time I got to him."

The sailor stood up and checked his hand, making sure the obol was still there. "That's odd. I could swear I just saw him walk out of Lusilla's."

"Big ugly bearded bastard?"

"No, he was thin and clean shaven."

Skaphis gave him the obol. "Give my regards to Dionysus, he's an old friend of mine."

"Thank you sir, you're a gentleman." The sailor's face lit up as he popped both coins under his tongue for safekeeping: small medicine for a chronic condition.

"By the way, why didn't you wait around for your payment the first time?"

"I was afraid of what might happen to me. It was dark in the tavern and I heard a crashing noise from upstairs. The first obol was good luck. I didn't want to push it."

Skaphis wondered what fate was worse than the life of an indentured sailor, landlocked and destitute. Perhaps death. Perhaps.

The tavern had settled back to normal after the altercation. More drinkers had filed in from the street and were noisily arguing over the wine mixture. Noise, but good-natured noise. The girls were in a knot in the back of the tavern chattering with each other. Skaphis nodded his thanks to Thrassia and sat down at an empty table.

Lusilla joined him, bringing a jug of wine and a platter containing a half loaf of thin bread and a heap of nondescript vegetables, stacked like the remains of a doused campfire.

Skaphis ate while Lusilla poured wine for both of them.

"Was he the messenger?"

"Yes, but he didn't come directly from Barysthenes, he stopped to drink his commission first. And unless he was completely drunk to start with, which I wouldn't put past him, he didn't come from Barysthenes at all."

Lusilla raised her eyebrows.

"He described Barysthenes as thin and beardless, in fact not unlike that bastard Orthagoras."

Skaphis drained his wine cup and continued. "Lusilla, what would you charge me to hire Thrassia for the day tomorrow."

She frowned at him, "You know I don't allow my girls to consort with lodgers, it's not healthy, even if they pay the going rate."

"That's not what I'm talking about. I need to talk to someone up in the market tomorrow, but I don't want to risk breaking this ban. I thought she could slip in for me and get the information I need. She managed to find that messenger. She's pretty quick witted."

"In that case, I'll lend you her for tomorrow, so long as you get her back by nightfall."

"And if I don't?"

"Three obols a day and she's yours."

Skaphis shuttled a silver coin onto her side of the table. It stared up at them like a small and unregarded planet.

"Four days, then and mind you - day work only. What I said about lodgers still goes, and a murderer might not find it too easy to put a new roof over his head."

Her sharp words were blunted by the trace of a smile.

"If you need any night work, lover, you know where to find me."

chapter **10**

Skaphis was wakened by a tentative knocking at his door. A pale light suffused the room. It was impossible to tell if it was the remnant of moonlight or the first pale presage of dawn.

"Mistress told me to go to bed early last night, that you had work for me today."

Thrassia stood by his open door, dressed in an unornamented cloak. A veil was thrown back from her face. She kept her eyes on the floor while Skaphis threw his chlamys over his shoulders. The weights sewn into the hem of the garment settled against his thighs like the gentle prodding of infant fingers.

"You did well bringing me the messenger. His information was important."

A look of pleasure crossed the girl's face at the praise.

"I have some similar work for you to do. There is someone in Athens I want to keep track of, but I have to be in the Piraeus; so I need you to follow the Athenian. Do you think you can do this?"

Thrassia nodded enthusiastically.

Skaphis handed her the fragment of pottery.

"I also need you to find who bought this. Come on, the agora will be open for business in a couple of hours."

Skaphis left Thrassia at the boundary of the agora and made his way to his client's house.

"It's early, I'll go see if Madame is receiving visitors."

The maid showed him into a downstairs room and climbed the stairs to find her mistress.

Skaphis could hear muffled talking through the heavy silence of the house. One of the voices was male. He quickly stepped out into the hall and opened the door to the street in time to see a figure emerge from the back alley. The man's rolling gait was that of an athlete, and looked vaguely familiar. Half furtively he turned to glance behind him as he left, and Skaphis recognized Euboulos, the ubiquitous dice player.

Euboulos caught Skaphis' eye and winked at him, touching his forefinger to his temple. A gesture, Skaphis supposed, intended to convey a mild embarrassment at being seen in a somewhat compromising situation, and asking Skaphis to keep the information in his own head. Alternatively, Skaphis thought as he closed the door, a gesture reinforcing that information was a commodity of value, and could be acquired here.

"It's early, but this is a good time to do business. I don't usually entertain guests until after noon."

Psamathe showed him back into the downstairs room. A small window opened into an interior courtyard. A shaft of sunlight threaded its way through the aperture to illuminate the dust particles which, otherwise unnoticed, filled the room. She lounged in a high backed chair with her back to the light, her shoulder casting a sharp shadow on the floor. Skaphis sat facing her.

"I've hired an assistant to track Protonikos. The cost will be a drachma a day. I've hired them on for four days. I'm hoping that should do the trick. I wanted to confirm your approval."

Psamathe smiled, "And collect an advance payment?"

She stood and lifted a box from a table in the corner of a room. She opened the lid and delicately plucked two coins from its interior. She held the coins in her hand and settled back in her chair. They sat in silence for a few moments. Skaphis observed that her beauty had a dynamic quality. Much of the excitement her presence generated was a property of motion. From the grace of her walk to the gentle animation of her features when she laughed, each movement served to draw your attention away from individual features and towards the whole woman. At rest, her lips were a shade too full, her chin certainly too strong, her brow too broad. The smallest motion defocused your attention and forced you to regard the whole woman. And the whole woman made you want to pick apart the strands of your life and thread them together in a pattern designed with her alone in mind.

"Wasn't that Euboulos I saw leaving when I came in?"

"Skaphis, I am paying you to see things, to find information for me."

She held up one of the coins with the Athenian owl, eyes unnaturally large, facing Skaphis. She closed her fist, then opened it again. The coin had disappeared.

"I know some parlor tricks too. The other side of the coin is that I'm also paying you not to see other things."

She closed her fist and opened it again with a fluid motion. The coin reappeared. Instead of the owl looking at him, the coin showed a head in profile, looking at the wall.

Psamathe tossed the coin to Skaphis along with its twin. "You know I heard a story about a scam involving selling the same cargo to several different insurers. The key to that business deal was to maintain the illusion with each insurer that he was the sole owner of the goods."

"No," said Skaphis, "the key to that proposition was that the goods should disappear and everyone be left empty handed."

She leaned towards him and spoke in a sultry whisper, "But you are good at making things disappear, are you not?"

"They always seem to pop up again somewhere else."

She smiled and leaned back in her seat. Her face grew serious again.

"You told me you met Barysthenes when you were fighting on Munichia Hill. What did you do before that?"

"I was mostly out of town with the fleet. My ship went down at Arginusae, but I was lucky: I was picked up before the storm built up. Twice lucky, I was picked up by Conon and absorbed into his crew to replace battle losses. It was one of the fastest and best disciplined ships in the fleet. And one of the handful to escape the Spartan ambush at Aegospotamoi. Otherwise I'd be feeding Creosote bushes from a shallow grave in the Dardanelles."

"So you returned to a city in chaos, Spartans blockading the port, and a gang of Spartan sympathizers running the place?"

"They never really managed to consolidate their grip on the Piraeus."

"And you joined up with the democrats?"

"The fleet's always been democratic. A ship, in its way is a miniature image of the state. There's a rich guy who gives the orders and is nominally in charge. There's a tough and experienced sailor who steers the boat. And there is a mass of rowers who provide the power. The thing with the ship is that it is obvious who actually propels it. But why this interest in the war?"

She leaned forward, animated.

"*Who* was the war fought between? Us and the Spartans, you say - but you're wrong."

Skaphis raised an eyebrow. "Seems like I remember a few Spartans on the ship decks at Arginusae, but I was busy at the time, maybe I was mistaken."

"Oh there were Spartans involved, but the war itself was really a class struggle. The cavalry class always had a soft spot for Sparta. They'd wear their hair long, Spartan style, and treat the rest of the population like serfs. Meanwhile, the war was relentlessly pursued to the bitter end by populist politicians, despite several chances to halt it on favorable terms. Why? Because they saw that with Sparta in the background, they would never really be safe from their own upper class."

"Or maybe they saw there was profit to be made from war."

"No, Skaphis, the war was a class struggle and its final battle was not Arginusae, but Munichia Hill: was not a defeat, but a victory. But did you ever ask yourself what Barysthenes was doing there?"

"He lived on Munichia Hill."

"No, I mean, how did he manage to survive the purges?"

"Barysthenes was a survivor. I suspect he had friends in the right places. Either that or he kept his head down."

"It's a pity he lost it."

"What?"

"His knack for survival."

"It would certainly have made my life simpler. First I find he adopted me as his son. Now I've been accused of his murder."

"I had heard that." She stood, as if she had come to some decision. "You should talk to my friend Lysias."

"The Piraeus arms manufacturer?"

"He used to be, but his wealth was stolen by the gang of thirty. Now he writes speeches for the law courts."

As Skaphis stood to leave, she touched his arm. "Skaphis, he's good. And I think you might need a good lawyer."

The river of commerce was approaching flood stage at the agora. Thrassia was standing in an eddy by the boundary stone. Veiled, her eyes downcast, she was ignored by the passing streams of market-goers. It struck Skaphis that slaves could stand unnoticed for hours with no need to create a pretense of activity for cover; their very servitude being a sufficient reason for being in a place.

Nobody would consider the presence of a mule standing tethered in a street to be suspicious.

Skaphis swept the odious comparison to the back of his mind and addressed Thrassia gently,

"Did you find Mnesia's booth?"

"Yes it was quite easy, and he immediately recognized the pottery. Seemed disappointed that it had been broken, and wanted to know how I had come across it."

Skaphis had the uneasy feeling he was being watched. A tall figure lounged inside the agora leaning against one of the pillars of the stoa. A spear rested casually in the crook of his elbow and against his shoulder. He appeared to be taking an interest in Skaphis' conversation, or perhaps he was just bored, waiting for a tardy companion to arrive.

Skaphis steered Thrassia away from the market place and they walked through the bustle of the Panathenaic way in the direction of the side streets, which led to Stephanos' house.

"I told him my master had brought it home with him from a drinking party but could not remember where. They had started at one place but then moved on to several others, and he was hazy about the details. But the pitcher broke and he wanted to compensate the owner."

Skaphis smiled at her inventiveness. "Did he remember who he sold it to?"

"Quite clearly, he said he sold a set to Huginos from Piraeus."

Skaphis led Thrassia off the busy Panathenaic way and into the deserted alleyways leading to Stephanos' house. He glanced back to see if anyone had followed them. The alley behind them was empty of anything except the hard shadows of the looming buildings that enclosed it.

The name was unfamiliar to him, but Thrassia said that he was an occasional guest at Lusilla's and that she would know where he lived.

Skaphis stopped in a doorway with a view of the entrance to Stephanos' house; himself in the shadows, while Thrassia stood in the street.

"There is a young Cyzican staying at the house at the end of the road. He traveled to Athens with a certain Aristophon, who we are trying to find. I want you to follow the Cyzican when he comes out of the house, and let me know where he goes. Aristophon is a corn trader from the cavalry class, in his middle years. If you think he has met up with Aristophon, you should follow him. Do you understand?"

She nodded.

He pulled her into the shadows, tucking her small frame under his forearm. The slave emerged from Stephanos' house and strode purposefully down the street for a dozen paces. When out of the immediate vicinity of the house, his pace slowed to an idle saunter. Skaphis put his finger to his lips and held Thrassia close to him bowing his head over the top of hers so that his lips almost brushed the top of her head and his face was certainly invisible to the street. The strength of her back muscles surprised him, as she momentarily resisted his sudden embrace. Her hair had a faint and exotic perfume.

When the slave had passed, he relaxed his grip.

"Thrassia, be careful. Aristophon is the one that Barysthenes was supposed to tail the night he was killed."

She looked up at him, but her face contained neither fear nor excitement, just a transient sadness.

chapter **11**

Psuchion's Tavern was empty in the early afternoon, and the barman had never heard of Aristophon. Skaphis nursed a bowl of cheap wine for a couple of hours watching the desultory clientele, but nobody fit the description of Aristophon. At the point where a second bowl of wine would be necessary to justify his continued presence in the tavern, he decided it was a waste of time and he would come back later.

The Piraeus streets were hot now, devoid of traffic except for the occasional muttering slave. Skaphis' throat felt like a desiccated sponge on a windy beach. He was unsure whether this was caused by too much or too little wine.

Lysias' house was a short distance inland from the tavern. The character of the streets changed. Warehouses and grumbling mule drivers became houses and silent water-girls. The houses, at first mean, grew gradually better appointed as he climbed away from the wharves and trading zone of the port. Halfway up the hill, Lysias' house was not quite at an altitude Skaphis would describe as opulent.

An old slave showed him into a cramped front room and gestured for him to sit. In the corner of the room a large man stood behind a chest-high podium. A pen was in one hand, and a papyrus scroll overlapped the podium, held in place by a bronze statue of a martial figure, helmeted, armed and used as a paperweight. The man raised his penless hand, as if to keep stray ideas from wandering into his document. Skaphis sat silently. The man wrote for a minute or so, scrawling fluently with his pen, dipping it in ink in a rapid motion, which reminded Skaphis of a pigeon pecking at a feeding trough. He thought for a moment, added some more writing, then he wiped the pen with an old piece of rag and placed it on his podium, blotted his new work with a torn scrap of papyrus, lifted the bronze warrior and slid up the scroll. For the first time he looked at Skaphis.

"You have to finish with a direct appeal to the Jurors' self-interest. They may have sworn a solemn oath to uphold the law, but if you can give them a reason to believe a verdict for you lies in their own interest they'll vote for you and the law be damned. So you tell them that the price of grain in the market will be cheaper with this price manipulator out of circulation, or you flatly tell them that they have been aggravated for years by this character lording it over them, and now they have the chance to turn the tables on him."

The slave reappeared with wine, premixed in two goblets. Lysias offered one to Skaphis and reclined with the other on a couch that crowded between the podium and the door. Skaphis still bobbed in the wake of a passing headache. He decided that more wine would help to fend it off and drank from the proffered cup.

"It takes more thought to explain why their wives and daughters will be safer with an adulterer back out on the streets."

A smile edged across Lysias' face.

"But you have legal problems of your own. I'm busy, but I can always squeeze out a few more words for a good cause. And I'm a democrat - any cause can be made to look good to me if there's money in it."

"Psamathe thinks I need your help. I'm accused of killing my partner."

Lysias sat up. Stretched across the length of the couch there was a feline quality to his recumbence. Eager now, he faced Skaphis, his ears seemed to twitch and his tongue inched out of his mouth as if already rehearsing the articulation of a famous defense speech.

"Accidental or deliberate homicide?"

"They're claiming murder, and it certainly looks like murder to me, only I didn't do it."

Lysias tilted his head slightly, as if dismissing this as an overly technical detail.

"Your partner was a citizen?"

Skaphis nodded.

"You say Psamathe sent you. What were you doing in the late political disturbances?"

"Is that so important to you?"

"Oh it doesn't matter to me personally. It's no secret I'm a democrat, but you know the old Solonic law - the only crime in a time of civil unrest is not taking a side. And it has a bearing on your defense."

"I've always been a Piraeus man."

"A fellow democrat, well I'm heartened."

His face looked more thoughtful than heartened.

"You know, murder, of a citizen at least, is treated as much as sacrilege as a crime, hence the ban on entering the Agora. Instead of a Jury court, murder cases are tried by the Areopagus. The juries are filled with men who are prepared to work for three obols a day - not the cream of society - and these days prone to look the other way if you fought for the democracy. But the Areopagus is a law unto itself. Fair, by its own lights, but very conservative.

"Still, to the Areopagus, you must go. First there will be three preliminary hearings, at monthly intervals. There we can argue for a change of jurisdiction, if we can come up with a reason. Perhaps we can argue unintentional homicide - that would pull it down to a lower court. And there's always the other option. But come, you'd better tell me what happened."

Skaphis recounted the events surrounding Barysthenes death, leaving out the discovery of his knife at the murder scene. Lysias listened without interrupting, gradually slouching back into his couch and lay still for a few moments after Skaphis had finished.

"How long had Barysthenes been in the private investigation business?"

"I had the impression he got into the business when he came back from fighting in Sicily. That is when he moved to the Piraeus. Before then he had been a soldier pure and simple, it seems. So that would put it about twelve or thirteen years ago."

"And yourself?"

"Barysthenes hired me on after the war ended. I've been at the trade for a couple of years now."

"What experience do you have in the courts?"

"Not very much, we tended to do investigation for clients who were involved in court cases, rather than speculative prosecution on our own behalf. What prosecutions we did, Barysthenes handled, and were usually settled out of court."

"Well, you will soon have court experience. And if you survive it, there may be some business we can do together. One thing which interests me about Barysthenes though is this - how did he survive the purges?"

"Psamathe asked me the same question."

Lysias sat up again.

"The Governing Council was made up of wealthy conservatives. Old money aristocrats always had pro-

Spartan leanings and were the most willing to collaborate during the occupation. The one thing families with money detest is redistribution of wealth. So over the years they had developed a hatred for freelance prosecutors - they viewed these as little better than extortionists, and worse, they were a method of redistributing wealth from the rich to the opportunistic. Their first action on taking power was to kill them all off. Barysthenes survived, and it would be interesting to know how."

"He was a survivor, I guess. He came back from the Sicilian expedition too."

Lysias finished his wine and put the cup on the floor beside his couch.

"The other group they hated was new money, people who could create their own wealth without inheriting it. And particularly wealthy foreigners, such as my family. We owned a shield factory. Employed over a hundred slaves. My brother and I were summarily arrested on trumped up charges. They were really after our money, which they confiscated. I managed to escape, but my brother was executed.

"The war is over now, though Skaphis, and the new battles are fought not in the planes of Sicily or in the waters of the Hellespont but in the courtrooms. The shields men need are not made of wood and bronze, but of words. And I am a good craftsman of word shields. Give me a couple of days to mull over our strategy and we can start working on our preparation for the preliminary hearings."

He paused for a moment, then continued.

"This Barysthenes interests me. You should find out more about his history."

Skaphis finished his wine and placed the cup on the floor beside Lysias'. He stood up to leave.

"You mentioned another option, what is it?"

"You could always leave town."

Chapter *12*

Psuchion's tavern was busier, but Skaphis was able to occupy the same seat in the corner. His headache appeared to have backed water, but was still hovering within ramming range. Over a couple of hours he poured a bowl of wine into the intervening space, but still it edged closer. He tuned his ears into the conversations at the neighboring tables, closing his eyes to focus his concentration. The talk at the table in front of him was loud and involved storms at sea and exotic island ports. The table behind talked in low tones, of business, it seemed. Skaphis tried to filter out the background noise, but was only able to make out the occasional word. It seemed the discussion centered on the price of grain.

Skaphis dropped off to sleep.

When he woke, the tavern was crowded, the accents around him were foreign and the talk was of women. His wine bowl had been refilled, though he did not recall ordering it. The wine kept him there into the evening. He talked to a couple of men who loosely fit Aristophon's description. He talked to some of the regulars and came to the conclusion that if Aristophon frequented this tavern, he didn't leave much of an impression on the other customers.

He left and trod the night streets to Lusilla's. Thrassia had returned an hour earlier and came down sleepy eyed at Lusilla's bidding to report to Skaphis.

"The Cyzican stayed at the house until afternoon. I then followed him to the market, where he bought fresh fish. He returned to the house. I stayed until dark and nobody came or left, so I walked back home."

"I was no more successful at Psuchion's. Can you go back tomorrow, I have a feeling we are more likely to find Aristophon by following the Cyzican than by watching the tavern. Nobody there seems to have heard of him."

"If she's trudging back up to Athens again she'll need to get her sleep." Lusilla draped a motherly arm around the girl's shoulders and shepherded her out to the back stairs.

Skaphis' headache had finally stopped maneuvering for position and rammed home. He knew it was caused by too much wine in the heat of the day, but the only cure he could think of was more wine in the cool of the evening.

Lusilla brought wine in a pitcher, and two cups. She filled each and sat beside Skaphis.

"I'm very fond of that girl you know lover, she reminds me of myself when I was that age. I wouldn't want any harm to come to her."

"The person she is following is a foreign youth. There's no danger in him as far as I can see, and besides, Thrassia seems able to take care of herself."

"I would have said the same about Barysthenes."

"Lusilla, how long have you known Barysthenes?"

"He's been coming in here for years. Let me think, it seems he turned up in the Piraeus some time after the Sicilian expedition. Come to think of it, I must have first met him very shortly after he returned. He was saved from the quarries by a wealthy Syracusan family who kept him as a house slave. Eventually they must have freed him, or he escaped, and made his way back to Athens. But I noticed that he had picked up a little of the Syracusan accent. Nothing too obvious, but I have an ear for Greek. You get more different nationalities through these doors in a month than you'd find in a Persian army. Anyway, I remember he had a way of lengthening his vowels, a little like you'll hear amongst the Piraeus dock-hands. But it wasn't Piraeus in him, it was pure Syracuse. He lost it fairly soon, so I must have first run into him when he was freshly returned from Sicily.

"I got the impression he was involved in some sort of trading, at first. He seemed to get his start in legal work doing jobs for some of his trading partners. I guess he found the legal work more profitable than the trading. I suspect his specialty was the pre-trial negotiation, with a healthy measure of strong arm work."

"I met him at Munichia. He told me to come join his business after the war; there would be no end of investigative work to be done. And he was right. A couple of people have asked me how he managed to survive the purges."

"Private prosecutors were not popular then, and I didn't see any of Barysthenes. I supposed he'd gone to ground amongst his friends in the Piraeus. But I was up at Athens for a funeral one day during the regime, and I was sure I saw him. He was with a group of armed men. I thought at first he had been arrested, but they were not restraining him, and he seemed to be working with them. I spoke to him, but he looked right through me as if I didn't exist. I later was unsure that it had really been him."

Skaphis finished his wine. It had not cured his headache, but had succeeded in dulling its effect.

"I'm sure there were a lot of reasons for someone to kill Barysthenes." Lusilla stood up. "That wife of his, for example, she's the sort of pretty little thing that can turn a man's head."

"Be careful what you say, you're referring to my mother."

"Well, your mother was here yesterday looking for you."

Thrassia had left for Athens by the time Skaphis woke. He wondered if he could be sure the Cyzican lad was harmless. He had been in the Piraeus the night Barysthenes was killed.

Huginos lived close to the corn market. His house formed a hollow square round a tight courtyard. There were no doors on the outside of the square. The courtyard was entered through a narrow close. An acrid smell loitered in the close like an unwelcome party guest. Two entire sides of the courtyard appeared to be taken up with storerooms. Windowless, these had entrances both on the ground floor and up external stairs. The house occupied the other two, shaded sides of the courtyard. The morning shadows were deep, and the house was shuttered and still.

The storeroom was chained closed, but Skaphis was able to peer through the gap between the two wagon-width doors. Against one wall of the storeroom, massive ceramic storage jars were stacked three deep, filling the space from floor to ceiling, like the hold of a well-loaded ship. The bottom of each jar tapered to a conical point. A single jar could not stand on its own. As a tightly packed phalanx, hemmed in by the storeroom wall, or by the hull of a ship, they stood firm, each supported by its neighbor's shoulders. The benefit of this amphora design was apparent with the second stacked row: the pointed base of each amphora slotted neatly into the interstices between the members of the bottom row, the way the legs of the rowers in the top tier of a fighting ship slotted between the shoulders of the rowers on the lower tiers. The handles were distinctive, squared off at the top. These occupied about a quarter of the warehouse. The remainder of the space was filled with bulging sacks stacked like headless corpses outside a defeated city.

"The master doesn't like spies."

Skaphis was tall but the slave loomed above him. Thessalian, by his sibilant speech, and looked like he would be a handy fighter with a spear handle. He held a spear handle in his right hand, its base resting in the dirt by his foot.

A slight sound scuffled in the dirt by Skaphis' feet, attracting his attention. A rat half under the storeroom door, startled by the bright light and the human presence in the courtyard, turned and scurried back into the gloom. Without turning, Skaphis kicked hard at the base of the Thracian's staff. As the top of the shaft rocked towards him, he grabbed it with both hands and twisted it out of the slave's grasp.

"Your master probably doesn't like you roughing up guests either, so I'm sure you're safer without this."

Skaphis laid the shaft in the dirt. The slave stared at Skaphis with a look of smoldering, but impotent resentment, rubbing the hand from which Skaphis had wrenched the spear.

"But you are no guest of mine."

A man emerged from the house, buckling his robe over his shoulder. The slave stepped back deferentially. Closer, Skaphis noticed, to the grounded staff.

"What business is my storeroom of yours?"

"I was looking for life, but did not want to wake you up if I was too early for the house. I thought a slave might be holed up in there."

The man smiled. "Well you succeeded in waking the house at that. What is your business?"

"My partner was murdered close to here a week ago, I found this under his body." Skaphis handed the pottery fragment to Huginos. He examined it closely and gave it back to Skaphis.

"And what has this to do with me?"

"You bought this pot at the agora in Athens a month ago at the stall of Mnesicles."

Huginos laughed. "There must be thousands of pots with a design like this."

"Actually, no, this is high quality work, only for the most discriminating, and wealthy customers. It was part of a set. Oedipus at the crossroads and so forth."

"You seem to be quite a pottery expert."

Skaphis followed him into the house. The slave picked the spear shaft out of the dust and lurked in the courtyard.

"We're a bit late getting going this morning. I had a symposium here last night and, well, you know how these affairs go."

They sat in the men's room. A stale wine smell permeated the place, like Lusilla's in the morning before the girls had drawn water and mopped out the detritus of the previous evening.

"I did buy a set of pots as you describe, especially fancy for a big celebration I was planning. One of the pots was missing the next day. I assumed it had been broken and the houseboy got a beating for it. But he swore blind he didn't know what happened to it. The party did get a little unruly towards the end. There were a number of gatecrashers I didn't recognize, but I was in a hospitable

111

frame of mind, and did not have them ejected. I'd guess one of them walked off with the pot, or maybe one of the dancing girls did."

"Who supplied the dancers?"

"We had a harp girl and a couple of aulos players from Polyctor the Samian. He has a school a few blocks from here. He also laid on the dancing girls. I've been meaning to ask the scoundrel if one of his people is a pot the richer.

"On the other hand, perhaps your partner crashed my party and walked off with the pitcher, what was he like?"

"A taciturn bastard, beard, full head of hair, fiftyish, war wound across his forehead."

"You're describing half the Piraeus."

"That's about as close as I've got to his killer too."

Skaphis stood.

"Be careful what doors you peer through, pot man. Not all of the Piraeus is as easy going as I am. And some have more effective help."

"Advice somebody should have given my partner."

Polyctor's music school occupied the shaded side of a courtyard less cramped than Huginos's and a small distance away. The harsh buzzing sound of a swarm of auloi being played in unison guided Skaphis' steps from four hundred paces out. Around the entrance to the courtyard, a knot of young men lounged in the street, chatting amiably. They did not seem to be particularly interested in the music. The sun cast a sharp shadow across the diagonal of the courtyard. In the triangle of shade, a handful of musicians sat on short three legged stools. An instructor walked between them, tapping out time by beating a stick against his leg. The musicians were all young women.

Each girl played the twin aulos pipes. A leather strap looped around the back of her neck and over her cheeks, providing pressure to blow against. Despite this, the girls' faces were red, and Skaphis could see the veins bulging on the neck of the closest girl with the effort of blowing.

"Unison, please, unison."

The instructor tapped with his stick against the wall of the courtyard. Each hand played its own pipe, left and right fingers moving in an identical pattern. The tune was a slow rhythmic one, a battle march. The loud wailing of the pipes playing a simple sequence of intervals in concord brought a chill to Skaphis' spine. The insistent melody seemed to push onwards to an unwavering enemy, the rhythm coordinating the footsteps of an advancing spear-line.

"Drone the left hand now."

The girls held closed the holes on the left pipe and continued playing with the right hand. The resulting music had a more primitive sound, the left pipe emitting a single low note, wavering only as the girls breathed. The right pipe held a high skirling melody, and Skaphis could hear his shield line walk, heedless, into the first unimaginable horror of a heavy infantry clash.

The nearest girl sat on the shadow line; her legs were in the shade, her arms and head in the glare of the sun. Her hair had been stuffed into a net, but tendrils escaped to worry her face. Above the playing-halter, her cheek bulged like an oarsman's forearm over his bandaged wrist. A narrow rim of sweat darkened the top of the halter.

"That's not bad, take a break girls, and we'll start work on a new dance."

The instructor had a board mounted on an easel, on which he began scratching with a stylus. At first, Skaphis assumed he was writing Greek, but as he got closer, he saw that the letters were unfamiliar. They reminded him of Phoenician. The girls had stood up and placed their instruments on their stools, the one girl moving her stool deeper into the shade. She had slid the leather halter down from her mouth so that it hung like a yoke around her neck. A light red weal marked its former position across her cheek. She was tightening the drawstring of her hair net, packing in the escaped strands.

"I'm looking for Polyctor."

"You've found him, but I don't rent out my musicians just to anybody off the street, you'll need to be referred. I run a respectable music school, and only take my players to proper occasions. House parties, yes but only house parties of the thoughtful, restrained sort."

"Like Huginos's?"

"Huginos is an old client, did he refer you to me?"

"He told me you supplied music for his party a week ago."

"I was there with two of my better aulos girls and a kithara player. I also supplied dancers, although I subcontract those from a Melian dance-master. Supple wenches they are too."

The girls had split into two groups. One group stood in the shaded corner of the courtyard, drinking water and chattering with each other. A smaller group was close to the entrance to the courtyard, trading glances and muffled words with the young men in the street. An invisible line across the threshold of the courtyard seemed to separate them, boys from girls. But that line was much thinner than in most of Athenian society, outside the mercenary freedom of the brothels.

"He also tells me one of his pitchers, an expensive piece, went missing after the party."

"And he's blaming me. Typical, that is. The whole affair was unruly and a number of young men came towards the end. They had already been at another party and were well gone with drink before they arrived. Any one of them might have taken a pitcher, especially if it was full of wine."

"Did you recognize any of them?"

"The invited guests were all business associates of Huginos's, men who are well known around the Piraeus, and who would not take kindly to being accused of thievery."

He mentioned a handful of names, none of which were familiar to Skaphis, with the exception of Kotos.

"And the young men who gatecrashed the party, did you know any of them?"

"Not by name, although I'm pretty sure I've seen one of them hanging around here. The youths these days don't seem to have anything better to do with their energy than to hang around the music schools ogling the girls. In my day, we were under arms and off at the frontier watch posts, or guarding the long walls."

The music teacher smiled.

"Well, when I say 'we' I mean as a group, we were doing these heroic things. Personally, I spent most of my time under a tree practicing the kithara."

Skaphis found himself liking this tiny self-deprecating musician.

"Cattana, come here a moment, please."

A girl walked over to the music teacher from the group by the entrance.

"At Huginos's party last week, remember the drunks who came in late. One of them looked familiar to me, do you know who I mean?"

The girl nodded.

"I know who you mean. I think he left with Mione. She would know him."

"Mione was the kithara player." Polyctor answered Skaphis' unspoken question. "My musicians are paid well for their performances. What they do afterwards is their own business."

Skaphis faced the girl. "Did they take a pitcher of wine away from party?"

Cattana paused and looked down briefly before answering.

"I didn't see."

But her pause contradicted her answer. Skaphis believed the pause.

"Mione will be here an hour before sunset. Meanwhile we have a tune to learn."

He turned back to his board and continued scrawling unintelligible symbols. As Skaphis passed through the gateway into the street, he was gathering his musicians together again.

"Come ladies, you see the notes, here is the rhythm."

He tapped out a rhythm with his stick against the leg of the easel. Skaphis was down the block and had turned his stride in the direction of Munichia and Barysthenes' house when the first quavering tremolo of the aulos reeds cut through the noontime languor of the street.

His intent to visit Astra declined with every step in the direction of her house. She represented a host of complications and questions, none of which he felt close to being able to answer. His status, both as heir apparent and accused murderer of her husband, added a layer of ambiguity to a situation that did not lack ambiguity to start with. When his route took him close to Lysias' house, Skaphis found it easy to persuade himself that he needed to talk to his lawyer.

"I've been thinking about your case, come in and take a seat."

Lysias offered him wine, but Skaphis declined. He had decided to experiment with the effect of abstinence on his feeling of well-being. It was too early to anticipate the results of the experiment, but he had survived the racket of massed aulos pipes without a hint of yesterday's headache returning, so the early indications were good.

"Your preliminary hearing comes up next week in front of the Basileus. As we discussed before, they will determine which court has jurisdiction. First-degree murder, and the case will go to the Areopagus. Now, as you know, the Areopagus is made up of all the living ex-archons. The archonships are just beginning to open themselves up to the broader citizenry."

"A lesser charge of homicide would go to a lower jury court. Those juries are chosen by lot from the available pool and paid a couple of obols a day for their time. That is barely a subsistence wage, so nobody with a better use of his time would show up for that duty. So, the juries are stacked with older men of the poorer classes: exactly those who fought against the governing council. A Piraeus man such as yourself, particularly with a good war record and creditable service to the democracy during our recent troubles, can expect much better treatment at the hands of a jury than in front of the Areopagus.

"So I suggest this strategy: at the preliminary hearings we claim that Barysthenes was killed in a fight, which, incidentally, he started. That would make it unintentional homicide, and in the jurisdiction of a jury court. Then for the jury trial, we paint a picture of Barysthenes in the worst possible light. We draw a contrast between you, the war hero fresh returned from restoring the democracy and Barysthenes, the long time private investigator, skulking around the Piraeus, and no doubt an agent of the thirty. A good speech, and we'll have them eating out of the palms of our hands."

"There's only one problem."

"What is that?"

"I didn't kill Barysthenes."

Lysias gave Skaphis the look a schoolmaster might give a slow but promising student for a particularly obtuse answer.

"Skaphis, my dear fellow, it is a mistake to let the truth get in the way of a good defense. Unless someone saw Barysthenes killed, all the jury has to go on is probability. A good prosecutor will point out that you have benefited from his death by inheriting his estate; he will ask who in Athens is more likely to kill him than the one who stands to gain by his death. They'll ask who is more likely to commit murder than a man who sees a little too much of his partner's wife.

"Yes, I have heard a rumor to that effect. And, true or not, put out by the prosecution themselves or not, it can add the weight of probability to their case."

"But I didn't gain much, most of his money is out on loan somewhere and I haven't been able to track it down. And besides, I didn't know I was going to inherit."

"They can make hay out of that too. The very disappearance of the money can be pointed to as a sign that you were already defrauding your partner, that you and his wife were stashing away his resources for the day that you would kill him and abscond. No, there is too much that points to you as the probable killer for a court to ignore. Your best strategy is to make a strong play to move the jurisdiction to a lower court, and the surest way to do this is to admit the killing but give a convincing story that it was in the course of a brawl, and not premeditated. In the lower court we can play on the jury's prejudices and tell them a story which makes them want to thank you for taking the trouble to kill Barysthenes and save them the effort of doing it themselves later. Of course, there is one other option."

"What's that?"

"Find who really killed Barysthenes."

Astra seemed not to be at home. Skaphis peered into the kitchen, then sat in the men's room and waited. He recalled sitting here with his partner's body laid out on a low table. Now the room had an emptiness at its center. Missing was an essential maleness. The furniture was the same as he had remembered it, but the couches had been pulled to the periphery, giving a feeling of space rather than the cramped comradeship of their usual disarray. A female touch, Skaphis thought. He pulled the end of one of the couches towards the middle of the room and reclined. He had forgotten how cool Barysthenes' house was in the afternoon.

He heard a faint noise from upstairs, but ignored it; perhaps the scuttling of a housebound mouse. A fly settled lazily on the doorframe. A second sound was louder and more persistent. Skaphis balanced his way up the stairs. Astra was sitting at her loom with her back to him. She was working with an easy rhythm, swaying gently on her stool as she passed the shuttle back and forth between the longitudinal warps. Skaphis noticed the cloth was different to the last time he had been there. The hoplite armor and weapons were gone.

She turned her head and a small smile quartered across her face. She kept working but inclined her head to a second stool.

"I've been trying to improve my weaving. I used to be quite good at it, but haven't needed to do so much recently."

Skaphis folded himself onto the second stool, leaning his back against the wall.

"Have you made any progress at finding the money?"

"Nothing definitive, but I'm working on it. You came by Lusilla's yesterday?"

"You could stay here you know, you don't need to be paying rent there."

She kept working with her hands deftly weaving the shuttle between the gently oscillating warps.

"Astra, I've been arraigned for Barysthenes' murder. It would look bad for me to be too fast to grab his estate."

"I had heard. What will happen now?"

"There will be a trial first, though there will be preliminary hearings at monthly intervals. The thing is, Astra, the prosecutor is a hack named Orthagoras. He works for hire. I need to know who is really behind the prosecution. Most obvious would be someone from the family who would inherit if Barysthenes had not adopted me. Who is the closest relative?"

Astra worked in silence for a few moments till she reached the end of a row. She then slackened a stretch of wool from her shuttle and hung it on a hook on her weaving frame.

"I told you, there was a cousin in Italy, he turned up around the time when my husband was imprisoned in Sicily."

She turned from her loom and faced Skaphis, her knee less than a handbreadth from his. Skaphis shifted his weight uneasily on the tiny stool. He had sat on many a hard rowing bench in his time, but none matched the discomfort of this weaving stool.

He stood.

"I need to go Astra, I may finally have a good lead on someone who can shed some light on Barysthenes' murder."

She turned back to her work and unhitched her shuttle.

"Ignorance is sometimes a good thing, Skaphis."

chapter **13**

Skaphis was at the entrance to Polyctor's music school before he was able to hear the sound of kithara practice. The aulos was loud and, to Skaphis' ear, the music of war. The warships of the fleet had used the aulos as the melody against which the straining orchestration of the oars beat in rhythmic counterpoint. The instrument had enough penetration to be heard above the creaking of two hundred oars pulled in unison, above the barked commands of officers and the muffled curses of marines trying to maintain their precarious foothold on a drenched and pulsing deck. The kithara was everything the aulos was not: quiet, melodic, thoughtful, an instrument of peace.

Mione was Polyctor's only student. Master and pupil sat at right angles, Polyctor's back to the courtyard entrance. The youths no longer lounged in the street, as if the harsh afternoon heat had baked them dry and they had crumbled like arid stonework into the city dust.

The U shaped wooden frame of the kithara rested on Mione's lap. At its base was a square sound box from which seven strings stretched to a dowel that reclined between the two arms of the U. Her left forearm passed through a strap on the sound box, her left fingers gently touching the strings. Her right hand held a small white plectrum, which was attached to the kithara frame with a leather chord. As she strummed, she lightly touched strings with her left hand, damping out their sound. The effect was, as she changed the combination of damped strings, the overall sound of the instrument changed.

Inside the courtyard, the individual notes of the tune became more distinct. The instructor played a repetitive sequence of low notes. The rhythm was complicated: it kept seeming to settle into a pattern, then, having established it, broke it and started over. Mione was now plucking single notes on her Kithara with the index finger, while damping strings with the other fingers of her left hand and strumming with the plectrum grasped in her right hand.

Skaphis found his feet shuffling to the rhythm of the tune in the dust of the courtyard. Mione touched the strings differently with her left hand, not damping them, but dividing them in two. The touch raised the pitch. In addition to being higher in pitch, the quality of the tone changed: the note rang purer, but in some way seemed more hollow. The melody spiraled upward, shaking off the earthy resonances of the bass line and ended with notes so soft and high that Skaphis was unsure whether he had heard or imagined the last phrase.

Skaphis clapped his hands in time with the now ceased rhythm. Polyctor hung his instrument on a wooden frame.

"An aficionado, I see. Mione, this music lover is interested in Huginos's feast, or at least in a pot which he thinks went missing from it."

The girl laid her kithara in her lap, sliding her wrist out of its strap. The ivory pointer dangled from its chord tracing a slow arc above the dirt.

"I didn't take the pot."

"Nobody is saying that you did. Do you remember the night?"

"Yes. The party started quiet. Mainly older men, and the talk was all business. I played an ode which they liked: it was one of the old Dorian ones, easy to play, but a crowd pleaser for men of a certain age and a certain level of sophistication."

"She's being polite," Polyctor interjected, "She means it was the kind of rustic folksong that the uncultured masses mistake for music."

Mione continued, "Nevertheless, they liked it and asked me to stay around so that I could accompany them in their singing later on."

She had reeled in the plectrum and as she talked was soundlessly touching the strings of the kithara playing the silent intervals of a tune heard only in her head.

"I waited in the kitchen while they drank. When I came back in to play again, there were twice as many men in the room, sitting and standing. Huginos wasn't there anymore, but some younger men had joined the group. I'd seen a couple of them before, hanging around here." She nodded towards the courtyard entrance.

Huginos came back while we were finishing the song, and a bit of an argument developed. One or two of the older men left. I slipped out with Herakleides, who I had met here. He said he knew another party, where they were sure to need some music."

"And he took the wine jug?"

"He said he had brought it with him. A couple of the older men seemed to be going the same way: we followed them through the streets, but after we had gone a couple of blocks, Herakleides seemed to lose interest in the party. He told me to get on home, and tipped me a half drachma. He kept the wine though."

"Do you know where he lives?"

She looked up from the kithara, which she had been nursing on her lap like a sleeping baby.

"No, but I'm pretty sure you'd find him here tomorrow about this time."

Mione turned her kithara over and slid her hand through the leather strap at the top of the sound box as if she had turned her infant on its stomach and was gently massaging its back.

"So you'll get another chance to indulge your passion for music." Polyctor lifted his kithara from its stand.

"Good, I don't seem to have been indulging many passions recently." Skaphis shambled out of the courtyard to the complicated tones of an anapest: emphatically not folk music.

Euboulos was at Lusilla's when Skaphis returned. On his table were an almost empty mixing bowl and three wine cups. He beckoned Skaphis over to the table. Skaphis sat by one of the wine cups. In the cup was the dregs of a wine draught. Lusilla cleared the dirty cups away and gave Skaphis a clean one. Along with the wine cup she gave him a dirty look, which he was unable to parse. At a gesture from Euboulos, she brought more wine and water in separate pitchers. She poured the wine first into the bowl, then a greater quantity of water. She mixed them with a single adroit curl of a ladle, then served the liquid into their separate cups.

"Sometimes I think business would be impossible without wine to lubricate it. But I believe I'm wrong, it's life that would be impossible."

Euboulos pushed a plate of olives over to Skaphis.

"Are you still looking for your grain dealer?"

"He seems to have gone to ground, but I still have hope of finding him."

"I hear you are under indictment for your partner's death."

"Yes, my lawyer says I should admit to unintentional homicide."

"Perhaps a good strategy; Barysthenes had enemies, you can count on the jury containing a few. It would not be too hard to imagine an argument with him turning violent. I've been thinking about your grain dealer, though, he puzzles me. Why go to the Black Sea to buy grain, why not wait here and bid for it on the dock? You make money as a dealer by turning stock over, not by traveling with it around the Aegean."

"According to the ship owner, he bought the grain for half the price in Cyzicus that he would have paid at the dock, even when you figure in shipping cost."

"Right, so it was a good business move, but how could he know it would be? What if the prices dropped in Athens while he was away?"

"He was apparently getting into maritime insurance."

"Insurance is a way to make extra money work for a passive investor. It'd be an unusual departure for an active trader. You need your money at home, ready to make a play on the market. No, I think his behavior makes no sense unless he knew the prices were going up in Athens."

"How could he know the prices would go up, you said yourself the market could just as easily have dropped."

"Unless he got some unusually unequivocal and accurate information from an oracle, there's only one way he could know that: if he was manipulating the market by hoarding grain himself."

Skaphis finished his wine and refilled the cup from the mixing bowl. The outside of the bowl showed a scene celebrating labor: stevedores each back-bowed with a single man sized amphora climbed the gangplank from a deep-breasted cargo ship. A deck cargo of amphoras was stacked two deep. The artist had been successful in conveying the weight of the amphora and the heaviness of the toil through the coiled posture of the workers. Each man's load seemed to pose an imminent threat of buckling his crouched legs and squashing him onto the dock.

"When we were on the road to Athens, a mule train passed us, and you were able to identify the type of wine they carried, how did you do that?"

"Easy – the shape of the amphoras told me the island they came from."

Skaphis dipped his finger in his wine and traced a shape of the urns he had seen in Huginos's storage room.

"I saw amphoras like this stacked in a warehouse, what would they contain?"

"From the shape, they're from the Black Sea. Can't guess what they'd contain, though, amphoras are used to transport everything from wine to pickled fish. Everything except wheat, that is, which comes in sacks."

"Funny you should say that, the remainder of the storeroom was filled with sacks."

"Now, that is interesting."

He sat in silence for a moment, taking an olive and nibbling thoughtfully around the pit as if scraping the flesh of an oyster from the periphery of a large and precious pearl.

"You were in the navy, Skaphis, I believe, where did you fight?"

"My last action was more of a massacre than a fight, the navy was caught by surprise on the beach, with most of the crews out foraging. I was lucky, I suppose, our crew was close at hand. The boatswain was a hard bastard and a stickler for protocol. The result was, we went hungry, but were close to the ship when the Spartans sailed into the bay. We escaped by a hard row."

"Aegospotamoi: Goat Rivers, a bad name for Athens. But what were the Athenian and Spartan fleets doing in the Hellespont in the first place, hundreds of miles from either city?"

He paused to sip his wine. Skaphis assumed Euboulos would answer his own question, so remained silent.

"Of course, the Hellespont is the entrance to the Black Sea and the grain trade. The Spartans were interested in cutting off the grain supply, the Athenians had to keep it open. So by placing a fleet across our grain route, the Spartans were able to force us into a strategic battle."

Lusilla was scowling at Skaphis from behind the bar. He caught her eye, but was unable to decipher any meaning in her look. Euboulos continued his dissertation on recent Athenian history.

"Now where was the other great disaster of the war?"

He paused only briefly before answering his own question.

"Sicily - as far west as Aegospotamoi is east. What on earth were we doing invading such a large and remote island? Well, Sicily is a great grain producer; we were simply trying to acquire an alternate source. The history of Athens in the last fifty years is largely a history of us trying to secure food supplies for a burgeoning population. Of course, the effect of these military disasters, along with disease, has been that our population is not burgeoning any more. But we are still very sensitive as a city to perturbations in our grain supply."

"How much do you know about the Sicilian expedition?" Skaphis asked.

Euboulos filled his wine cup and took a long drink before answering, as if loosening the flecks of memory from the back of his throat.

"A disaster from start to finish. We were beaten in battle and in siege warfare. We attempted to wall in their town, they walled in our wall. Then they blockaded our ships in the harbor: instead of the besiegers, we became besieged. We were finally forced to retreat across country: night marches over unfamiliar terrain. By day, their cavalry harried us mercilessly. Our foragers were unable to get far from the main body of troops without being cut down. I was so hungry and exhausted, I'd have welcomed the relief of a spear thrust or sword stroke: the whole retreat was a living nightmare."

"You were there?"

"I came in the second wave, but I was there to the sorry end."

He paused and drank more wine, slaking, it seemed, a remembered thirst.

"Which was death for most of us. Our columns were initially strong, but we became fragmented in night marches and were cut down at the river crossings. A fraction of the expedition was taken prisoner, but our troubles didn't end there. They imprisoned us in the stone quarries. The conditions were terrible: cramped and dirty, no protection from the heat of the day or the cold of the night, and they kept us underfed. Disease was rampant, and we died like flies."

He paused again, as if the ghosts of an army reprimanded his inconstancy in not sharing their common fate.

"Ironic, it was not the strength of my shield arm, or the prowess of the sword arm that saved my skin, though I was proud of both. The Syracusans were very fond of drama, but had little exposure to the more modern plays. My knowledge of Euripides saved me. I was bought as a house slave by one of their wealthier citizens and trotted out at parties to recite speeches for the benefit of guests."

Skaphis wondered what other quiet talents perished in the wanton slaughter of the fighting retreat or the slow wasting of the stone quarries.

"Anyway, the point of this is that we are, as a city, very sensitive to fluctuations in our grain supply. In war, constricting our supply can bring us to fight on unfavorable terms. In peace, constricting the supply can bring vast profit. It can also bring harsh punishment: the penalty for manipulating the grain market is death."

"And you suspect Aristophon of manipulating the market?"

"He couldn't do it by himself, the volumes are too big, and it would be too obvious. No, it would need a group of traders working together as a cartel. But secrecy would be absolutely imperative. There are many eyes in the market place, not just the official ones of the market regulators, but all the other buyers and sellers. Any hint of collusion would invite a private prosecution for anti-competitive behavior."

"So maintaining the security of the operation would be of paramount importance?"

"The stakes would be high. Enormous amounts of money to be made if the plan is successful, but prosecution on a capital charge as a potential downside."

Motive enough for murder, Skaphis thought.

"Did you know Barysthenes in Sicily?"

"No, I ran into him a few years ago. There are not so many survivors of that expedition in the city. I bought him a drink and chatted about old times. But he seemed reticent and unwilling to drag up old ghosts. Those wheat sacks, where did you see them? Maybe I can do a deal."

"You're still looking to buy wheat?"

"There's money to be made in wheat trading, sure enough, but there's also money in knowledge, applied right."

"You mean you want to blackmail cartel members with threatened prosecution?"

Euboulos smiled, and picked another olive to worry with his teeth.

"Look at it this way, it would be doing my city a service to break up a wheat cartel. A service which has cost us fleets in the past."

"And making a little money into the bargain."

He picked another pair of olives from the plate and rose to leave.

"Be careful, Skaphis, where there is money there is often also danger."

chapter *14*

Skaphis woke to an insistent tapping on the door of his cell. Dawn was yet to give more than a wan hint of a new day lurking beyond the eastern sky, but a late moon spread its diffuse light through the tiny aperture in the wall.

"Skaphis, get up you bastard, I need to speak to you."

Skaphis threw his cloak over his shoulders and unlatched the door to let his landlady in.

"You're making too many night visits, the tavern might start talking."

Lusilla had an earthenware lantern in her hand. Her face flickered in its low light.

"She hasn't come back yet. I should never have let her get involved with you."

Skaphis wondered, unkindly, if her concern was that of an owner over potential loss of her property. But her face belied that assumption. Skaphis sat on his couch and tied on his boots.

"I'm sure she's fine. She was probably too late up in the city and decided to stay up there rather than walk back to the Piraeus in the dark."

"But where would she stay? She doesn't know anybody up there."

"Don't worry, Lusilla, I'll find her. I need to get her back today, after all, I only paid for three days."

But as he left the room, an uneasy feeling developed in the pit of his stomach.

131

Dawn traffic clogged the road to Athens. All was going in the same direction: up from the sea to the markets of the city. Skaphis strode with a steady stream of pedestrians along the verge of the road, in which a long mule train threaded up to town like a string of wooden beads on a cheap hempen necklace. Each mule carried a pair of sacks slung like panniers and a couple more balanced on top of its back, held in place by a wicker frame. As the mules braided with slow deliberation up the road, the loads swayed in sympathetic rhythm like awkward shadow riders.

The last mule in the string had a tendency to stop or to stray sideward from the road. When this happened, the whole column shuddered as each animal was pulled by the rope which bound it to its neighbor. A muleteer would then launch into the flank or haunches of the refractory beast with his switch while calling down the wrath of all the gods and several by name on the ancestors of the hapless animal, on its previous owner for a swindler and on the cargo. He admitted to being behind on his sacrifices but would renew them forthwith if he could only get up to market in a timely fashion. Skaphis wondered which god liked mule meat.

"Mule driver, what is your cargo?"

"Wheat, from the Black sea. There's god knows how much of it on the road today."

Skaphis doubled the slow moving mule column. He couldn't help feeling that he was going the wrong way. He was sure that the reason Thrassia had not returned last night was that she had got onto the trail of Aristophon. And he felt in his gut that Aristophon's trail lay in the Piraeus. But its start was in Athens. The mule driver was right though: before he reached the city he passed three similarly laden convoys.

"You've found Aristophon?"

Stephanos let Skaphis directly into his sitting room. The slave boy was nowhere to be seen. Without the slave, the master seemed more hospitable.

"Not quite, they've never heard of him at the tavern where he said he could be contacted."

Skaphis took the proffered cup of water and slice of bread. The bread verged on stale. The water was tinctured with wine, a pale red suffusing the liquid like blood in the ripples on a summer beach.

"Have you heard from him?"

"No."

Stephanos poured himself some water.

"But I'm very worried."

Skaphis believed the second statement at least. "The Cyzican youth who sailed over with Aristophon. He was here last time I was up. I'd like to talk to him."

"You've seen service in the war, Skaphis, you must know the kind of bonds of comradeship which can form in combat."

"Perhaps in the cavalry, rowers smell too bad to bond with."

"Aristophon and I did our military training in the ephebes together. Then we were in the same cavalry unit. The heavy infantry consider the cavalry to be soft, because we don't fight it out shield to shield with the enemy. But we spend time in the field when the infantry is safe inside the city, patrolling the outposts, scouting, raiding."

"A tiring branch of the military profession." Skaphis remembered the utter exhaustion with which he would lay himself down on a beach, his back clenching and a dull ache from old blisters in his hands.

Stephanos missed or ignored the sarcasm in his tone.

"After our navy were defeated, the Spartans had us at their mercy. The only rational course was to come to some sort of rapprochement with them. And it seemed more likely that they would give favorable terms to a government run by a small number of leading figures: one more closely resembling their system."

"The Spartans have never been great admirers of democracy, I'll give you that."

"On the other hand, democracy is deeply rooted in Athens. Even while decrying the coarse habits of the Piraeus mob, while complaining about the cheap rhetoric of the rabble rousing popular politicians, the Athenian middle class as a whole will defend the democracy to the hilt. So, in order to establish a non-democratic government, it was necessary to push into exile the more radical democratic elements. You have to understand though, it was a matter of the survival or annihilation of this great city. The Spartans could have razed it to the ground, killed all the men and sold the women and children as slaves. In the face of this reality, the discomfort of a few had to be sacrificed for the survival of the many."

He looked down at his hands, in which a piece of bread had been wrung into crumbs.

"It seems that shared guilt as well as shared combat can strengthen a friendship."

"And the Cyzican?"

"He's in the Piraeus. He went down yesterday to try and arrange passage home. He didn't come back last night. I expect he stayed down there. I told him to look up Aristophon's friend Alexis, as he might have a ship sailing in the right direction."

Skaphis was right; the trail did lead back to the Piraeus. Being right didn't make his feet any less sore.

Chapter **15**

A noontime sun baked the ascent to Alexis' house. A pebble had worked its way into Skaphis' boot, and as he climbed the hill he tried to maneuver it into the crook of his big toe where it would cause the least hurt. Gravity gnawed at the muscles of his legs, just as anxiety gnawed at his mind.

Skaphis sat down outside Alexis' house and untied his boot to remove the stone that had been annoying him. In the sea below, white caps seemed as remote as the sudden frown on the face of a sleeping lover. Before entering, Skaphis circled the house, in case Thrassia was lurking in the vicinity, but there was no sign of her.

Alexis was discussing business with two vaguely foreign sounding Greeks. Skaphis waited outside until they left, and then was shown into Alexis' sitting room. The model ship that Alexis had been carving sat on a shelf leaning on its curved keel, like a ship drawn up on the beach with its oars stacked by its side and crew foraging for their evening meal. Beside it, another completed model was supported on a pair of V-shaped stands so that it seemed to sail even-keeled on an invisible sea. Alexis had attached miniature oars to the model - three banks stacked one on top of the other, thirty or so to a bank. This was a trireme: a ship of war, nigh on 200 rowers able to project it across a maritime empire without let or hindrance from contrary winds. The long sweeps were horizontal and slanting backward, so that the ship seemed poised in that dripping instant of stillness after the oars have been pulled out of the water and before the recovery stroke begins.

"The 'Owl': the ship I took to Sicily."

"You were in the Sicilian expedition?"

"The first year only, thank God. We campaigned around the coast of Sicily trying to pick up allies against Syracuse. But the locals seemed to resent us more than they resented the Syracusans and the welcome they gave us was lukewarm at best. I remember the fleet as it set out across the Ionian Sea, though, 134 triremes, some fitted out for naval combat, others with heavy infantry pulling the oars. Those were old ships, slow and leaky in the best of times, but comic with a crew of landlubbers. Spread out behind us were merchant ships and boats of all sizes: a whole floating city of carpenters, stone workers, bakers, shopkeepers. I have never seen such a sight. Nor will I ever again.

"We had reliable allies in Naxos, fifty or so miles up the coast from Syracuse, and more reluctant allies at Catana, closer in to the city. The fighting ships sailed from there on down to Syracuse; the whole damned fleet in a single line. I think the hope was to lure the Syracusans out to fight a naval battle. The Owl was one of the ten ships that were sent into the grand harbor to see if there was a fleet being made ready, and perhaps to tempt them out to fight. The harbor was superb: a steep sided circular bay protected from winds in all directions, and with a fine landing beach. We cruised around in grand style noting fortifications, or lack of them, and seeing no apparent sign of naval opposition. The consensus on the deck was that this would be an ideal place to base an attack on the city, but I did not agree."

The old man gestured to a pair of couches in his sitting room, and they sat down.

"The harbor had a narrow entrance, which could be stopped by a line of ships, and any fleet within could be caught like fish in a trap.

"But you didn't come to talk about old wars. Are you still looking for Aristophon?"

"I seem to be looking for half of Athens at the moment, but yes, Aristophon is on my list."

"A friend of his was here yesterday, a young Cyzican chap, he was looking for passage home. Apparently he sailed over here with Aristophon. It would seem that you were right in saying that he was back in Athens."

"Did you find him a ship?"

"No, it's getting late in the season. There are still ships going out, but I don't choose to risk my boats for a little extra profit. I referred him to a business associate - a Syracusan as a matter of fact - he has a hunger for trade and is not so concerned for his crews."

"Have you seen Aristophon yourself?"

"No, but according to the Cyzican he is staying in the Piraeus with a corn trader by the name of Glaukos."

"At least you didn't tell me he was up in Athens. So how did you get out of Sicily?"

"The state galley Salaminia came to recall our general Alcibiades. He was under indictment for sacrilege, to do with some drunken and ribald activity the night before expedition sailed. The people did not like their gods being mocked, especially by long-haired generals with outspoken leanings towards the Spartan way of government. The Salaminia's helmsman had taken sick on the way over, and I was transferred. It was a significant honor to serve on the Salaminia - an all citizen elite crew. We were to escort Alcibiades back to Athens, but of course he jumped ship in Thurii. We searched for him for days before we gave up."

"And then Alcibiades joined the Spartans?"

"You can't really blame him from a personal point of view - the Athenian assembly would probably have put him to death. But that's the problem with this city; the upper classes find it too easy to side with the Spartans against their own people. Anyway, that is all ancient history, and irrelevant now."

Skaphis wished he could be so sure.

Skaphis checked out the Sicilian trader. Protonikos had indeed been there yesterday looking for passage home. The trader's ships were scheduled for trips in a westerly and southerly direction, but he had advised the boy to ask around the docks, that being where you found ships after all. Skaphis circled the trader's house looking for signs that Thrassia had been there, but found nothing conclusive.

He had no more luck at Glaukos's house. A slave came to the door and informed him that his master had left early that morning. Indeed there were a couple of house guests: one had been staying for a couple of days, the other, a younger man had joined them yesterday evening. They went with his master in the morning. No, he did not know when they would return.

Again Skaphis looked around the house for any sign that Thrassia had been there. Across the street from the entrance to the merchant's house was an alleyway, which was where he would choose to lurk if he wanted to watch the house while not being seen himself. He could perhaps convince himself from the indentations in the dirt that someone had stood here for some time, but he could equally well convince himself that this was the result of intermittent traffic in and out of the courtyard beyond. In the dust at his feet, there a dozen pebbles, which zigzagged in a way that reminded him of the tattoos on Thrassia's arms. Maybe they had been deliberately arranged that way by a bored girl on a long surveillance. Or perhaps Skaphis was seeing a pattern that did not exist. Occupational hazard for an investigator, he thought.

Skaphis was in a quandary as to what to do next. He could stay at Glaukos' house till the master and possibly his guests returned, in the hope that Thrassia was still trailing them. But it was approaching the time when Mnesia practiced at the music school, and he wanted to talk to the man who had taken the pot that was under Barysthenes' body.

He compromised by checking back at Lusilla's tavern to see if Thrassia had returned. She had not, and Lusilla was not happy. Skaphis told her he'd have her back by nightfall, and slipped away hoping that he sounded more confident than he felt. Glaukos' house was not too far from the tavern. If Thrassia had followed the boy to the house and he appeared to be spending the night there, why had she not come home?

Mnesia and her instructor were playing a duet. Polyctor was strumming a sequence of chords on his kithara, the beat a regular marching rhythm, or perhaps that of the deliberate entrance of a tragic chorus. Skaphis noticed that there were three different chord sounds that repeated endlessly, two strums to the chord. Mnesia wove a musical fabric by teasing a long thread of single notes in and out of these chords. The whole sounded good to Skaphis. It also clearly sounded good to the young man listening from the street. He was tall and good looking, except for a circular scar about the size of a four-drachma piece on his face, near where the front of a helmet's cheek guard would be.

"Good isn't she?"

Skaphis nodded in agreement. Even without the scar, he would have recognized the young man as a soldier. He also recognized him as the hooded individual who had silently listened to his last conversation with his partner.

"Herakleides, we need to talk, but not here."

The color drained a little from the soldier's face as he looked at Skaphis. Clearly he was trying to remember where had met him before, but not succeeding.

"Do I know you?"

"Mnesia told me your name, come let me buy you a drink."

"I was waiting for Mnesia to finish her practice," he paused, and something in Skaphis' demeanor seemed to complete his thought for him,

"But she'll be practicing again tomorrow."

There was a tavern a few doors down the road from the music school. Apparently it did a good business slaking the thirsts of young music lovers. Skaphis recognized the faces of a couple of the customers from Polyctor's school the previous day.

"You don't remember me, do you?" They were sitting over a bowl of well-watered wine.

The soldier looked at Skaphis and shook his head.

"Lusilla's tavern, I was talking with Barysthenes, you were sitting at the next table. Later that night someone stabbed him."

With a knife I left lying on that table, Skaphis thought.

Herakleides glanced at the door of the tavern as if weighing his chances of getting out without being stopped, but Skaphis was between him and the door. He leaned forward and talked in a low monotone, which Skaphis strained to pick out from the background clatter of the tavern.

"I've been a soldier since I was barely more than a boy. Soldiers are not in high demand just now, and I thought I should try my hand at investigation. I got wind of some irregularities in the corn market, and was trying to pin down the scheme exactly. I was sure that Kotos was involved, but I was trying to find out how widespread the plan was."

Herakleides lowered his voice farther. Skaphis had to lean forward across the table to hear his mumble.

"I'm new at this investigation business, but I have survived a long time in a dangerous profession," he fingered the scar on his cheek, "going after Kotos himself would be suicide, like charging a phalanx with a few light infantry. I wanted to find an outlier to attack - someone less well connected who might be amenable to settling out of court to make a charge go away."

"Kotos was trying to corner the wheat market?"

"I suspected something of the sort. I'd picked up some talk of a cartel that had sucked in most of the wheat supply, and was controlling its distribution to manipulate the price. Kotos was at the center of the scheme, but I was exploring its fringes. Your partner set up a meeting with Kotos for later that night, but I couldn't hear where. I didn't follow Kotos out of the tavern, it would be too close - too dangerous."

"But you caught up with him later at a party?"

"I wasn't invited, but Mnesia slipped me in. I missed Kotos at the party, but I followed out a couple of his associates in the hope they'd lead to the meeting. They met at a warehouse across from Ktesiphon's barber shop, I slipped into the door of the shop to stay out of sight. I was out of sight, but I was too far away to hear what they were discussing. Your partner joined them, and another man. I'm pretty sure I heard Kotos's voice, even though I couldn't make out what he was saying. They left one at a time: Kotos first, but not your partner. I stayed hidden in the door of the barber shop; I wanted to move closer but didn't want to be seen. I have stood night sentry duty in my time, it was not too arduous to stand silent in the doorway."

"And you had a flask of Huginos's wine for company."

Herakleides looked up at Skaphis in surprise. "How do you know that?"

"I found the broken pot."

"Time passed, but the moon got higher and I was able to see more across the street. Barysthenes was leaning against the side of archway, he seemed to be eating something. He was waiting for somebody.

"Another man joined him and they talked briefly. The man walked away from Barysthenes in my direction. When I looked back at Barysthenes, there was someone else in the shadows beside him. Barysthenes seemed to know the newcomer and they talked for a few moments, then the stranger turned and walked briskly up the other side of the road. He was hooded and walked fast, despite being in a full robe.

"Barysthenes stood stock still against the wall for a moment, then sank to his knees, silent all the while. He staggered out into the street, and I could see that he was hurt. I went to help him: dragged him to my doorway and looked to tend his wound. He had been stabbed. He begged me for some wine, and I gave him my pitcher to drink from, but he dropped it and soon after passed out. I've seen stab wounds before, and there was nothing I could do for him, so I left him there, I didn't want to have to explain my presence to the authorities."

"Did he say anything?"

"He tried to speak, but he was pretty delirious and didn't make much sense. He seemed to be talking about the stars, although with the moon out, there was scarce a star to be seen. I did make out a name though, or thought I did."

"What was that?"

"It sounded like 'Clytemnestra'".

The sun was beginning to set when they left the tavern. No music came from Polyctor's studio. Mnesia was nowhere to be seen. Herakleides shrugged and ambled down the street, his shoulders hunched against the evening chill.

"I'll come by tomorrow."

Skaphis turned in the opposite direction towards Glaukos's house. If Aristophon and his Cyzican friend were spending the night, sunset might bring them back, and if Thrassia was still on their trail, sunset might bring her back too. This thought was too optimistic to keep at the front of his mind.

Skaphis wasn't sure the extent to which he believed the young soldier. After all, he had been in Lusilla's tavern and could easily have picked up the knife, which he had left lying on the table. He admitted being at the scene of the murder. What if Barysthenes had spotted his surveillance and come across the road to accost him? An argument could easily lead to knife thrusts. But that didn't fit the evidence on the scene, the blood, the marks in the street and the discarded weapon, all pointed to the fact that the killing had been done on the other side of the street. On the other hand, if the soldier was trying to hear what was being said, was it likely that he would have remained out of earshot on the far side of the street? Would he not have tried to get closer, perhaps leaving the wine jug in the barber's doorway?

The shadows in the street were lengthening when Skaphis reached Glaukos's house. Instead of approaching directly, Skaphis ducked into the alleyway across the street. A smell of fish frying seeped into the alley and piqued his salivary glands. He couldn't remember when he ate last. Wine he'd had though. A lamp was lit in Glaukos's window. Skaphis had the feeling that the master was not home. He settled down to await his arrival. Tuna, the fish smelled like, seared in olive oil, flavored, perhaps with a little garlic, although the latter was unnecessary. He could almost taste the rich flesh, and his stomach tinged in reflex anticipation.

A noise behind made him turn, but too late: a hand was on his arm before he could reach for his hidden blade.

"Master, it's me."

The hand let go of Skaphis' arm and a figure emerged from the shadows of the alleyway sufficiently for Skaphis to recognize Thrassia. She had a shawl hunched over her head and he could read tiredness in her eyes, but she was alive and a smile played with the corners of her mouth.

"I found him, master. The Cyzican left Athens yesterday and I followed him all the way back to the Piraeus. I stayed well back on the road between the cities, I'm sure he didn't spot me. But he walked quickly and I had to run to catch up. He was slower when he got into the Piraeus, he seemed unsure of where he was going. I was able to keep up and stay at the side of the street. I followed him to a couple of places, then he came here."

"Why didn't you go back to Lusilla's last night?"

Her face betrayed annoyance at having to pause her story.

"After the Cyzican came here, another man arrived, older and with the bearing of the upper classes. I thought it could be Aristophon. I wanted to follow him so I stayed here. But they didn't leave the house. It got dark and late and I worried about finding my way home safely, so I just stayed here."

She tilted her head at the ground below Skaphis' feet. Her face brightened as she continued with her story.

"Anyway, early this morning, they all came out: the Cyzican, the house owner, who I found out is called Glaukos, and Aristophon. It was Aristophon—I heard Glaukos address him by name. They walked together down towards the docks, and then split up. The Cyzican stayed by the docks while the other two headed up into the warehouse district. I followed Aristophon. They appeared to be organizing a mule train, hiring drivers and organizing them to pick up goods at a particular warehouse. There was a good deal of haggling with the drivers. Glaukos stayed with the mule men, to supervise the loading, I supposed, but I followed Aristophon."

Thrassia's face glowed with enthusiasm as she recounted her story.

"He spent the rest of the day down around the docks and warehouses. He had meetings with a number of different people. The meetings tended to turn into arguments. He had lunch in a tavern down by the docks - 'Psuchion's' it was called. I didn't follow him in, but he was there till late in the afternoon. He may have been meeting someone. I was beginning to worry that he had left by a back door, when eventually he emerged, and I followed him here."

"Lusilla was worried about you when you didn't come home, Thrassia, and aggravated as hell at me for losing you."

145

The girl looked crestfallen at this cool reception for her triumph.

"You did well, though, very well."

"There he is now, Aristophon, look."

Skaphis watched a man speak a parting word to someone inside Glaukos's house, then march up the road through the gathering evening dark.

"Back to Lusilla's with you - now. I'll take over here."

Thrassia started to object, but Skaphis put his finger over his mouth and gave her a look that brooked no argument. Then he darted out into the street and followed the elusive cavalryman.

Aristophon knew where he was going. He wove his way through a skein of tightly packed alleyways. Skaphis was quickly lost, but sensed he was getting closer to the water. He hung back as far as he dared, but had to stay near his quarry for fear of losing him in the twists and turns of his erratic course through the back streets of the port. Once or twice, Skaphis had the impression that he in turn was being followed. However he could not catch a glimpse of anybody on his tail, and Aristophon was moving too fast for him to worry too much about his own back.

Eventually Aristophon slowed down. They were in a section of town that was unfamiliar to Skaphis. The houses were larger here and stood back from the road shielded from the gaze of passing traffic by courtyard walls and high wooden gates. There was no passing traffic. Aristophon knocked on one of the gates. Skaphis stepped round the corner of a building, and pressed himself flat against its wall. Aristophon was admitted to the house across the way and the gate closed behind him.

Skaphis waited, still as a wall: an old one, mortar starting to crumble, and one or two bricks loose at the top. A minute later a hooded figure slipped silently through the shadows at the fringe of the street. At first Skaphis thought that Thrassia had followed him against his instructions, but the figure was a little taller than the slave girl, and there was a squat masculinity in its gait. Skaphis must have made a sound, for the hooded man turned sharply to face him, in his hand a long metallic gleam. Skaphis moved quickly: he stepped sideways to avoid a knife thrust, while smashing his forearm with all his strength into his attacker's arm. The speed of the attack must have caught the hooded man off his guard, for the knife fell softly to the ground and lay there useless as an autumn leaf. Its owner meanwhile lunged at Skaphis, trying to pin him against the wall and beat him against it.

Skaphis twisted away from the main thrust of the attack and his angular momentum spun the two round until his attacker had his back to the wall. Skaphis' arms were pinned so that he could not reach for his own knife. The hood slipped from the stranger's head and he smiled a gap toothed grin at Skaphis. His breath carried a smell of rotting fish. Skaphis pulled back slightly, and as the knife-man balanced forward in reaction, Skaphis planted a head butt square on the bridge of his nose. The pain shot all the way from Skaphis' forehead down his neck and back to the soles of his feet. But he heard the stranger's nose crack and he sank to his knees, blood gushing from his abused face and mixing with the dry dust of the road. Skaphis bent to pick up the discarded knife, and was hit from behind by something the size of a battle-ship's ram. He felt a second blow on the back of his head before lapsing into unconsciousness.

chapter **16**

"Well spade-man, I told you to stick to the sea. Digging up the past is an unhealthy occupation."

Skaphis lifted his head off the table over which he was slumped. The movement caused a shooting pain to sear his back as if someone was stroking it with a red-hot poker. He rested his head back down on his arms and waited for the pain to subside. It centered on his neck and throbbed a lazy rhythm in the back of his head. He was afraid he was going to be sick.

"A lucky injury: Brochos would have killed you for what you did to his face, if he'd had the chance."

Skaphis tentatively raised his head again. This time the pain was less, although a wave of nausea rippled through his stomach. He rested his chin on his arms and peered through a haze of defocused vision across the table. Kotos was picking his teeth thoughtfully with a sliver of wood.

"He wasn't in much shape for killing anything last time I saw him."

Kotos laughed.

"And you are the picture of health and vivacity yourself."

Skaphis sat up. The pain shot through his head with such intensity that his vision blurred and his stomach again threatened to disgorge its contents. But he stayed up and the pain, if it did not subside, at least became familiar. He touched the sleeve of his cloak. It was fine linen: not the coarse woolen garment he had been wearing.

"Your clothes got a little dirty last night, but I'm having them washed. It would be inconsiderate to disturb the good citizens by dragging unconscious drunks through their streets, so we put you in a wagon."

He stopped picking his teeth and smiled.

"We have the contract for cleaning the effluent from the city streets. Not a glamorous franchise, but a profitable one, and an undoubted service to the democracy."

"It's amazing how much civic spirit one comes across these days."

Kotos reached down to his side and lifted a wine goblet from a low table. He did not offer any to Skaphis, but drank a long draught himself.

"I've brought you here to tell you a story, oar-man, and it's one in which civic pride plays some part."

Skaphis straightened in his chair. The throbbing pain in his head was beginning to recede to a dull ache.

"Imagine two young men growing up in a great city in the western sea. It is a city of merchants, a city of warriors, a democratic city. The citizens are descended from settlers from the Peloponnese, so in the war between Athens and Sparta, they are naturally aligned with the Spartans. But they are a democracy, and there is as a result an underlying empathy with the Athenian people. Besides, as I said, this is a city of merchants and Athens is a great customer for what they have to sell."

"What they have to sell is wheat?"

"This city is on an island with broad fertile plains. Good territory for wheat and for horses. Horses are the love of these two young men. They ride when they have the chance, and they frequently have the chance, for their fathers are from the merchant class, rich and happy to provide fine animals for their sons. The sons are more like brothers than friends, and when they are old enough for military training, eagerly join the cavalry.

"In the evenings, however, they eat together at the house of one of their fathers or the other. And there they meet visitors of all kinds: Carthaginian merchants, sailors from the Greek colonies in Italy, other Sicilians, but especially travelers from Athens. The Athenians seem a race apart: men who are equals of the Syracusans in business and in rhetoric, but also men who can quote the latest plays and recount the latest trends of thought. The boys fall in love with a city of ideas beyond the sunrise that they have never seen, except in the eye of the imagination.

"Then comes the news that an Athenian fleet is stationed across in Italy with the intention of attacking the boys' city. At first this is regarded as far-fetched in the extreme, but reliable reports trickle down the coast that a large fleet has put in at a city up the coast. A cavalry detachment is sent along the shore on reconnaissance, and the boys see a sight that inspires and frightens them. A fleet of warships, stretched in single file back to the far horizon. There seem to be ships beyond counting, their oars beating the water in a steady, unstoppable rhythm. Commands bark through the still air and the skirling music of a hundred pipers sends shivers of dread through the watching cavalrymen. They gallop back to their city in time to see a handful of enemy ships sail unopposed into its harbor. The speed with which these massive ships slide through the water surprises the boys, as does their responsiveness, the whole squadron stopping and turning in concert on a couple of shouted phrases. The sight inspires the boys: to defend their city against this powerful enemy, but also to see the city that can send out such a magnificent fleet."

"The Sicilian expedition? The boys are from Syracuse?"

"Yes, and soon they are involved in a life and death struggle for their city's existence. In heavy infantry combat the Athenians are more than a match for the Syracusans. They have been at war with the Spartans for twenty years and managed to hold their own, and the Spartans, man for man, are the best heavy infantry in the world. But the Athenians have no cavalry. Now the Syracusan cavalry is useless against heavy infantry in pitched battle, but pitched battle, the boys find out, is only a small part of warfare. Most of warfare is finding vegetables to feed the troops, and wood to supply their campfires. Day in and day out, the Syracusan cavalry are in action attacking Athenian foraging parties. Initially, these are lightly armed, and the cavalry rout and disperse them easily, killing and capturing many of the foragers. Eventually, the parties are always escorted by detachments of heavy infantry. This makes them harder to attack, but also means they cannot range far from their base camp. Soon, the area around the Athenian encampment is bare of food and fuel. They rely increasingly on supply from the sea.

"The war drags on into a second year, and the Athenians are reinforced by another expeditionary force as splendid, or even more splendid than the first. They also have brought cavalry. However, cavalry is a difficult commodity to transport by boat, and these new arrivals are no match for the native Sicilian squadrons. While the Athenians are trying to supply themselves with cavalry, the Syracusans are trying to supply themselves with a fleet - and with more success. They build themselves a battle fleet and use it to block the entrance to the harbor. With the Syracusan cavalry ranging inland and supply from the sea cut off by their blockade, the Athenians' fate is sealed.

"They try to escape across country to their allies to the north. But, on the move, they are defenseless against the Sicilian cavalry. Eventually, the sorry remnants of the great Athenian invasion surrender to Syracusans who are sick of the killing. The boys find themselves in charge of a group of Athenian prisoners. Two of the prisoners are brothers, and both are sick. Disease has been rampant in the closely confined Athenian camp. The boys are under orders to take their prisoners to the stone quarries on the outskirts of town. These quarries form a steep sided natural prison where the Athenians can be encamped and guarded. However, they take pity on the two brothers, the younger of whom is their own age, and smuggle them instead into their own homes."

"Let me guess, the brothers' names are Barysthenes and Barybromos."

Kotos narrowed his voice to a thin command.

"It is rude to interrupt the story teller, Skaphis. Even if you have already heard it before, and I doubt very much if you know the plot of this one."

He poured himself another cup of wine and continued more expansively.

"Yes, the brothers were, as you have surmised, Barysthenes and Barybromos, and at first their health responded well to the good treatment they received in the boys' homes. However, their countrymen, herded like animals into the stone quarries, did not fare so well. They had little or no protection from the heat of the sun in the daytime, and from the cold of the night. The weaker ones died from exposure. Worse, though, were the sanitary conditions. They were defecating in the same water supply they were drinking from. Soon, disease spread like wildfire through the prisoners, and from them out into the population of the city. The Athenian brothers in the boys' care relapsed into sickness and both died within a week of each other. They were buried with full rights as if they were members of the family. But the boys had hatched a bold plan."

"They decided to impersonate the dead Athenians."

"Spade-man, you are beginning to annoy me. One of the Syracusans had a similar build to Barysthenes, and they had learned that he had been away from Athens for years. This Syracusan returned to Athens in Barysthenes' place, married Barybromos' widow and settled in the Piraeus."

"And the other followed later, setting himself up as a resident alien, trader, and dockyard strong arm man?"

"A resident alien needs an Athenian sponsor. Barysthenes sponsored me. In Athens, the courts are a natural extension of the market place for conducting business. Lawsuit and the threat of lawsuits are part of the normal process of doing business. While I was getting my business established, Barysthenes provided legal cover, usually in the form of counter-investigation or counter-suit. We learned in the cavalry the value of sharp and sudden counter-attack from an unexpected quarter. In recent years, we have seen less of each other, but occasionally I funnel work his way, or give him the opportunity to invest in some business opportunity.

"Such as your grain cartel?"

Kotos's eyes flashed angrily. He made a movement as if thumping the table with the edge of his fist, but when he pulled his arm away a long thin knife was embedded in the table top a few inches from Skaphis' chest, quivering with the residual violence of its sudden placement.

"Skaphis, I have told you this old story so that you will know that I did not kill your partner. He was like a brother to me. He did invest in a little grain-trading venture with me, which has just matured. I have the proceeds here, I understand you are his heir."

He produced a coin bag from inside his cloak and placed it onto the table beside the knife, which still wavered like a reed in the current of a rain-swollen stream.

"As for talk of a cartel: I have long experience in the grain trade, I time my trades carefully. I have to admit, prices have been climbing recently, but this is normal towards the end of the season. The grain market is tightly controlled, and collusion and price fixing amongst dealers punishable by death. These are not the sorts of accusations you should bandy around lightly.

"Besides, I've started to unload my wheat: I felt it my civic duty with prices spiking so high."

Kotos nodded to someone behind Skaphis. Skaphis started to turn round, but the movement caused the pain to shoot through his back again.

"Your clothes are ready: a little damp perhaps, but they'll dry off quickly in the sun."

Skaphis experimented with standing up. His legs felt weak, but they held. His stomach felt weaker still, but it kept its contents, probably only because its contents were meager in the extreme.

"The night Barysthenes was killed, you met him outside Ktesiphon's shop?"

"Yes, we talked in Lusilla's tavern in the afternoon, and arranged a business meeting later that evening."

"Do you normally do business at night?"

"Some types of business are best done in the dark. I left first: the last time I saw Barysthenes, he was alive and well and eating olives in the street across from Ktesiphon's."

"Was Aristophon at the meeting?"

Kotos looked up at Skaphis, something like surprise was in his eyes.

"No, but he was supposed to be. Do you think Barysthenes waited for Aristophon?"

"I'm sure of it."

"Do you think Aristophon killed him?"

"That I don't know. When you sat with Barysthenes at Lusilla's tavern, was there a Phoenician dagger on the table?"

"I'm sure there wasn't. The table was bare, there wasn't even any food, I had to order some. Why do you ask?"

"The dagger was mine: I left it at the tavern and it was used to kill Barysthenes."

Kotos gave a low whistle, or at least his lips formed into a whistle, the sound Skaphis may have imagined.

Every step he took shot a spear of pain up Skaphis' spine and into the base of his head. From there it spread outwards and throbbed into his temples. The sun had taken the chill off the mid-morning air and was beginning to build a heat, which abetted the dryness in his throat and the pain in the back of his head. The streets grew in vague familiarity as he walked into the sea breeze, more for the comfort the cool wind brought to his headache than for any sense that this was the correct direction.

However, he must have been unconsciously backtracking the route that he had been wheeled over the previous evening. He clearly recognized a spot where he had hugged the side of the road while following Aristophon. He turned and retraced his steps for a couple of blocks and found the corner where he had been attacked. The ground showed signs of the scuffle. The back of his head throbbed in painful resonance with the location of its abuse. He could see where they had dragged him across the side street, and where they had obviously tired of the task and laid him against the wall. An insensate drunk sleeping off a night of debauchery on a Piraeus corner would raise few eyebrows. He could see wheel marks, where they had fetched a wagon to complete their task.

Skaphis straightened up, a red flame of pain shooting up his back. Across the main street, a two-wheeled cart trundled behind a somnambulant donkey matching the slow gait of its master. It passed in front of the gate that Aristophon had entered the previous night. With his sense of direction re-established, Skaphis started for home, barely keeping pace with the slow lurches of the cart. After a few steps, however, he changed his mind, along with his heading.

The gate was a heavy wooden structure, eight feet tall and shaped to fill completely the coarse stone arch in which it was set. It was not latched though, and yielded to a casual nudge from his shoulder. On three sides of the high walled courtyard were squat, windowless buildings. Tracks of wheeled wagons scalloped in the dirt from the entrance to the perimeter of the courtyard. The doors on two of the buildings were closed, the third swung open.

A flock of birds spiraled into the air like a wind blown column of dust. A crow hopped away from the open door and flapped heavily into the air. Skaphis sidled into the building and paused to let his eyes adjust to the dark inside. The air had a heavy old smell. A faint light seeped through a high window under the eaves, by which Skaphis could see that the room was empty. Empty, that is, except for a small bundle of clothes hunched in the corner.

Closer inspection revealed the bundle of clothes to be, in fact, the body of a man curled in a fetal position. Skaphis recognized Aristophon from the previous night. A knife was lodged under his rib cage. The dead man's fists were locked around its handle, but whether convulsed in a moment of steely resolve to end his own life or in a futile attempt to extract the blade, Skaphis could not tell.

Skaphis instinctively felt for his own dagger. It was where he expected it to be, sheathed against the outside of his thigh. This corpse at least had had the decency to get himself killed with someone else's knife. Skaphis crouched beside the body. The knife had been thrust upwards under the ribs and into the chest cavity: a well-planned trajectory or a lucky one?

A gold coin lay on the ground beside the dead man. Skaphis picked it up and held it to the light from the open door. It had Persian writing on it - a gold Daric - the coin of preference for trading in the east. He couldn't decide what significance such a coin had lying by a dead grain trader in an empty warehouse in the Piraeus. He pocketed it all the same.

Skaphis' eyes had fully adjusted to the room's lack of light, although his brain had not yet adjusted to its contents. The building was devoid of furniture, and had clearly been used as a storeroom. Wheel marks in the dust of the courtyard suggested that the storeroom had recently been emptied. Apparently Aristophon was in the process of getting his grain out onto the market. If Kotos started liquidating his supply, the market price would drop precipitously, there would be a premium on getting to the market quickly: hence the urgency in Aristophon's quest for drayage. Skaphis presumed that the premature breakup of the cartel would leave the last to market holding the bulk of any financial loss. Kotos did not strike him as the sort of operator who would be last to market. He wondered if Aristophon was left holding the bag.

Skaphis could see no apparent signs of a struggle, apart from the stark evidence of the dead man's body. He tried to pry his hands from the hilt of the knife, but they clutched it as if determined to carry the offending implement with them beyond the grave. He ran his own hands down the side of the body, and gently rolled it over onto its other side. He patted this side of the body in turn, but did not find what he was looking for. What he was looking for was a dagger, and it was not lying on the floor of the warehouse either. Skaphis suspected that it was Aristophon's own knife that he clutched to his belly.

The stones underneath the body were stained a dark brown. Skaphis touched the stain: it was still slightly sticky. He tried again to pry Aristophon's fingers off the knife, but they were clamped with the uncompromising rigidity of death. He did, however, notice something else between the fingers and the knife: a torn fragment of fabric. By working the knife hilt to and fro, Skaphis was able to inch the fabric free. It was a scrap of papyrus. By the light shafting in from the open door, Skaphis could decipher two words of Greek on the parchment. He read

"The best man died."

A short and somewhat cryptic message from a dead man. Of course aristos - best - was the first part of Aristophon's name, was this a play on his own name?

The back of the papyrus contained four letters:

'A E

'B Γ

Skaphis was unable to extract any meaning from the letters. Perhaps the papyrus had been torn from some larger document.

158

He left the body where he had found it, and quickly checked the other two buildings. Both were warehouses. Both were full of grain. Neither shed any further light on the death of its owner. As he slipped his way out of the courtyard into the glare of the street, the heat of the sun rekindled the embers of his headache. The ashes caught and the whisper of warm wind blew it into a full blaze of pain as he retraced his steps along the deserted street. Overhead a pair of crows squabbled in the branches of an olive tree.

Lusilla smiled benignly at Skaphis when he entered the tavern. Thrassia had clearly returned safely and was sitting in the corner spinning yarn with another girl. Skaphis' intention was to experiment with the effects on his headache of a horizontal orientation and squeezed through the midday clientele to reach the back stairs to his room. Half way through the room, however his stomach drew attention to the fact that he had not eaten for the best part of a day. He sat at a table with the hope that Lusilla might infer his hunger and bring him some food.

Instead, Thrassia sat across from him.

"You are late back, master, I was afraid you had been hurt."

"I was hurt all right, but I'll get better. A little food wouldn't do any harm."

He looked wistfully in Lusilla's direction, but she was deep in conversation with a couple of foreigners at the bar.

"Thrassia, you did very well in tracking Aristophon. You aggravated the hell out of Lusilla by staying out all night, but you kept on the trail. You'd make a fine investigator."

The girl beamed at this praise. Skaphis reached across the narrow table and touched her fingers with his. He held her hand briefly and transferred a silver coin from his palm to hers.

"You hired her for a job, Skaphis, don't get over-familiar with the help."

Lusilla was smiling. She also held a broad platter of fresh bread, which she placed in the center of the table. Thrassia withdrew her hand, her fist clenched round the small coin. Lusilla sat beside the girl and tore a corner off the bread. Skaphis sheared a segment from the swollen rim of the loaf and gnawed hungrily on it. Thrassia picked up a timid portion of the bread with her coin hand and put it to her lips. Skaphis imagined that he saw her slip the tiny silver disk beneath her tongue.

"Skaphis, you look like yesterday's sacrifice."

"I do feel like someone wants to offer me up to some god or other. Right now, I think I'd give myself up to Hypnos."

"Just make sure you stay away from his brother, they're sometimes difficult to tell apart."

Thrassia tugged at her mistress' sleeve.

"The ignorance of you mountain girls will never cease to amaze me. Hypnos is the god of sleep as you know; surely even in Thrace you learned that he has a twin brother Thanatos - death."

Thrassia looked down, but did not leave the table. Neither did she pick any more bread off the loaf. Her mistress did.

"Your client was here last night, Skaphis, looking for you. She wasn't happy when you didn't appear. She waited until Thrassia turned up and told her that you were out following Aristophon."

She slid her legs out from under the table.

"Oh and also, Barysthenes' little widow deigned to set her dainty feet in the tavern again yesterday. You haven't been neglecting her, have you? It's not right to neglect your parents."

"She wants me to stay at the family house." Skaphis replied. "But I suspect I'd miss the sumptuous fare here." He divided the remains of the bread into two uneven pieces. He took the largest piece himself, and pushed the remainder over to Thrassia. Her mistress gone, Thrassia grasped the bread eagerly.

"Thrassia, why did you think I might be hurt?"

She looked down at her lap and chewed her bread in silence. Eventually she answered, her voice a tentative whisper in the swirling noise of the tavern.

"I didn't come straight back here when you left me. I followed you. I hung back in the shadows a long way. I became aware of some men who were also trailing you. I was afraid, but I don't think they saw me. I stayed out of the way and came back here. But I was worried they intended you harm."

"They intended harm to me all right, but fortunately they work for a stern master, and he wanted to talk to me. Mind you, I didn't come away unscathed, my head feels like it spent the last week being used as a cobbler's last."

He threaded his way out from the table and up the back stairs to his tiny cell. There he slid the foot of his cot sideways to uncover a wooden slat, which had been concealed by the leg of the bed. He lifted the slat to reveal a shallow hole sculpted from the floor. The hole was empty, and just large enough to hold the purse, which Skaphis squeezed into the space. He twitched the lid back in place and jolted the bed frame to its customary position before sliding gratefully into a sleep that resembled closely its twin brother in all but the fact that he woke up several hours later, hungry and with a mouth as dry as a Theban funeral oration.

chapter **17**

The tavern was in the late afternoon lull between clienteles: the market goers had passed through on their way home, but the evening's revelers had not yet stepped out onto the night streets. There were several empty or near-empty tables. Skaphis made for the nearest one. Euboulos was sitting at a table in the corner, and beckoned Skaphis over. In the middle of the table was a krater full of wine mixed with water.

Skaphis sat, ladling some of the wine mixture into a fortuitous empty beaker. He sipped the beverage, but it was less diluted than his thirst warranted. He gestured to Lusilla, who brought over a pitcher of water. To Skaphis' taste, the wine was mixed one and two or one and three. He added more water to the liquid already in his cup to approximate one in eight. He swirled the cup in his hand to mix the fluids and drank deeply. At this ratio, the physiological effect was of water, but the flavor was tinged with a sharp remembrance of fruit. After a second drink his throat began to rehydrate. The back of his neck no longer throbbed with pain, and his stomach tightened with hunger untainted by nausea. In short, he was back to normal.

"It is virtuous to be moderate in all things."

Euboulos poured wine from the mixing bowl into his own cup. He did not add further water, however.

"Including moderation?"

Euboulos drank from his stronger cup.

"Including virtue. It would seem that it has now become a buyers' market for grain. There was any amount of the stuff to be had the last couple of days, and the price went through the floor."

"So you have lost an opportunity."

"The market is like a ship. With a wind from the quarter, it will heel over at a constant angle and sail steady day after day. But sometimes the wind will drop, and the market will be left becalmed and wallowing in the swell. As each wave sweeps under the hull, it will roll first to leeward then to windward. On deck, at the extreme point of the roll, you can feel as if the boat will never right itself, but eventually the weight of hull and cargo counterbalances the surge of the wave and the ship rights itself. More than that—it swings back in the other direction. There's always opportunity of one sort or another."

"But you no longer are looking for grain to own?"

"No, I've recently acquired an adequate quantity. And at a good price."

His smile was cold and sly, like a fishmonger who has just passed off a piece of worthless rockfish as high-priced tuna.

"I hear you had an interview with our friend Kotos last night."

"His position was that the rising price of grain was due to normal market fluctuations, and totally unconnected with the fact that he and a few associates were attempting to corner the supply. I found his position convincing— backed up as it was by some fairly heavy-handed gentlemen of the street. He also pointed out that he had just released a substantial consignment of wheat onto the market."

"The cartel was too wide - too difficult to maintain security and too much danger of prosecution, so he decided to cut his losses. Still, I'd wager Kotos was the first cartel member to get his grain onto the market, before the prices collapsed. He wouldn't make the killing he was looking for, but I'm sure he made a tidy profit. Different for the other plotters, especially if they were over-extended, they'd be forced to sell at a loss to whatever buyers they could find. Something of the kind would seem to have happened to Aristophon. He was found today in his warehouse, apparently he killed himself."

Skaphis examined Euboulos' expression for signs of irony, but saw none.

"Rumor has it he sold at a loss and couldn't bring himself to face his creditors, one of whom is, I believe, your client, the lovely and costly Psamathe."

"I don't suppose she'll be paying me to look for him any more. Still the job had as much trouble as reward. Barysthenes didn't see the other end of it. Without some luck in court I may not either."

"Surely Aristophon's death provides you with a useful legal strategy. He was, after all the target of your investigation, involved in illegal trading activities with death the penalty if caught and convicted. And here is Barysthenes, well known court informant, observing a cartel meeting. That would seem to be reasonable justification for murder."

"It could even be true."

"Oh, I don't think Aristophon really killed Barysthenes. Any more than he killed himself."

Euboulos looked into Skaphis' eyes. Skaphis returned his stare, and either Euboulos saw what he was looking for or gave up, for he broke first and looked down at his wine cup, which was empty.

"If Aristophon didn't kill himself, who did?"

"An interesting question."

Euboulos refilled his wine cup, and poured a portion for Skaphis, who mixed in water: this time in even quantity to the liquid in his cup. His urge was to dilute the conversation, but he made do with strengthening his drink.

"Even more interesting is why. If we suppose for a moment that Aristophon did indeed show up at the meeting that Barysthenes had staked out, but that he did not in fact kill him, then he may have seen who did. Which could be motive for murder."

Euboulos cupped his wine in both hands and peered into Skaphis' eyes.

"Aristophon's warehouse is only a few blocks away from Kotos's house."

The conversation was steering in a dangerous direction. Skaphis thought for a moment in silence before responding.

"You said you didn't believe Aristophon had killed Barysthenes, why not?"

"Because he told me he didn't."

Euboulos slipped an olive into his mouth and rolled it with his tongue into the hollow of his cheek like some bald rodent.

"I met up with him last night and bought a consignment of corn. He was having trouble finding transshipment for it."

"Let me guess, some cartel had cornered the market in mules."

"Mule trains are susceptible to robbery. It's in the mule drivers' interest to stay on the good side of certain Piraeus figures, or they find they start having trouble with lost goods, with sudden illness in the stables, with nocturnal theft and banditry. I imagine it's possible for Kotos to put a moderately effective temporary embargo on shipment of wheat from any source but himself."

Skaphis found himself thinking of the functional similarities between young cavalrymen harassing an invader's foraging parties and middle aged gangsters extorting protection money from a city's supply trains.

"He told me the meeting at Ktesiphon's was supposed to set the timing for the second phase of the cartel operation… the sell off. It had to be carefully managed so that the price was kept artificially high, but at the same time, they had to make their profit before next year's sailing season, and all without their collusion becoming apparent. It was an important meeting. But Aristophon was late, and the principals had gone by the time he arrived, all that was left was Barysthenes - a minor member of the cartel."

He paused and looked at Skaphis. If he was looking for a reaction, Skaphis gave him one: his left eyebrow raised a hair's breadth.

"Yes, ironic that Barysthenes should be paid to watch a meeting he was scheduled to attend anyway. I certainly wouldn't say it was outside his usual ethical envelope. Barysthenes and Kotos go a long way back and I'd guess Kotos would cut him in on this deal. In fact it was Barysthenes who introduced Aristophon to the cartel. They were looking for more financing, and Barysthenes had known Aristophon in his better days. He wasn't aware the boy had squandered away the bulk of his inheritance."

"You seem to know a lot about Barysthenes."

"He worked with Aristophon up in the city for a spell and he and I moved in the same circles."

"During the rule of the thirty?"

"As a matter of fact, yes. Anyway Barysthenes apparently filled Aristophon in on the planned schedule for wrapping up the cartel. When I talked to him, Aristophon was under the clear impression Barysthenes had misled him. He left Barysthenes across from the barber's and went into town to a party where he thought he would find Kotos. But Kotos had left already, and Aristophon returned to the docks."

"He could just as easily have killed him himself."

"Possible, but I don't think so."

Euboulos delicately positioned another olive on the end of his tongue and curled it to its slow doom inside his mouth. Skaphis waited for him to elaborate, but he didn't.

"What did you pay Aristophon for his grain."

I got it for a good price, I told you.

"Did you pay him in coin?"

"Persian Darics. That's why I don't think he killed himself. The money wasn't found on the body."

chapter **18**

"An interesting story: a bit hard to swallow though; do you think Kotos would give you a deposition?"

Lysias lay on his back studying the ceiling, his legs drawn up in an ungainly arête on the foot of the couch. Skaphis reclined, in more conventional posture, across the dining room. An elderly slave cleared away the remains of a lunch which Lysias had described as "Some light refreshment," but which would have passed for a wedding feast at Lusilla's, if ever a wedding had been sufficiently low in tone to hold itself there.

"Highly relevant though, from a legal point of view."

"Barysthenes had a much more colorful background than I imagined, and I suppose there would be a plethora of reasons why someone might want to kill him. But he is still dead, and I'm still accused of his murder."

"My dear fellow, under Athenian law it is one thing to kill a citizen, quite another to kill a resident alien, even if he wasn't here under false pretenses."

Lysias hunched himself up into a reclining posture and turned his gaze from the ceiling to Skaphis.

"The penalty for killing a citizen is death. The penalty for killing an alien is exile."

"So the worst that can happen to me is that I'll be escorted to the boundaries of Attica and put on the road to Thebes?"

This didn't sound too bad to Skaphis, especially when compared to a hemlock breakfast in the state prison on the morning after the trial.

"They don't escort you to the boundary, they just issue a proclamation that if you are found inside it then you can be summarily executed. That usually does the trick. But Skaphis, here you are a citizen of the greatest city in the world, city of playwrights and philosophers, of democracy and empire, hell, even the ladies of our streets are famous. Surely leaving this city is akin to leaving life itself?"

Skaphis regarded his empty cup.

"They have wine in other cities, don't they?"

Lysias smiled.

"They also have wine in my cellar."

The old slave must have been listening at the door. He appeared shortly and filled Skaphis' cup, then turned to Lysias, who dismissed him with a gesture.

"As I told you before, citizen murder trials are held at the Areopagus: a body which prides itself in its fairness and deems itself worthy to try the gods themselves. For mortals with lives to lose, however, and particularly democratic ones, they can be a touch too conservative. Non-citizen murder trials are put on in front of the Palladion. This court used to consist of a smaller group of the Areopagites and so had the same aristocratic leanings. After the revolution though, there was a move to make the courts more democratic: one result of which is that the Palladion is now comprised of ordinary citizen-jurors and is likely to be a much more favorable venue for your case."

"I would have thought that the soundness of our defense case would have some bearing on the result. You seem to be concentrating on the composition of the court."

"Skaphis, my family was originally from Syracuse in Sicily. My father was a friend of the great Athenian general Pericles, and became a resident of Athens. My family became wealthy supplying arms to the Athenian war-machine. When the Athenians invaded Syracuse, I was studying on the mainland of Italy, but I saw the fleet on its way down the coast: an impressive sight, and one to strike terror into the hearts of a maritime adversary. But the expedition was a disaster. Why?"

"They had no cavalry, and the Syracusans did?"

"Exactly, they picked the wrong enemy and the wrong place to fight. The Athenians had honed their fighting skills over nearly twenty years of war against the Spartans. They were expensively equipped - the ideal mobile expeditionary force for fighting on the rocky shorelines of the Aegean islands. They were also used to fighting a conservative, predictable foe. In the Syracusans they found an enemy as quirky and innovative as they were themselves. And one whose cavalry dominated the planes of Sicily."

"So I should be careful in choosing the legal battlefield on which my case will be fought?"

"I have generally found that skill at playing a sport is less of a factor in winning than judicious selection of opponents. In due course, we will attend to getting ourselves in training for the competition. For now we will concentrate on picking the right venue. The only problem I see is that the story is so wild. The opposition can presumably bring people in to swear that Barysthenes was who he said he was. We do need a deposition from Kotos. Do you think he will give you one?"

"I can always ask."

Skaphis wondered if he could reach Kotos's house unaided by knife wielding longshoremen and dung-carts. His head throbbed an echo of the previous day's pain, and, perhaps because of this phantom pain, he turned and headed in the opposite direction. It was mid-afternoon: time for Mnesia's practice. He had some questions for her admirer.

The usual cluster of indolent youths loitered outside the music school, but Herakleides was not one of them. Inside the courtyard, a group of younger girls plucked tentatively at their kitharas under the indifferent tutelage of their music master. The lack of musical talent did not deter the youths, however. They maintained an ardent discussion on the other merits of the performers, who by their sideways glances showed they were not oblivious to the attention.

Mnesia would practice later, apparently. Skaphis found himself in the nearby tavern. He sat in a dark corner of the room facing the door and ordered a pitcher of wine. The tavern was busy for mid afternoon. Skaphis recognized the faces of some of the young men whom he had previously seen hanging around the music school.

There was also a rougher crowd: mule men and carters drinking after their day's labor in the sun, replacing, Skaphis mused, the sweat shed on the road to Athens with cheap Piraeus wine. Year by year, Skaphis imagined, a Greek body would contain less and less water and more and more wine. Eventually your sweat would stop tasting salty and take on a flavor of fruit. And what then? Ripe, you'd be plucked by war or pestilence. Or, with luck, you'd be left to wizen on the vine and fall unnoticed to the earth among the first frosts of death's long winter.

Skaphis drank to that.

Herakleides came through the door, blinking in the tavern's gloom like a marine sent below from the sun-swept fore deck. He noticed Skaphis and came directly over to his table.

"They told me you were looking for me. I was inclined to turn round and go on home. But I have to admit to a bit of a thirst."

Skaphis tilted his head in assent. The soldier beckoned to a serving girl, who brought him a wine cup, which he filled from Skaphis' pitcher.

"I wanted to ask you about Barysthenes death. You told me someone met Barysthenes and left just before he was killed? Did you recognize this man?"

"I got a good look at him as he was leaving. The moon was shining brightly on his face. I don't think he saw me in the shadows."

The soldier drained the wine from his cup.

"I didn't recognize him, though. Anyway, he wasn't the killer. The killer seemed to come out of the alleyway."

"All the same, it would be useful to know who it was. I'd like you to come to Athens with me."

"Why?"

"To look at a body."

"No, I meant, why should I come to Athens with you. I told you about my suspicions of a wheat cartel, and now I find the market is flooded. As I said, I'm new at this investigation business, but I doubt that a prosecution for hoarding wheat would go anywhere with the prices dropping and the citizens fat and happy."

"Aristophon was killed yesterday. It was made to look like suicide. He was supposed to be at the meeting with Barysthenes. He could have seen the murderer, or he could have been the murderer himself. With two suspicious deaths, there are ample opportunities for a private investigator to find some traction. Or even a client."

Skaphis poured another cup of wine for himself, and emptied the pitcher into his companion's cup.

"If Aristophon killed Barysthenes, and then killed himself, then there is nobody to prosecute."

"If he knew the identity of Barysthenes' murderer, perhaps he was killed to keep him quiet. In any case, if he was the man you saw leaving, then he wasn't the killer."

"How are we going to get to see the body?"

"Aristophon was a soldier and a trader. He must have had many acquaintances who would want to pay their last respects."

"So you want me to pretend to be a grieving former comrade of a man I never met to see if he could be a murderer?"

"You wanted to be an investigator."

Skaphis straightened the scrap of paper he had found in Aristophon's dead hand onto the table.

"What do you make of this?"

"It could be some sort of code, I suppose. Is it relevant?"

Skaphis reached across for the paper.

"Wait a minute, let me look at it again. Look - the marks by the A and the B - I've seen that before. You know, it could be music. Mnesia sometimes carries her tunes written down."

Herakleides seemed pleased with his investigative prowess and became expansive.

"The music seems to be written in a foreign script. I've teased her before about carrying love letters from barbarian admirers. But I've seen some songs written in honest Greek. I suppose in its way it is a code - each letter represents a single pluck of the string. And they do use marks beside the letters like the marks beside the A and the B."

He handed the scrap back to Skaphis who folded it carefully away

"Tomorrow morning, early at Lusilla's."

Skaphis wondered if the soldier would show up tomorrow. Perhaps he should have taken him up today. There would be more chance of slipping in to view the body unobtrusively tomorrow. The first day after the death would see all the close family and friends in attendance. Besides he had to go see Kotos.

He raised his finger to the serving girl and ordered another pitcher of prevarication.

More young men had drifted into the tavern, along with a large group of laborers - slaves possibly, or lower class citizens. They all knew each other and talked loudly about drink. They appeared to categorize wine by the price required to reach oblivion, and the cost exacted on the return trip. Most of the mule drivers had left; a couple, dryer than the rest, perhaps, lingered.

Skaphis caught the eye of one of these muleteers and motioned with his wine pitcher. The man's lips cracked into a smile, which revealed a matching pair of missing teeth, top and bottom. Skaphis had never known a mule man to refuse a free drink. He sat on the stool that Herakleides had occupied and poured himself a liberal draught from Skaphis' jug. His companion proffered his cup, and without pausing for permission, he filled it to the brim.

"Thirsty work today boys?"

"Mules are aggravating bastards. But we've been working these beasts hard the last few days and they are getting tired. They need a day of good fodder in the stables to get their strength back, and restore their tempers. I can restore my temper with this."

The mule men both drained their cups and refilled them at Skaphis' expense.

"I'd heard that mules were in short supply at the moment. Say I needed to transport a cargo up to the city in the next day or so, who should I speak to?"

The mule men looked at each other.

"We should be able to help you - what sort of cargo are we talking about?"

"Let's say a load of grain."

The muleteers drank their wine in silence before responding.

"Like I said, our mules need rested up or they will start breaking down. I doubt we'd be able to squeeze you in."

"But a moment ago you thought you could help me."

"Mule driving is a risky business. Strung out on the road in the early morning, anything can happen to your train. Robbery at spear point. Accidents which leave lame animals. Spilled loads - with amphoras of clients' oil lying broken on the road. Bad fodder which sickens half your train. You do what you can to reduce the risk."

"So carrying grain increases your risk of accidents?"

The muleteer leaned closer to Skaphis and spoke in a low voice.

"Your risk of accidents decreases sharply if you stay on the right side of certain Piraeus businessmen."

"And one of these has spread the word that transporting grain is bad for business?"

The muleteer nodded.

"A couple of weeks ago - the exception being of course for his grain. Not that there was any to transport. But now we're shipping grain till our mules wear themselves to asses. Only authorized shipments mind."

Skaphis' pitcher was empty. The muleteers rose to leave.

"You're sure that you were warned off grain shipments a couple of weeks ago?"

The mule man raised his finger to his lips and then drew it sideways across his throat in an unmistakable gesture.

Skaphis took this to mean yes.

The music studio was quiet when Skaphis emerged from the tavern. Polyctor sat in the corner of the courtyard. The twin pipes of an aulos hung on a leather strap around his neck.

"The best time of the day. Just before the sun goes down, the colors get brighter, the shadows sharper, and the air cooler. And there are no more students."

He took a reed from a box on his lap and placed it in his mouth. He blew through the reed, making a noise like a particularly irritable wild fowl disturbed in the nesting period. Apparently satisfied with this unearthly shriek, he separated one of the pipes from its socket and fitted the reed into its cylindrical bore.

He lifted the pipes to his lips and played: at first a low and slow melody undulating like the gentle waves lapping against the side of a beach-bound craft, then a higher, faster lilt danced from the instrument, culminating in a single note held in unison on both pipes.

"I like to play to the sun when it goes down. Maybe I feel that I can encourage it to come back again with music."

He smiled.

"Or maybe I need to hear myself after a day of listening to others play."

"Worth listening to, I'd say."

"So you are a music lover after all."

"But not an expert. Which is why I came to you."

He handed the musician his paper.

"This scrap came up in connection with a case I'm working on. I wondered if it might be music."

Polyctor let his instrument dangle again from the neck strap and studied the fragment.

"Unlikely. We do use letters to denote musical notes. Higher notes have a dash beside them - that could be the meaning of the marks beside the A and the B. Greek letters are usually used for vocal pieces though, so you'd expect to find them over the text to be sung."

"It couldn't be an instrumental piece?"

"We typically use different notation for those. But let's say we were using the vocal notation for an instrument. Those are unlikely intervals. Difficult to play."

He lifted his pipes again to his lips. Straining, he blew a high note: his cheeks bulging with the pressure and the reed cracking and warbling. He then relaxed his cheeks and the pipe rasped out a low note, which slid up slightly, then down, as Polyctor adjusted the aperture of one of the holes of the pipe by sliding his finger over it.

"Not easy on the ear either."

"I knew you were a music lover."

Chapter *19*

"I didn't expect to see you here so soon, spade man. It's fortunate for you that Brochos is still laid up. I wouldn't guarantee that you'd make it this far if he was on his feet."

"I came to ask you for a favor."

Kotos's eyebrow rose in a questioning curve.

"They are saying that Aristophon killed himself, oar-man, on account of business losses. Not far from where we, shall I say, encountered you, the other night."

Skaphis edged uneasily into the couch opposite the Sicilian.

"Quite convenient for you, it seems to me. A good line of defense would be that Aristophon killed Barysthenes and then killed himself. Of course the argument could be used backwards - Aristophon saw you kill Barysthenes and then you killed him to keep him quiet."

"You think I killed Barysthenes?"

Kotos laughed.

"If I thought you killed Barysthenes, oar-man, you wouldn't be lying there chatting with me."

"I was following Aristophon when your men jumped me. He had just gone into the courtyard, when I made my acquaintance with Brochos. After that I didn't see anything. You told me they fetched a cart, so they were in the area longer than me. Did they see anyone else go into Aristophon's warehouse?"

A low laugh suppurated from Kotos's throat.

"Perhaps Barysthenes did not make such a mistake in his choice of partner after all. I asked my men if they saw anyone else on the streets. Brochos saw nobody, but my cart driver said he did see a woman lurking in the shadows along the street from the warehouse. He assumed she was a whore or music girl, but he didn't get a good look, it could have been a man."

Skaphis thought of Thrassia. She had followed him from Glaukos's house. He wondered if you could mistake the slight slave girl for a man. In a dark Piraeus alleyway, small shadows did have a tendency to loom large.

"I walked by the warehouse when I left here yesterday, though, and slipped in to see what was inside."

Skaphis wasn't sure why he felt the compulsion to be open with Kotos. Perhaps it was the sense that the facts were, in the last analysis, unimportant to the gangster. His currency was will, not truth. If he willed it, mere facts could be made to point in any direction.

"What was inside was Aristophon's body. He'd been dead a while. Most of the night, I'd guess. I found this in his hand. What do you make of it?"

He placed the paper on the table. Kotos sat up and studied it in the poor light of an oil lamp.

"Well it's the first five letters of the alphabet with the delta missing. The first two have marks against them. It could be an acronym: the first letters of four words, or maybe four names - a client list, possibly. More likely it's a tally sheet, though - these are numbers. The dashes are written a bit sloppily, but look: 'A is 1000 and G is 3. 'B is

2000 and E is 5, so read as numbers we are looking at 1003 and 2005. Or you could read it as a fraction: the quantity on the upper line signifies the number of parts that the whole is divided into, the bottom number signifies the number of those parts which you have. Not a fraction you'd be likely to use, though, it's so close to 2 that the difference is not worth worrying about, except to a mathematician."

Absorbed in the abstract meaning of symbols and in the flickering lamp light, Kotos's face lost its harsh angles and seemed to shed a dozen years.

"Mathematics was a favorite subject of mine in my youth - that and horsemanship. The numbers are interesting in their own right. 5 obviously divides into 2005, so it can be represented by a rectangle of 5 by 401. 401: I know of no rectangle with this area, except of course the rectangle whose width is 1 and length is 401. And 1003, I don't know a rectangle of this size off hand. There certainly isn't one of width 2, or 3, 5, 7 or 11."

He paused and looked up at Skaphis.

"Some people put significance in such studies. For me, it is a pastime. More likely the numbers are tallies of grain shipped, or even a price list: 1000 drachmas for 3 shipments, 2000 for 5. But that would make no sense."

"Why not?"

"Simple businesses; usually when you buy more you pay less per unit. You'd expect to receive 7 shipments for 2000 drachmas, 6 at the minimum, but not 5."

"It could be the other way around, then: 1000 ears of grain for 3 drachmas, 2000 for 5."

Kotos laughed again.

"Sound economics, but your units of measure are idiosyncratic, to say the least."

He swung his legs back onto the couch. Skaphis recovered his paper from the table.

"Most people make the mistake of underestimating me, Skaphis. I fear you have been guilty of overestimating my capabilities. There are people in Athens that know a good deal more about codes and numbers than myself."

"There was another favor I wanted to ask of you. It would be a great help with my defense if you would give me a deposition attesting to the fact that Barysthenes was not a citizen."

"The story I gave you the other day was not for public consumption. I told you so you would appreciate why I would not have killed Barysthenes myself. I am a resident alien, and Barysthenes was my original sponsor. It would make my position a little delicate if it was known that my sponsor was here under false pretenses."

"I'm sure that is something you could manage one way or another."

"That may be so, but it would cost money and effort, and I don't see why I should expend either on your behalf. The man you call Barysthenes was like a brother to me. But you are nothing. You bring me an entertaining riddle but ask a high price for this diversion."

"I assume you'd like to see Barysthenes' killer brought to justice. If the crime has been pinned on me, that will be harder to do."

"If I find his murderer, I will have no difficulty bringing him to justice. However, there may be something in what you say. Let me think about it."

"Don't think too long, the preliminary hearing comes up next week."

Skaphis stood, arching his back to stretch the muscles that had been curled up in the recliner.

"I heard an interesting story from a mule driver. He said that an embargo had been put on ferrying grain to the city a couple of weeks ago. Maybe the cartel's collapse was planned in advance. Now I'm sure you could contain the effect of this information being conveyed to other cartel members, also. But perhaps this would cost some effort too."

Kotos exploded angrily. He uncoiled himself from his couch and stood face to face with Skaphis.

"I told you there was no cartel, spade-man. Mule drivers love to talk, but the substance of their talk is like the substance of air – it weighs nothing."

Kotos continued in a voice so low that, close as he was to the gangster's face Skaphis had to strain to make out the words.

"If I thought you were threatening me, Skaphis, I might get angry. I'm told that people do not like it when I get angry."

His voice modulated to a more readily audible level.

"I will think about what you have said, however."

It occurred to Skaphis as he was leaving that his threat was indeed a hollow one. The only members of the cartel he knew were already dead.

chapter 20

Somewhat to Skaphis' surprise, Herakleides did appear at the tavern the next morning at sunrise.   Lusilla was already up and about, directing the efforts of a pair of deliverymen, who were unloading vast amphoras of unmixed wine from a cart pulled up at the front door. They struggled them through the main room like the awkward bodies of drunken comrades and helped them down the cellar stairs to sleep it off in the cool darkness.

She gave Skaphis a crust of bread for his journey, which he split with his companion.   The men walked in silence up to the city.   Though smaller than Skaphis, the soldier loped with an easy stride that Skaphis found difficult to match.   Get him on an oar-bench all day in the airless swelter of a three-banked battleship, and he'd see who lasted the longest.

A water urn standing guard at the entrance to Stephanos's house advertised the presence of death within. Skaphis watched from the street as a group of men ladled water from the container over their hands: ritual protection against death's dark influence.   He slipped in behind the group, splashing a cursory scoop of water over his fingers: if death was going to pollute him, it would have done so years ago.   Herakleides didn't even make this perfunctory gesture.

Aristophon's body lay in state with his feet towards the door.   Two women were singing an ululating dirge to the rasping accompaniment of an aulos played by a third.   They withdrew to the corner of the room when the group of mourners entered. They did persist with the wailing, however. The intrusive scent from the flowers strewn around the head of the bier, and undoubtedly from the perfumes used to anoint the body, did not quite mask a sharper smell that pervaded the room. The closeness of the atmosphere, and the buzzing of the aulos amplified the wave of nausea that welled through Skaphis' stomach.

The music stopped, and the vocalization dropped to a low mumble, seemingly in deference to the visitors, who had each filed by the corpse and were now reminiscing about times they had spent with the live Aristophon. These times involved horses and women. They stood with their backs to the body. Herakleides had attached himself to the end of the line of ex-soldiers and paid his respects in turn. He now stood with the group, accepted as a fellow campaigner.

The aulos music started again, and Stephanos's slave strutted into the room carrying a table loaded with wine cups and a mixing bowl. He placed the table on the floor near the soldiers. As he turned, his eyes rested on Skaphis. The slave scurried back out of the room. The singing was rising again to a crescendo of grief. Skaphis was sure that these were professional mourners and the grief was mercenary. The real thing was seldom quite so extravagant. Real or feigned, the noise combined with the air in the room to set his head throbbing. He slipped back out into the street and ladled a little water from the urn onto the back of his neck. The water was still cool, and made his skin tingle to the touch. He flattened himself into the shade of the wall and waited, wishing for a breeze of some kind.

"Infernal racket in there. Damned women are paid to mourn, I wish they'd do it a little more quietly."

One of the ex-soldiers had emerged into the sunlight. He took up residence in the shade beside Skaphis.

"Served with the fellow during the war for a while, patrolling the border to the north. Didn't have much time for him after that though. Those other chaps knew him better. I notice you didn't stay long."

"I'm from the Piraeus. Aristophon has been spending a lot of time down there recently."

"I don't get down to the Piraeus much any more. I was based down there for a while a couple of years ago."

"During the revolution?"

"Just because you are well-born, doesn't mean you are anti-democratic. My family has a proud history of standing up for the democracy, and a long history of opposition to Sparta in the assembly. When the regime of thirty seized power with Spartan backing, most of the cavalry joined up with them more or less willingly. I thought it best to leave town. My family had a place in the Piraeus, and I stayed there for a while, but things were getting dangerous, so I slipped across the border to Thebes."

A compact balding man turned into Aristophon's house, pausing briefly to sprinkle water on his hands. Skaphis recognized Euboulos.

"Aristophon, there, was in one of the snatch squads that went out daily to grab victims of the regime. There was him and a fellow we called Gyllipus. We gave him that name because he admired the Spartans so much, it's funny, we called him that for so long now that I can't remember his real name. There were a couple more in the squad — one, apparently was a private investigator who had avoided the purges by helping the regime.

"Anyway, they had orders to pick me up in the Piraeus. Aristophon managed to slip away the previous night and get warning to me. He told me about the work he was doing. How they were picking up whole families at the whim of the thirty to be put to death on fabricated charges. I urged him to come with me into exile, but he was not a strong-willed character. Getting warning to me was as much of a rebellion as he could muster."

The group of ex-soldiers blossomed from the doorway into the sun-lit street, talking volubly now that they were putting walls between themselves and death. Herakleides followed a moment later and loitered by the water stoup.

"But for that small rebellion, I owe him a debt, and so I listen to that damned singing and look at his dead face."

He turned to join his companions.

Herakleides sidled over.

"That was the man who left the meeting before Barysthenes was killed."

"You're sure of that?"

"I told you, the moon was bright and I got a good look at him. I'm sure he was the man. I'll tell you what though – they don't believe he committed suicide."

Skaphis raised his eyebrow.

"They don't think he had the nerve. They also believed that his friends would have helped him out if he was in financial difficulties."

"It's easy enough for them to say that after he's dead. Were they so forthcoming when he was alive?"

"They certainly blamed his taking up trading for his death, and they traced his decline to unsavory characters he was thrown into contact with during the rule of the thirty."

Stephanos had come out into the street and was lurching towards them, anger in his gait. The slave stood in the doorway half in the house, half outside, his face curled into an ironic replica of a smile.

Herakleides continued, oblivious to the impending interruption, "A woman was also mentioned."

185

"You," Stephanos spluttered, "You have the audacity to come here and gloat over my friend's body. You plied me for information with some ludicrous story that you were working for a client who had a claim against that whore Psamathe. Where is your client? Where is the prosecution – I haven't heard of it, and you can be sure I have been listening. For all I know, it was your client who killed Aristophon. Or for that matter, you."

"I did try to find Aristophon, briefly, but made no progress. However, I interviewed Alexis, and from him got a sympathetic description of your friend. I just came to pay my respects. I apologize if I intruded on your grief."

Stephanos seemed somewhat mollified by this.

"I'm sorry, I can't help feeling that this is somehow my fault, I was a little harsh with Aristophon last time we met and accused him of frittering away our money on bad business schemes. I wonder if he was too ashamed to face up to me."

"You think he did commit suicide?"

"That is what it looks like isn't it?"

"I'm not so sure. With your permission I'd like to dig around a bit and find out."

Stephanos' face brightened a little. With the brightening, the irony returned to his voice.

"And with my permission you'd also like some of my silver."

"I've already got some of your silver, and didn't deliver anything for it. What do you say if I keep that owl you gave my last time in my care and I'll see if I can turn anything up in return?"

"Perhaps I misjudged you."

"People are always misjudging me. I do have a question for you, though. A cavalryman whose nickname was Gyllipus: what is his real name?"

"You think he had something to do with this?"

"I'm not sure if there is any connection at all."

"His name is Kallictor. If that bastard had anything to do with killing Aristophon... But I should get back inside. I know where some more owls roost if you can produce some information I can base a prosecution on."

The slave darted back into the house as his master returned.

"Slick, the way you hired him on as a client. But you didn't ask him where to find Kallictor."

"The cavalry class are never hard to find. It's the lower classes that can be difficult to pin down."

"Aristophon was in the cavalry class, I believe."

"You have a point there."

Barysthenes' aunt was sitting at the shaded side of her tiny central courtyard. Her slave recognized Skaphis from the funeral and showed him through, bringing a stool from the house for him to sit on. The slave unfolded the stool in the sunshine opposite the old lady. Skaphis sat and squinted into the sun's glare. He wondered if he had been deliberately positioned so that it was a strain for him to see his hostess, while she had him sharply illuminated. He thought it was a good bet.

"There was a day when it would have been a major scandal for me to casually entertain a gentleman caller, unchaperoned in the middle of the day. My father, or later my husband would have punished such impropriety severely. Now, I'm afraid, no-one would believe anything improper was going on. A benefit of age is that you can associate more freely than when you are young, because nobody considers you a threat. This benefit, though, is vastly outweighed by the stark fact that you are indeed no threat."

"Do you know that I have been accused of killing Barysthenes?"

"Did you?"

"No."

"I have been accused of things in the past myself."

"I am trying to find out who is behind the accusation."

"Young man, I know no more about the law than a well-bred Athenian lady should, which is I know to fear it as an arbitrary agency, which like war and pestilence can take your loved ones away from you with little warning. But I had the distinct impression that the prosecutor has to formally issue a summons to the accused. Surely this has happened?"

Skaphis nodded.

"Then you must know the identity of the accuser."

"Yes, but he is a prosecutor-for-hire, and I don't think he is going after me on his own in the hopes of collecting a bounty from the state. I believe someone is behind him."

She sat silently for a while, and then leaned forward in her chair. The shadow carved a line through the top of her head. Her face was in the sun, and her eyes smiled.

"I do believe you think it is me."

"I have to admit, it crossed my mind."

"The law courts are not a place a respectable Athenian lady goes, even by proxy. I can assure you I had nothing to do with it."

"You did say that there were no remaining male members of the family."

"Ah well, there I may have over-simplified a little. My younger sister was married to a colonist and moved to Italy. She had a son by the name of Zenothemis. I didn't count him because I assumed he was abroad. It turns out I was wrong; I had a visit from him a couple of days ago. He is in Athens on some trading venture. I can hardly imagine he would be behind your accusation, though. He has lived most of his life in Italy. As far as I know he never met Barysthenes. What would he gain by prosecuting you?"

"You said yourself it was a family's responsibility to find a murderer. Perhaps he feels it is his duty."

"Not that one, duty is the last thing that would motivate him to take some course of action which involves him in any trouble."

"Money, then, Barysthenes has a little and it would fall to him as the next of kin if he could discredit his adoption of me."

"I still find it hard to believe, he's only been in Athens once before, to my knowledge and that was years ago. What would he know about the law courts? And why wouldn't he mention this to me?"

Skaphis thought, but could not come up with a satisfactory answer.

"You told me that you barely recognized Barysthenes when he returned from Sicily, he had become so taciturn. I wonder if I could ask you to write me a statement to that effect. It would help my defense."

"I know I do not understand the law, but I cannot imagine how that would help you."

"I'm trying to give the jurors an image of Barysthenes' whole life, before I met him and after. To be honest, I'm trying to show that there are many people who had a motive to kill him."

"Including Zenothemis?"

"Sometimes the best form of defense is attack."

"Zenothemis is my sister's son. I have not seen her in half a lifetime, but when he smiles, he reminds me of her and for that I should love him."

"You said he was in Athens once before?"

"It was during the Sicilian expedition. Along with our fleet, an armada of merchant ships sailed carrying supplies and equipment. They returned to Athens with their holds filled with cargoes of Italian produce. Zenothemis hitched a ride on one of these ships. He was quite young, and an ingratiating sort of a lad. He persuaded me on the strength of his kinship to let him lodge with me. He stayed on for the entire winter eating at my expense and never offered to pay a single obol towards his upkeep. Whenever I was on the verge of throwing him out onto the street, he would smile at me and there would be the image of my far off sister. My longing for her got the better of my good sense."

She called for her slave.

"Milyas here can write, I'll have him prepare a statement for you."

"Why did he leave in the end?"

"Why did who leave?"

"Zenothemis."

"He left when Barysthenes returned."

chapter **21**

"Skaphis, I thought you had been avoiding me. Mind you, given your success at finding Aristophon, I assumed your embarrassment kept you away."

"I've just come from seeing Aristophon."

"Finding him when he's dead doesn't count. How will I get my money back from him now?"

They were sitting in Psamathe's downstairs room.

"You could always sue the estate."

"They say that his debts forced him to kill himself. It doesn't sound like there would be much of an estate to sue."

"Do you believe that?"

"He was certainly in debt to me."

"Do you believe he killed himself?"

"I wouldn't know one way or another."

"You knew him well. Does it sound like something he would have done?"

"I suppose it does take a certain amount of strength of will to kill yourself, and Aristophon was not a strong character. But, Skaphis my dear, despair can lend a person unnatural resolve. Although, sometimes I believe it takes more courage to go on living than to do away with yourself."

"You were down in the Piraeus the night that Aristophon was killed."

"I came by Lusilla's looking for you. I was rather annoyed by your lack of progress. However, they told me you had finally found Aristophon, so I returned to the city expecting to hear back from you soon."

"You seem to spend a lot of time in the Piraeus."

"I told you, I have friends there."

She stretched her legs forward, hooking the footstool on which they had been resting back under the chair with her ankle, then stood up.

"Excuse me for a moment, Skaphis my dear, I'll be right back."

Watching her stride across the room, Skaphis reflected that her particular lifestyle afforded her an independence that most women lacked. This showed up even in her gait, which was purposeful and confident, almost manly. He wondered if she feigned demure when the occasion demanded it. But no, he supposed the beguiling attraction of a woman like Psamathe was the very contrast she afforded to the more respectable wives and daughters.

Psamathe returned and placed a bag onto the table. She picked up a dowel, which had been propped in a rack beside her seat. The end of the stick was swaddled in raw wool, like the bound stump of a newly amputated limb. She couched the distaff under her left arm and, licking her right thumb and forefinger, began to tease the wool into a thread. Skaphis found the nimble motion of her fingers uncomfortably arousing, as she twisted form into the chaotic structure of the raw fiber.

"You are surprised, Skaphis? I am skilled in all the women's arts and then some more."

Her voice dropped a tone in self-mockery.

"And especially in the one which involves spinning men's unorganized desires."

She smiled, and her voice raised again.

"I see you are not immune."

"Where do you stay when you are in the Piraeus?"

"I find spinning to be a relaxing pastime. It puts the fingers to use and leaves the mind to think. You could think of your life in woolen terms. Some people are like a clump of raw wool, with threads going this way and that in a disordered clump. Useless, other than as stuffing for a pillow. But twist and coax the different strands of a life so they align in the same direction and you can spin it into a thread, and that thread can be woven into a useful or decorative garment."

"My life is more like a clump of sodden flax."

"You'd be surprised at what a woman's fingers can do with sodden flax, Skaphis."

No, Skaphis thought, not surprised.

"My father thought of spinning as a metaphor for the state. He used to come into the women's quarters and talk with me while I worked. He talked about men's topics: politics, war, the law. I had a brother, but he was young and only interested in archery and swordplay. My father preferred to chat with me. He would describe the debates in the assembly, and I would venture my opinions as to what course of action the city should follow. At first he found this amusingly precocious, but he encouraged me nevertheless, and eventually, I believe, he respected my opinion. He was a good man. But Skaphis, why do you look so amazed."

"I didn't realize you were a citizen."

She smiled and stopped spinning, laying her distaff across her lap like an infant replete from feeding. She kneaded the palm of her right hand with the fingers of her left.

"I'm a little out of practice. Yes I was a citizen. You don't think this life is right for a citizen woman?"

"I just thought it was – unusual."

"Think of the alternative for a young girl of fourteen: marriage to a boor twice her age and then a life of seclusion trapped within the four walls of her house except for the occasional religious festival or funeral. By the time you are in your twenties, if you are lucky, you have survived a handful of childbirths and your husband has been off at war enough to keep you from risking more. Your husband consorts with his cronies, with younger boys and with whores. But if you entertain a lover, you risk death for both of you."

She replaced the staff in its retainer on the floor.

"I don't think my father wanted to lose me, and so put off arranging a marriage. And then other events intervened. My life, at least, affords a certain freedom of action."

She lifted the small bag from the table and teased a coin out of it between her thumb and forefinger.

"In the end you were unsuccessful, but I appreciate the work you did for me. I believe this should cover your time."

She handed the coin to Skaphis.

It gleamed golden in the dull light. He slipped it inside his cloak.

Lusilla's tavern was busy. She caught Skaphis' eye when he walked through the front door and beckoned him over to her.

"That hairy chap in the corner, he's asking for you."

She indicated a swarthy man, whose beard seemed to sprout not just from his chin and upper lip, but also from his neck and cheeks.

"Any chance of a bite of food? The road to Athens is as long as it used to be and I find looking at dead bodies gives me an appetite."

"Skaphis, I should raise your rent, the amount you eat."

She smiled.

"Away with you, I'll send a plate to your table."

The hair on Skaphis' visitor really did seem to grow from every inch of his face. His eyes peered out from the mass of hair with the startled glare of a nocturnal animal caught in the light of a bonfire.

"I was told to bring you this."

He handed Skaphis a papyrus scroll. Skaphis unrolled it, but was unable to make out the lettering in the dim light of the tavern. An oil lamp sat unlit on the table. He caught the eye of one of Lusilla's girls, who brought over a taper and nursed the lamp to sputtering life. The writing was cramped, and the shadows from the flickering lamp played over the surface of the text, but Skaphis was able with some difficulty to decipher it.

It contained the story of Barysthenes' and Barybromos' deaths in Sicily, and the subsequent impersonation of Barysthenes by a young Sicilian. It went into significant and quite convincing detail, but made no mention of Kotos. The author of the document was apparently a Syracusan by the name of Diomedorus, who had encountered the man who was calling himself Barysthenes on a visit to the Piraeus. He had recognized him from their days in the Syracusan cavalry together. At first Barysthenes had maintained that Diomedorus was mistaken, but they drank together, and eventually he had admitted the whole story to his old comrade in arms.

"You are Diomedorus?"

The man nodded.

"You know what this says?"

Diomedorus' eyebrow raised in a non-committal arc.

"I was told to bring it to you."

He finished his wine and was pushing back his stool when Lusilla bustled to the table carrying a generous plate of bread and cheese. At the side of the plate was an anonymous yellowing slab of salt fish.

"That mother of yours was back round here looking for you. She seemed to think you were neglecting her in favor of one of my girls."

She was speaking softly so that Skaphis' companion could not hear. Skaphis' companion did not look interested in the slightest. He was busy tearing off a chunk of the bread into which he rolled the bulk of the fish.

"I told her it was against the rules for you to favor anyone but me in that way," she winked mischievously, "you'd better attend to your dinner Skaphis, before your guest attends to it all for you."

The Sicilian had stuffed the remainder of the fish and half the bread into his mouth.

Skaphis lifted the scroll, "You'll testify to this in court?"

"I am shipping out for the west in the morning. Good fish that."

He indicated the space on the platter where the fish had been.

He left Skaphis clutching his testament and allaying his hunger with cheese.

Skaphis reread the document. On the face of it, the tale seemed fantastic. Listening to Kotos' intense description his youth in Syracuse, their encounter with the two Athenian brothers, and the subsequent bold plan to impersonate one of them, Skaphis had found the story completely believable. He wondered how good a substitute this deposition would be. The first hearing was coming up in a day's time. The lamp flickered and Skaphis looked up from his reading. Thrassia stood holding a plate.

"The mistress told me to bring this. She said that next time you should be more careful who you share your food with."

She put the plate on the table in front of him. It contained a small piece of the same yellow fish the Sicilian had devoured and a strip of bread. He gestured for her to sit down in the seat the Sicilian had recently vacated. He pried a few flakes from the fish and chewed on them. Its taste was sharp and salty and it left his fingers smeared with oil. He tore off some bread. The bread had absorbed some of the fish oil, and tasted good. He glanced up to catch Lusilla's eye and lifted up the bread in a silent motion of thanks. She responded with a gesture formed by inserting her thumb between the first two clenched fingers of her right hand, which Skaphis could only interpret lewdly.

Skaphis offered the food to Thrassia. She peeled a single flake from the fish and nibbled tentatively at it.

"That night, when you followed me, did you see the men ambush me?"

"I was frightened, and ran back to the tavern."

She looked down.

"I'm sorry, I should have stayed. Perhaps I could have helped."

Skaphis shrugged, "Not much you could have done against those ruffians."

"I told Lusilla when I got back to the tavern, but she didn't seem too concerned. She said that you could look after yourself, and if you couldn't then she needed better quality help anyway."

"Was my client here?"

Thrassia thought for a moment. "Now that you mention it, she was. She said that it sounded like you wouldn't be back any time soon. So she left."

Thrassia pushed back her stool and stood.

"I must get back to work. The mistress will be looking for me."

Skaphis turned and surveyed the tavern. There was no sign of Lusilla. There was a sign of Astra, however, holding her robe clear of the floor like an ambassador disembarking from a beached ship.

"Skaphis, why don't you come see me. You spend all your time down here, consorting with these.... girls. I need you at home with me."

Thrassia had scurried into the storeroom. Skaphis guessed she'd be occupied in there for a while. Astra sat opposite Skaphis, and he offered her the remains of his fish. Initially she refused, but on second thoughts she reached over and seized the whole piece.

"Astra, you know I have been indicted for Barysthenes' murder. I explained before, that it would not look good for me to take up residence in his house with his wife under these circumstances."

"I get lonely. And I'm worried about the future."

"I did find out a little more about Barysthenes' business dealings. He had some money out on an investment, which recently matured. I have the proceeds upstairs in my room."

Her eyes brightened.

"Wouldn't it be safer to keep the money at the house? There are all kinds of people wandering around this place."

The proclivities of the taverns clientele were all too easily guessed at, mused Skaphis, and therefore easy to guard against. Preserving the cash at Astra's house was a different matter entirely. However, he didn't feel particularly proprietorial towards the money, and it might make Astra feel more comfortable to have it in closer proximity.

"I'll get it if you like."

She smiled a demure assent. He lit the way to his room with the guttering lamp leaving her glancing nervously round the dim tavern as if fearful that if she caught the eye of an individual patron, she would reveal by her glance the imminent presence of silver and awake in him a slumbering larceny.

Skaphis dug the purse that Kotos had given him out of its hiding hole. He poured the coins from the purse onto his bed and divided them into two unequal piles. He took a square of cloth from a box at the foot of his bed and folded it around the larger pile, tying it off with a piece of string to form a makeshift money bag. He replaced the smaller pile in the purse and stuffed the larger money bag back in the hole.

He was about to close up the hole, when he recalled the coin that Psamathe had given him. He took this out of his pocket and examined it in the light of the oil lamp before adding it to his cache. It was indeed gold. In fact it was a Persian Daric: a twin for the one he had salvaged from the floor beneath Aristophon's corpse.

Astra was sipping nervously from a cup of wine when Skaphis returned downstairs. He handed her the purse, which she secreted in her garment, glancing skittishly round the room, as if anticipating an imminent assault.

"Did you know that Zenothemis is in town?"

She studied her wine in silence for a moment.

"Who is Zenothemis?"

"Barysthenes' Italian cousin. I talked to his aunt today: apparently Zenothemis stayed with her before – at the time of the Sicilian expedition. But you spent a lot of time with his aunt around that period, surely you met Zenothemis?"

"It's a long time ago, and I was nearly out of my mind with worry for my husband. Skaphis, you're not going to let me walk home alone carrying this?"

She touched her robe where she had concealed the purse. Skaphis shrugged but accompanied her out of the tavern. They walked in silence through the gloaming: to all appearances man and wife returning from a visit to a shrine. The few people they encountered en route were intent on their own business, scurrying home to dinner before dark.

Strange, Skaphis thought, how you always assumed the banal. A stranger hurrying through the streets could be a foreign ambassador on an important state mission, or a murderer attempting to flee the scene of his crime. But you assumed he was just an ordinary fellow late for his supper. That couple strolling in silence that you assumed were comfortably married could be bound by a difficult web of wordless contradictions.

Their pace quickened as they approached Munichia hill. They kept the pace up as they ascended the hill, and arrived breathless at Barysthenes' house. Astra turned to face Skaphis at the door. Her cheeks glowed red with the exertion of the climb and with the reflection of the setting sun.

Unexpected as the jolt when a ship beaches on an unseen sandbar, she lurched forward and grabbed hold of him. Her embrace was surprisingly strong. She stretched herself up by pulling on his neck with one hand and kissed him, her body a taught cable warped along his length. As suddenly, she relaxed her embrace, and without a word, slipped into the house.

Skaphis hoped that the two men loitering across the street were indeed carousers waiting to rendezvous with a drinking partner and not spies paid by his legal opponents to watch Barysthenes' house.

chapter **22**

"This first hearing is a bit of a formality, really. Either side can submit evidence orally or in the form of written depositions. These will be entered into the record and may be read out at trial. However, they also have the option of withholding such statements for later hearings."

Lysias had decided to accompany Skaphis to the proceeding, and chatted as the pair joined the intermittent stream of commuters on the road to Athens. He had explained that, while it was incumbent on Skaphis to conduct his own defense, it was quite legitimate for him to take professional advice. As the law courts operated in public, Lysias had every right to observe.

"In lesser cases, a major goal of the pre-trial procedures is to attempt to arbitrate a settlement short of the expense and risk of a trial. This can sometimes happen in a homicide case too. If an indictment is made more out of personal enmity than a dispassionate analysis of the evidence, having a strong defense laid out at the pre-trial can persuade the prosecutor to withdraw his case."

"In murder cases, there are three pre-trial hearings, held a month apart. We can elect to enter new evidence at any of these hearings. The Basileus has jurisdiction. Murder, you see, has a strong religious overtone – it is an act that brings pollution to a citizen and by extension to the city itself. So it makes sense that the Basileus, whose duties are primarily of a religious nature, should preside.

"He also has to decide which court to assign the case to. Cases of intentional homicide are assigned to the Areopagus. This is an ancient court, a direct descendent of the pre-democratic justice system. There are four lesser homicide courts, though: the Palladion for unintentional homicide and for killing of a slave or resident alien, and the Delphinion tries cases of justifiable homicide. The court meets on the beach in Phreatto in cases where the killer is already in exile and cannot set foot on Athenian soil. He pleads his case from a boat offshore. Finally there is the Prytaneion, which hears cases where the death was caused by an animal or an inanimate object."

Skaphis touched the hilt of his dagger under his cloak. Perhaps it should be prosecuted for his partner's murder; hard to imagine it accomplishing this on its own, though without human intervention.

"There can't be much money in writing defense speeches for those cases."

Lysias smiled.

"A slate falls off a roof and kills someone. It does seem strange at first glance that the state should bother to put the slate on trial for its life. But the victim's relatives have the responsibility of bringing his killer to justice. If the court establishes that no man's hand was behind the homicide, then the relatives can be shown to have fulfilled this obligation. Besides, these cases are short and only involve the Basileus himself and four subsidiary officials.

"My suggestion is that we hold back the evidence that Barysthenes was not in fact Barysthenes for the next hearing, or even for the last one. That will give the prosecution less time to dig around for contradictory witnesses. In this hearing, you should confine yourself to a brief statement to the effect that you did not kill

Barysthenes.   You should also account for your whereabouts on the night of the murder."

"Over the course of the hearings, we will get to hear what evidence the prosecution is basing its case on. This will give me the raw material to write your trial speeches. Then the hard part will be done."

"And the easy part?"

"The easy part is for you to deliver my speech and wait for the court to rule in your favor."

He stepped aside to avoid a pungent heap of recent mule droppings.

"Or otherwise, as the case may be."

The Royal Stoa, where the Basileus held court, was on the northwest corner of the agora, where the road from Piraeus intersected the Panathenaic Way, the grand thoroughfare along which the annual Panathenaic procession pulsed its way from the Dipylon gate to the Acropolis. On their way through the city, they had skirted the Areopagus hill, where the senior homicide court sat. Lysias had also pointed out the state prison, where a condemned man could expect to spend his last night before a final state sponsored breakfast of hemlock.

Skaphis recognized Orthagoras and the two witnesses he had brought to the summons loitering in front of the Stoa. He glared at Skaphis, but did not speak.   In addition to serving as the Basileus' office, the royal Stoa was the state's law library. Around the three walls of the building large marble blocks were arrayed on which were inscribed the laws.   Two men were absorbed in an analysis of one of these blocks, which appeared to have writing carved in both sides.

The Basileus was a willowy gray-bearded man by the name of Onesippus. He carried a blue cushion under his arm, which he placed on a limestone throne in front of the Stoa before bending himself into the seat. A court recorder sat on a lower stone seat, with a table and writing implements. At his feet were a number of earthenware jars. These could be used to seal testimony submitted at a preliminary hearing for later use in trial. Lysias had drifted away and was standing with a small cluster of bored onlookers in the shade of an olive tree at the margin of the Panathenaic Way.

The Basileus started by verifying that the summons had been correctly given according to the appropriate format, and that Skaphis had indeed appeared to answer the summons. He then turned to Orthagoras,

"Your kinship with the deceased?"

"Your honor, here stands dead man's next of kin," he pointed his finger at Skaphis, "And he should, by all our laws and customs be relentless in the pursuit of his murderer. But he killed Barysthenes with his own long-bladed dagger. We could hardly expect him to bring himself to trial."

"Nevertheless, it is the duty of the family to prosecute a homicide case."

As a member of his phratry, I have taken the duty of prosecution upon myself. An unresolved homicide pollutes more than just the family; it pollutes the state as a whole."

Onesippus raised a skeptical eyebrow.

"Very well, but let me put you on notice. I do not approve of prosecutors for hire, least of all in murder cases."

"Ridding my city of the stain caused by an unanswered killing in the only reward I ask."

The hearing turned out to be largely a formality. The Basileus established dates for the subsequent hearings and

Orthagoras outlined his case. His case rested largely on the fact that Skaphis was the obvious beneficiary of Barysthenes' death, along with some thinly veiled hints that even before his partner's death, he had been trespassing on his estate by a too close relationship with the dead man's wife. He also made great play on the fact that Skaphis had been the one to discover Barysthenes' body.

Following Lysias' advice, Skaphis kept his speech simple and short. He described Psamathe's visit and his trip to Athens on the day of the murder. He recounted how the body had been stiff and cold when he had found it. He concluded by stating that he had only found out about his adoption by Barysthenes after his death.

The Basileus suggested Skaphis bring witnesses, or witness statements to the next hearing, and closed the proceedings with a gesture for the clerk to bring in the next case.

Orthagoras and his cronies disappeared as soon as the hearing was over. The plaintiff on the next case was already loitering by an ancient cut limestone block that adorned the entrance to the stoa. Skaphis joined Lysias under the olive tree.

"They didn't have much in the way of evidence, did they?"

"I wouldn't say that," Lysias responded. "Nobody saw you kill Barysthenes, but nobody saw someone else kill him either. There would seem to be every reason for you to kill him, and an Athenian jury tends not to make the fine distinction between the one who was most likely to have committed the offense and the one who actually did. They can make a good case just based on likelihood – who is more likely to commit murder than the person who will most immediately benefit?"

"An inheritance would seem to be a dangerous thing."

"Look at all this."

The two men studying the law inscriptions had swollen during the course of the hearing to a dozen or more. In front of the stoa a small group were preparing for the next hearing. Down the road, they could see a throng of potential jurors preparing to file into the law courts.

"Half of this legal activity involves inheritance in one form or another."

In spite of Herakleides' pessimism, Kallictor was not hard to locate. Lysias knew the family, and pointed Skaphis in the right direction. The right direction was down the Panathenaic Way, backtracking the route of the annual religious procession. The thoroughfare scythed through the teeming residential districts, the further away it got from the austere temple of the Acropolis and the grandeur of the civic buildings surrounding the Acropolis the shabbier it became, at once noisier, dirtier and livelier, until it plunged before the Dipylon gate into that teeming anthill of enterprise and iniquity called the Kerameikos. An inverse redemption this: a downhill slide from a high moral bastion to the low ground brimming with life of a questionable virtue.

The Panathenaic procession itself was an uphill struggle: the entire citizenry filing up the hill bearing obeisance and new clothes for the lonely goddess. But it was only once a year. The more usual pilgrimage was in the other direction, to the Kerameikos. And the goddess to be worshipped: not the maiden Athena, but her more prodigal kinswoman Aphrodite.

Kallictor lived fashionably close to the Panathenaic Way and unfashionably close to the Kerameikos. An elderly slave led Skaphis to a tiny courtyard that burrowed through the center of the building. The slave was unsteady on his feet. Skaphis assumed he had been dipping into his master's wine supply. A certain amount of wastage could be expected in the process of admixing water to a wine flask opened in the heat of the day. Kallictor sat on a folding stool, his back to the earth encrusted wall of the building. A mixing bowl yawned like an exhausted volcano on a table by his side, a ladle leaned against its arid sides. Kallictor was drunk, which explained how his slave could afford to siphon his master's wine in the middle of the day.

"I blame Conon and his set," he said, continuing a train of thought that he seemed unaware Skaphis was not party to, "Trading in their horse harnesses for rowing pins and calling themselves patriots. That's when the rot started. Saved the city from the Persians, they claimed, and built us an empire in the sea - but for what? They made us dependent on the sailor rabble - foreigners, people of no account."

He spoke with a lisp. This had been a popular affectation of the upper classes, aping the affliction of the trend setting Alcibiades. They said that Alcibiades, as a youth, had been an entirely talentless player of the kithara, instruction in which was a standard part of the young gentleman's education. He let it be known that he considered the kithara effete and an unsuitable instrument for a man of culture. His influence on fashion was such that the kithara dropped out of the curriculum and his lack of talent went unobserved.

"Put your faith in the wooden walls the oracle was supposed to have told Themistocles - meaning the fleet. Phah, the Spartans have no walls at all, they put their faith in their men."

Kallictor's hair was long and braided in the Spartan style. This had been popular with the upper class youth a couple of decades ago, but looked incongruous in a middle aged Athenian in these democratic years.

Kallictor continued parsing the past century's history.

"Themistocles had an interest in shipbuilding contracts more like. And did our fleet save the city? Of course not - the Persians burned it. They only went home after they were defeated on land at Plataea: by Athenians and Spartans fighting side by side."

Skaphis had heard this sort of pro-Spartan rhetoric before, though not recently. The rigid, militaristic Spartan society was put forward as a model of moral rectitude and contrasted with the chaotic free-for-all that was Athens. More attention to the Spartan virtues of courage, discipline and fiscal restraint were touted as cure-alls for the moral degeneracy that was continually perceived to threaten the city. Never mind that the final Spartan victories were not won by their vaunted legions on land, but by a new mercenary navy. And the key to the success was not Spartan discipline in combat, but Persian money, used to raise the sailor's daily wage from 2 obols to 3 and thus lure away a significant component of Athens' manpower. The Persians clearly feared the unpredictable Athenians, in the end, more than the rigid Spartans, and used their cash resources to tilt the balance once and for all in favor of the latter.

"Athenians and Spartans fought side by side more recently than that, though."

"That we did. And if we'd stuck to our principles, we'd have straightened the city out once and for all. Power was formally centralized in the elite families … those with a few years of history, who could be trusted to act in the best interests of the state as a whole. There was a fear that the power base was too small, that we weren't strong enough militarily; so we enfranchised the middle class: three thousand in all. Rich enough to equip themselves for the heavy infantry, if not for the cavalry. The theory was that with the heavy infantry behind us, we could keep the rabble under control. Too many of those bastards are democrats at heart, though and they undermined our regime. You'd think that they'd be happy with a share of the power and be civic minded enough to pitch in for the good of the city, but they never think of anything except their personal advancement. They achieved that by allying with the lower classes, making up in quantity what they lack in quality."

Kallictor spoke of the infantry classes as if they were an alien race. He reached for his empty cup. Some wine still puddled in the base of his crater. Skaphis tipped the bowl sluicing its contents into his garrulous host's empty cup.

"Stephanos asked me to look into Aristophon's death. He doesn't believe it was suicide. You were in the same unit with him during the regime?"

Kallictor took a healthy swig from his replenished cup and leaned backwards against the wall. His eyes drooped closed in the sunshine. Skaphis was afraid he had fallen asleep; he could hear the old slave moving around inside the house. His coordination had apparently not improved any, from the clatter he was making. In time, Kallictor spoke, though his eyes remained closed.

"As I was telling you, we lowered the bar too far and enfranchised a legion of malcontents and grumblers, and outright democrats. We were forced to apply harsh measures to the traitors in our midst. Don't forget that if our regime hadn't presented them with a viable alternative, the Spartans would likely have sacked the city."

True, Skaphis mused, to the Athenian in the street, the Spartan was an uncultured, unsophisticated, dangerous lout. Yet those louts had spared Athens the awful fate of a conquered city out of apparent deference to its history and culture.

"We operated in pairs: a cavalry officer, who had at his disposal whatever troops might be necessary to make an arrest, and a second team member who typically had some legal experience."

Kallictor slumped back in his stool, his legs splayed like two alternative views of history.

"I worked with a hustler from the Piraeus by the name of Barysthenes. A private investigator, and earmarked for arrest in the purges, but he worked off his debt to society by helping us locate miscreants."

Kallictor went on talking, but Skaphis wasn't listening. His mind was racing with the potential ramifications of Barysthenes' involvement in Kallictor's activities.

"Did Barysthenes ever work with Aristophon?"

"As a rule, we worked in pairs. Occasionally, though we'd team up, and Aristophon and his partner went out with us."

The alcohol which had caused Kallictor's talkativeness seemed now to have the opposite effect. He slumped motionless in his stool, seemingly unconscious except for the occasional swat with his arm at a circling fly, which could have been reflex at that.

"You said you worked in pairs."

Skaphis interpreted the answering grunt as affirmation.

"Who was Aristophon's partner?"

The mumble was soft, but Skaphis was certain of the name he articulated:

"Euboulos."

Kallictor's arm slipped from his lap and pendulumed down, his cup tumbling out of his sleep-numbed fingers onto the hard packed earth. Good Athenian pottery, fired in a side street of the Kerameikos no doubt, it rolled on the floor but did not break. Skaphis was reminded of the oil flask Astra cast into his partner's grave. He tried to remember if Euboulos had been at the funeral or not.

Euboulos was not at home when Skaphis called. On a hunch, he tried Psamathe's residence, but Euboulos was not there either. Psamathe was, though, and after having Skaphis wait downstairs while she 'fixed her appearance', summoned him to her upstairs quarters. If there was anything that needed fixing about Psamathe's appearance, Skaphis couldn't see it. She stood with her back to him looking out of a small window cut high in the wall.

"You can see the corner of the Acropolis from here. I like to imagine our lady Athena sometimes looks down and sees me here."

She had lifted her hair up at the back and was fixing it in place with a comb. Her elbows were lifted above her head, and the folds of her dress had slipped back towards her shoulders. Skaphis watched the sinews working in the narrow elbow joints as she teased her hair into conformity. He was reminded of the motion of mooring cables sprung along the side of a docked merchant ship stretching taught in the swelling tide. Innocent joints, elbows: asexual. Hers nagged him with a forsaken domesticity.

"What do you think the goddess would say to us, Skaphis?"

"She wouldn't notice us. Up there on the Acropolis, the whole city lies spread out below you like a child's play fortress dug into the sand, the people just insects scurrying through its crevices."

"Skaphis, I'm surprised at you, I thought godlessness was a hobby of the idle rich."

"The poor have little reason to relish eternity. Anyway, I find it easier to believe in the gods than to believe that they take any interest in men."

"Oh, I don't imagine Athena would pay any attention to me personally."

She turned to face Skaphis. As she lowered her arms to her sides, the fabric rippled over her elbows.

"I do feel that Athena has a care for our people as a whole."

She smiled, "Don't look so skeptical, Skaphis, I am of the opinion that Athena takes an interest in the affairs of her city. When the people are free, I believe she is happy, and generous with her gifts. When her people are oppressed, she is angry and withdraws her favor from the city."

"My impression of the gods is that they were more capricious than democratic."

"Homer's gods. But life was more capricious in Homer's time. Gods, like humans, have to adapt to the times."

"As you have adapted?"

The smile dried on her lips and she shot a glance at him that warned him he had crossed a line.

"I make no apologies for my life, Skaphis." The flash of anger died almost as soon as it had begun. "But come, sit down, I hear you were in court today. How did it go?"

"Routine, I suppose. It would have been quite boring if it hadn't been for the fact that my life is in the balance."

"Our lives are continually in the balance, Skaphis, except we aren't usually aware of it. You choose to react with anger to a stranger who bars your way at the crossroads. You turn out to have widowed your mother, who will become your wife, thus damning you and your children. The only difference with the court is that you are aware of the risks at the time you take them."

"I've come about the court case, actually: I need to get witness statements to back up my account of my whereabouts when Barysthenes was killed."

She touched her fingers to Skaphis' arm. "Come with me."

She led him into an airless back room. Most of the room was occupied by a wide couch strewn with cushions like the casual dead on an abandoned battlefield. Light slanted from a high casement, onto a three-legged table on which stood a couple of rolls of papyrus along with writing implements.

"Now, what shall I say?"

Skaphis reclined amongst the fallen cushions on the couch while Psamathe sat at the table and began to write.

"I learned more than the female crafts when I was a girl. My father treated me as much as a son as a daughter. He saw no reason why a woman should be denied the pleasure of reading, or the freedom of writing."

"A radical attitude."

"My father was a radical in some ways. In other ways he was deeply conservative. He believed in traditional values - family, community, democracy."

"What became of him?"

She continued writing in silence. Skaphis was afraid he had again overstepped some unseen boundary, but eventually she replied.

"The times became dangerous for democrats, and my father did not adapt to the times as quickly as he might."

"He was killed by the thirty?"

She glanced momentarily at the ground.

"A lot of good men died then."

"And his family was disenfranchised?"

"That was a gift from the gods. The life of an independent woman has many advantages, which are denied to citizens. I cannot see myself suiting the role of an Athenian matron."

But Skaphis could, and he wondered if it was an ache for an idealized domesticity that drew men to this upper room at a cost that would be many times the going rate for mere sex.

Skaphis decided to try Euboulos again. When he reached his house, Euboulos was closing the door on his way out.

"Ah, Skaphis, I'm surprised to see you, I thought you were in court today."

"Preliminary hearing, it was over almost before it began. But they suggested I secure witness testimony to back up my story."

"Are you thirsty ... of course you are, the law is a dry business. I was just heading out to a local watering hole for a bite to eat. Join me and tell me about the case."

They walked a block down the street and into a narrow alleyway, then through a nondescript door in the side of the alley. No sign distinguished the door from any of the several along either side of the alley. Once inside, however, they found themselves in a well-lit, almost spacious dining room. A serving woman nodded to Euboulos, and they reclined at an empty table beside a window facing an interior courtyard. The courtyard was large enough to contain a couple of stunted trees, and the statue of a young boy, which seemed to cast a forlorn eye on the trees, condemned as he was to stand perpetually out of their shade. On top of this, he had the indignity of being used as a perch by the birds that flitted noisily between the trees.

Skaphis looked round the room. Men in pairs or small groups lounged and chatted at the different tables. They were not ostentatious, but something about their demeanor spoke to Skaphis of quiet wealth. Their talk lacked the frenzied hyperbole you heard amongst merchants who were discussing the day's market prices – a topic which would be out of date on the morrow. It lacked the noisy volubility of the scheming of the political classes, whose shifting alliances would be irrelevant before the year was out. Skaphis fancied these men had the leisure to discuss the big questions of life and human destiny: questions that would still be relevant in a thousand years. You didn't need to rush to get in the last word on an eternal topic. Or perhaps he mistook languor for philosophic detachment. Perhaps they were indeed discussing the market price of slaves.

"So how did the pre-trial go?"

"My opponent claimed he was prosecuting for the good of the city."

"An experienced speaker. That can cut both ways, though – too much professionalism can annoy a jury: they have been known to side with the less accomplished speaker out of contrariness."

"Or because he has the stronger case?"

"You're right; sometimes strength of case does have some bearing. How is your case?"

"Pretty weak."

"Let me explain how the water clock works. Imagine you are pissing against a wall. You start off full of water, and the stream comes out horizontally, hitting the wall at prick level. Gradually the pressure reduces and the piss slants further and further down the wall. Eventually the last few drops dribble straight onto the ground."

By way of illustration, he ladled wine into Skaphis' cup, transferring the last drops by holding the ladle upside down and shaking.

"The water clock works the same way. At first the top container is full, and the water comes out almost horizontally. As the pot empties, the water comes out under less pressure, and the stream slants downward more. By watching the angle of the stream, you can judge how much time you have left."

"You sound like you have some experience in the courts."

"Experience in courts to an Athenian is like experience oppressing subject peoples to a Spartan – part of our national heritage. Yes I've taken on a few cases, both on my own account and to benefit the city."

"So you have prosecuted for money?"

"In Athens, we have no state department of prosecution, apart from the eleven, of course, and they deal only with open and shut cases which do not need to go to trial. So the system relies on individual citizens being prepared to spend their own time and resources in court, pursuing justice on behalf of the city. It is only reasonable that such public spiritedness should be rewarded."

"The thirty didn't approve of private prosecutors."

"No, they tended to favor summary judgment over open courts. They did their best to dismantle the legal profession, both by restructuring the law itself and by more direct action."

"Which was?"

"They arrested and executed the prosecutors."

"But not you."

"Even summary arrests need functionaries to carry them out. I made myself useful to the regime. As did your former partner, I might add."

"You were teamed with Aristophon, I heard."

Euboulos raised his eyebrow.

"You are well informed. They paired us like that: a cavalry officer, ideologically attuned to the regime, along with a man who knew something of the law and how to locate people. Aristophon and I were paired up, Barysthenes worked with a fellow by the name of Kallictor.

"The legal basis for our arrests was admittedly a bit thin at times, but personal enmity towards the powerful has always been an indictable offence in Athens. It's just that the thirty had more personal enemies than most. They were also funding the regime with confiscations from those we arrested, so there was a strong bias towards arresting the wealthy, regardless of their criminality.

"It wasn't exactly pleasant work, but political arrests and confiscations were not invented by the thirty – they just streamlined the process. Aristophon didn't find the work to his taste though – he was happy enough executing lawyers: he saw them as enemies of the state, but he couldn't stomach arresting the politically suspect rich. He saw too much of himself in them. Personally, I feel a certain amount of pragmatic flexibility is my birthright as an Athenian. If that bastard Alcibiades can defect to the Spartans in the middle of the Sicilian expedition, and later be welcomed back as a hero, then I feel no compunction about having briefly worked for the thirty: they were at least Athenians."

The waitress had brought a dish laid out with dried fish: a tiny shoal whose search for safety in shallow water led only to desiccation and death. Euboulos paused to lift one of the miniature fish by the tail and drop it onto his tongue. He gestured to Skaphis inviting him to eat. The overwhelming initial taste from the fish was of salt, as if the essence of the ocean had been reduced into its lifeless body. Skaphis sipped some wine, which quenched the salt taste and brought out a complex of more subtle flavors.

"Good aren't they – they ship them sealed in amphoras from the western seas beyond Sicily. They have a tendency to ferment a little on the journey, and that gives them their special flavor."

They ate in silence for a while before Euboulos continued.

"The confiscations are what offended Barysthenes' sensibilities. He hated to stand by and watch all that money flow from the private sector into the public sector, and came up with a scheme to divert a little of it. When an arrest was imminent, he would approach the target, and tell him that his property would be subject to confiscation. He would then offer to hide some of his assets from the authorities, and bank them. If he survived the arrest, he could reclaim the assets. If not, they would be available for his heirs once the political situation had stabilized.

"Faced with the immediate loss of their entire estate, this was an offer they found hard to refuse, and Barysthenes was correct in his assessment that few of the targets survived long beyond their arrest, and that their families were subject to banishment, the end result being that few reclaimed their resources."

"Was Kallictor aware of this arrangement?"

"He had to have been. I'm guessing Barysthenes bought his compliance with a proportion of the profits. Aristophon, I'm sure, did not know what was going on. It is not something that would have sat well with his selective conscience.

"A month ago, Barysthenes was contacted by the survivor of one of these estates. He had been living in exile, but was now back in Athens and wanted his father's money back. Unfortunately, Barysthenes did not have ready access to the cash, having it out invested. He had gone to meet this man the day before he died in order to explain the situation. But he apparently did not show up."

"He told you this?"

"Yes, he was worried that the fellow might get upset that his money was not readily available and wanted me to chat with him about the realities of the banking and investment business."

"How was a descendent to authenticate his claim on the money?"

"Barysthenes had the accounts referenced by number. Presenting the account number to him would supposedly get you the money. On this occasion, Barysthenes was given a note with the account number on it and instructions to go to Panthumion's tavern in the Kerameikos and ask for "the Eel". He showed up at the appointed time, but when he asked for the eel, they thought he was ordering from the fish menu."

"And he asked you to follow up on this?"

"He wanted me to go back by the tavern. One of the serving girls was quite observant. She noticed a particular young man who seemed little interested in wine but strongly interested in the other customers. He watched Barysthenes keenly and left shortly after he did."

"He wanted to recognize Barysthenes?"

"That's what I thought, and a couple of days later Barysthenes was dead."

chapter **23**

Skaphis spent the best part of the next couple of days in Panthumion's tavern. He gained nothing from the experience but a sore head and an enduring contempt for the conversational skills of inebriated potters.

The serving girl remembered Barysthenes and the young man who had followed him, and had told Skaphis she would be sure to point him out. However, the youth did not show up. On further questioning, the girl admitted that though the lad had been a regular for a while, she hadn't seen him recently, but maintained she would recognize him if she did. Skaphis gave her a three obol coin and promised two more if she was able to give him a lead on the boy.

He returned to the Piraeus and heard no more from the girl. There were more stimulating ways to spend three obols in the Kerameikos, he reflected, though in the long run, equivalent wastes of money.

Lysias seemed surprisingly optimistic about the progress of the case. Skaphis laid out his theories

"According to our witness, Aristophon did not kill Barysthenes, but he could have seen who did, and was removed from circulation by the killer. Barysthenes had been acting as a banker for victims of the thirty, but had been using the money to finance his own schemes – motive for murder certainly. A young chap – perhaps a relative of one of his victims – had set up a meeting with

Barysthenes the night before his death, but seemed to use the meeting as a way of recognizing Barysthenes. Perhaps he had followed Barysthenes back to the Piraeus and waited for an opportunity to kill him. The opportunity had arisen when Barysthenes had attended a clandestine meeting of a corn cartel. Ironically, the purpose of the meeting was to achieve an orderly end game to their illegal market manipulation. This should have freed up the cash that would have allowed Barysthenes to pay back the loan."

The fact that the young man was nowhere to be found, and that they did not even know his name, did not appear to perturb Lysias.

"You have implicated Barysthenes in two highly illegal and anti-social activities: market manipulation and misappropriating funds from condemned democrats during the terror. Not to mention that he was impersonating a citizen – itself a serious offence punishable by enslavement. It hardly matters who killed him, a jury will see it as a service to the state."

Instead of wasting effort trying to track down a young man in a Kerameikos full of young men, Lysias persuaded Skaphis to find witnesses who could vouch for his own good services to the state and the democracy in war.

This proved a more difficult task than Skaphis initially thought it would be. The army he had fought in at Munichia Hill had been a scratch affair, hastily assembled from democrats returning from exile and Piraeus residents who had never left the city. There was little of the organization of a regular army – certainly none of the muster rolls and pay ledgers. Bound by a revolutionary zeal and a common hatred of the Spartans and their own upper classes, the army had coalesced, fought, won, then dispersed, all within the brief span of a few weeks. It was not easy for Skaphis to find anyone who remembered fighting beside him.

Harder still was the task of locating shipmates from his trireme. Fleet rowers in Athens were an underclass whose movements on land were barely noticed by the citizenry. At sea, they were an expense item in the accounting of a trierarchy. On land, they led a half-life in the taverns of the Piraeus and waterfronts across the Aegean. With the destruction of most of the fleet at Aegospotamoi, and the decommissioning of the rest – Skaphis had no place to start except those very dockyard taverns.

He divided his time in the next couple of months between the dockyard and the neighborhood of Munichia Hill where he had fought in the revolution. It seemed a massive waste of time, but Lysias maintained it was important to his case to contrast Barysthenes' anti-social anti-democratic activities and his own stalwart defense of the city and its institutions. Skaphis suspected the speechwriter had a taste for balanced clauses and was trying to match the case to his grammatical predilections.

The second pretrial hearing was less dramatic even than the first, and Lysias declared himself pleased with the result, although to Skaphis, the whole procedure seemed pure routine. Witness statements were collected from both sides and sealed in jars for later use at trial, but as far as Skaphis could see, the statements proved very little. He established his presence in Athens the evening before the murder, but had no witness able to swear to his whereabouts at the time of the murder. Prosecution witnesses established that Skaphis had found the body, and inherited the estate, but nobody claimed to have seen him at the time of the murder. On Lysias' advice, Barysthenes held back Diomedorus' deposition detailing Barysthenes' early life until the third hearing so that the prosecution would not have time to unearth counter-testimony. The speechwriter still considered the change of trial venue to be critical to the case.

Skaphis' search for shipmates led him to a dimly lit single room in the labyrinth of low rent establishments between the waterfront proper and the warehouse district. There he found Chromon, shipmate and fellow top-tier oarsman.

An Athenian warship was designed for one thing only: speed. The handful of archers and marines who fought from its surging upper deck were more for defense than offense. It's main weapon was the ugly bronze ram which curved forward into the bow wave, and the muscle behind this clenched fist was the hull filled to capacity with straining, swearing oarsmen. To maximize the amount of muscle per foot of hull length, oarsmen sat on three overlapping levels, the feet of the top oarsman being level with the head of the bottom tier man. The top oar struck the water at a greater angle than the bottom two oars, and was thus more difficult to handle. In the power stroke its shaft was high and awkward to pull, its recovery stroke was a deep arc. The strongest oarsmen were assigned to the top tier. Offsetting the harder work was the exposure to a clean breeze through the space between the hull and the upper deck. It was through this space that Skaphis and Chromon had watched the Spartans destroy the Athenian fleet on the beach at Aegospotamoi, as they rowed first in a sprint to gain sea room, and then settled in for the long pull into an uncertain future.

As the hull was full of men, there was no room for supplies on a trireme. Crews had to fend for themselves on land – buying provisions at whatever market the local population might set up, or foraging in hostile country.

The Spartans had caught the Athenian fleet on its way to buy breakfast.

In the way of old comrades everywhere, Chromon and Skaphis had first been garrulous, exhuming campfire jokes from their shallow memory, musing over the fate of shipmates, reliving the drudgery of fleet operations and avoiding, by silent consent, the moments of terror. As the wine ate away at the fringes of their consciousness a silence descended on them: a realization that they had nothing in common but an accidentally shared past. They parted with promises to keep in touch which both knew were lies. Skaphis got his affidavit.

Munichia Hill was even less productive. Skaphis found doorways he had skirmished from during the battle and knocked on them. But the inhabitants had been in exile, or in hiding, or didn't remember him. He watched women empty washing water over ground he had seen soak up a battle-line's blood. But nobody recalled him. On old man absorbing the brief warmth from the winter sun did remember him as Barysthenes' former partner. He went on to comment on the behavior of the widow, and how he'd seen her on several occasions recently in male company. But he did not remember Skaphis from the battle.

The third pretrial hearing began much the same as the previous two. Witness statements were collected and sealed as before. When it came to the part of the proceedings where jurisdiction was determined, Skaphis presented his evidence that Barysthenes was an illegal alien. This contention was greeted with scorn and anger by the prosecution, however, unprepared as they were for such a claim; they had no evidence on hand to refute it. After a hurried consultation between the Basileus and his assistants, the case was assigned to the Palladion. The plaintiff was told that, if he had evidence to the contrary, he could always file suit for illegal procedure.

Lysias was jubilant about the change of venue, and seemed to regard the trial as essentially won. He wrote a defense speech, big on patriotism and short on facts, to Skaphis' eyes, but under the speechwriter's tutelage, he practiced its delivery until Lysias warned him that he was in danger of becoming too polished. A certain amount of amateurism played to your advantage in an Athenian court.

As the days slipped by before his trial, Skaphis found himself prowling the streets of the Piraeus, where he had spent his youth, and much of his adult life, wondering if he would be banished forever from their comfortable familiarity. And wondering if that would be such a bad thing.

Then, three days before his trial date, Lusilla showed a girl up to Skaphis' room.

Chapter *24*

It was the serving girl from Panthumion's tavern. The youth had been in the tavern again. Better, when he left she had followed him home. She could take Skaphis there. Skaphis asked her to wait downstairs and pried open the small hole beneath the tattered rug and pulled out his moneybag like a tail-caught rodent. Not much meat on these bones, he mused, but teased it open and fished out several tiny 3 obol coins. The hole was empty except for the crumpled scrap of parchment, which he had prized out of Aristophon's hand. He replaced the money, but took the paper with him. He examined the letters written on the paper: A,B,G,E. Something occurred to him. Aristophon and Barysthenes were dead: A and B both with marks against them. Who then were G and E?

The girl walked with him to the city, and led him through the bustling streets of the Kerameikos to a side alleyway and an undistinguished door. This was where she had followed the lad from the tavern. Skaphis thanked her and passed her three of the small silver coins, which she slipped gratefully under her tongue before darting out into the main thoroughfare. With one glance over her shoulder at Skaphis, she disappeared into the stream of foot traffic.

Skaphis knocked at the door, but nobody answered. He settled in to the shadows across the alleyway and waited. He pulled out the paper. He was convinced that A and B were Aristophon and Barysthenes, both dead. A was paired with E. Could E be Euboulos, Aristophon's partner in the purges of the late anti-democratic regime? Then Barysthenes should be paired with his partner Kallictor – K not G; Kallictor, the unabashedly pro-Spartan aristocrat with the bibulous slave, spouting anti-democratic rhetoric.

A man turned into the alleyway. Skaphis' muscles tensed and his hand went for the hilt of his dagger. The man continued past the door and went on into the shadowed depths of the alley. Skaphis relaxed. Kallictor – so pro-Spartan that he'd been nicknamed Gyllipus after the Spartan general. AE was Aristophon and Euboulos; BG was Barysthenes and Gyllipus.

Skaphis left the alley and joined the crowds milling around on the main road. His stride was purposeful and directed towards Euboulos' house.

Euboulos was not at home, but Skaphis found him at his dining club. The remains of a substantial meal were arrayed on the table in front of him. His dinner companions had apparently left and Euboulos presided over a derelict fleet of decommissioned platters: a beached admiral in marooned exile.

"Skaphis, my good fellow, haven't seen you in a while – sit down."

"I've been practicing pissing into pots."

"Your trial is coming up?"

"Day after tomorrow."

Skaphis leaned towards Euboulos and spoke in a low voice, "You once pointed out to me that Aristophon's body was discovered in a warehouse close to where Kotos lives. As a matter of fact, I had been following Aristophon when Kotos's men jumped me. When Kotos released me I went back to the place I'd last seen Aristophon, but he was already dead. I didn't want to give the appearance of continually turning up bodies, so I left him where I found him."

Euboulos whistled. "So it was you who took the money."

"No, the money was gone, with the exception of a single coin."

Skaphis stretched the paper out on the table in front of Euboulos.

"I did find this though, but couldn't make anything of it. I thought it was perhaps a cryptic suicide note, or just a trading ledger. But now I think I know its meaning: it's a ledger all right – a kind of death tally. See the two pairs of letters: AE and BG, and the marks beside A and B. I believe A is Aristophon, and B stands for Barysthenes, both of whom are dead. The G is Barysthenes' partner

Kallictor, whom everyone knew as Gyllipus. Which would make the E you: Aristophon's partner."

Euboulos picked up the paper and examined it in silence. He turned it over and read the back, scratching his chin absently.

"Interesting theory. It's out of date though."

Skaphis raised his eyebrow.

"There's a story that is going the rounds of a group of youths in Agrigentium. They had been drinking hard at a dinner party, and fell into the shared delusion that they were in a storm-wracked trireme. They proceeded to lighten the ship's load by tossing the furniture out of the windows. The street was soon thronged with neighbors fighting over the furniture and carting it off home. The resulting melee attracted the city magistrates who promptly put a stop to the activities. The lads still hadn't sobered up in the morning when they were admonished for their behavior. They thanked the magistrates for rescuing them from the shipwreck."

Euboulos laughed at his own story. Skaphis parsed it for a moral that would apply to his case, but could not discern any. He waited, assuming the punch line was still to come.

"Kallictor died last week. They found him at the base of the city wall. It was assumed that he had drunk too much and was reliving his stints on guard duty as an ephebe. He fell off and broke his neck."

He left unspoken the observation that Kallictor might have been pushed. It would not be too difficult to push a drunk from the walls, once you had first lured him up there on some pretext or other. The death would be taken as an accident. Or perhaps it would be taken as suicide, like Aristophon's.

"It looks like I should stay away from high places, wouldn't you say Skaphis?"

"Or stay sober."

"Too late for that."

Euboulos spread his hands towards the empty wine bowl on the table.

"What do you make of the writing on the back of the paper: 'The best man died'?"

"That is what made me think it was a suicide note. A pun on his own name, or perhaps a plea for understanding: despite the evidence of his own actions, maintaining that at core he was a man of good values."

"Very philosophical, Skaphis, but doesn't the phrase remind you of something?"

"Is it from some play?"

"More immediate than that, do you remember your partner's funeral?"

And then Skaphis remembered, Barysthenes' gravestone had read: "A good man died".

"You think the killer left both the messages, but if these men were good, why kill them?"

"Perhaps the good man does not refer to them, but to somebody else, somebody whose own death is a motive for their murders."

"Someone whose death the four of you were responsible for. You said that there were occasions when your two teams joined up in an operation."

"There was considerable disaffection in the city. The rule of the thirty was seen as not only unduly harsh, but increasingly arbitrary and capricious. The democrats had established their base in Phyle and had started attracting supporters in numbers large enough to start posing a realistic threat to the regime. A particular political club was suspected of sympathizing with the democrats, and not only that, of lending them material aid, and of providing them with intelligence of activities within the city. The problem was, if we moved against one of the group, the others would realize they were targets and escape."

"As a matter of fact, they used to meet right here. In order to pick them up all at once without any trouble, we came up with a plan. I was acquainted with these men, and my connection with the regime was not general knowledge. I told them that they were on an arrest list, but that I was sympathetic to their situation and would help them get away. Barysthenes was to be my contact in the Piraeus, he would show up at the beach with a boat to take them across to Salamis.

"In that way, we got them all in one place, away from the city, where they could be arrested quietly and without anyone getting hurt."

"I'm sure they appreciated your consideration."

"Their fate was sealed as soon as they became targets. Remember, like them or not, the thirty were the duly appointed civic authority at the time."

"Duly appointed?"

A cynical half-smile played with Euboulos' features.

"Well, duly self-appointed at least. Sometimes an injustice to a few is required to serve the good of the many. The thirty were necessary to appease the Spartans, who had it in their power to destroy the entire city.

Euboulos had a knack for clothing the most venal of behavior in an armor of patriotism. Skaphis wondered just how extensive his experience in the law courts was.

"Anyway, clan affiliations are strong, and those men were well connected with the democrats who now hold the power in the city. The amnesty makes it difficult if not impossible to seek revenge the usual way, through the courts. Someone is resorting to extra-judicial proceedings."

"What became of the men's families?"

"Exile, I believe, and disenfranchisement. Although, they'd have been free to return I'm sure, when the democracy was restored."

"However, they might tend to hold a grudge."

"It certainly looks that way."

"One more thing, did Barysthenes offer to look after assets for these men?"

"The situation was tailor made for him. He visited the city the night before we were planning the escape, ostensibly to arrange details of the pick-up. He not only charged them cash in advance for the boat, but also offered his banking service to them. Only one took him up on it, though."

"Who?"

"Thersippos."

"Did he have a son?"

"He had a son by the name of Nikandor, I believe, too young for the thirty to bother with."

It was fully dark by the time Skaphis returned to the Kerameikos, and further pounding on the door elicited the same lack of response from within. He settled back into his niche in the alleyway, turning his new theory of the case around like a clay statuette, examining it from different angles to look for flaws.

Thersippos had been executed by the thirty, his arrest having been duplicitously orchestrated by Euboulos and Barysthenes in conjunction with the cavalry detachments led by Kallictor and Aristophon. To add insult to injury, Barysthenes had also scammed the family out of a considerable amount of money under the pretext of providing a banking service. The family, returned from exile, and a young kinsman, the son perhaps, approached

Barysthenes to get his money back. But he changed his mind. Maybe he realized that Barysthenes had absconded with the money, or maybe he intended to kill him from the beginning.

He followed Barysthenes to Lusilla's, and picked up Skaphis' dagger from the table. From there he tailed Barysthenes home and then to his nocturnal meeting. Did he recognize Aristophon at the meeting and follow him from there, once he had stabbed Barysthenes with Skaphis' dagger and left it as incriminating evidence? A young man entered the alleyway, and without hesitation, opened the door. Skaphis crossed out of the shadows.

"You must be Thersippos' son."

The young man turned, and Skaphis saw in his eyes a desire to run, or to fight. He held a lighted taper in his hand and for a moment, Skaphis thought he was going to thrust it into his face to cover an escape. He twisted his cloak around his arm in preparation to parry such a move. But the young man's stance relaxed. His face looked familiar to Skaphis.

"You knew my father?"

"He was a good man – can we talk, inside?"

Nikandor opened the door and they stumbled into a tiny room. He fixed his taper into a bracket in the wall. A couple of low wooden couches flickered in its stingy light. A bowl and cup lay on the floor by one of the couches. A sputter of light from the taper illuminated some scraps of food in the bowl. A rancid smell tinged the air. A tiny shadow flitted from the bowl and merged with the deeper shadows below the couch.

"A friend lets me use this place when I'm in town."

He sat, and Skaphis studied his face. Good looking, a tight mass of curls squeezed onto the top of his head, the outliers falling in lazy spirals down his brow. Skaphis ran his fingers through his own thinning forelock. Something about the young man's eyes seemed hauntingly familiar.

He tried to recall whether he had been in Lusilla's tavern on the night of Barysthenes' death, but he could not. That was the flaw in his thinking, the killer had to pick up his knife in Lusilla's, and he was fairly sure this lad had not been there. Could he have come after Skaphis left? Or perhaps, after all, Barysthenes had taken Skaphis' knife and had been carrying it when he was killed.

"How did you know my father?"

"I'm working on a law case. I was hoping you could help me. It involves the men who turned your father over to the thirty."

"The amnesty protects them from prosecution."

"It doesn't protect them from death. Somebody's been killing them."

Did Nikandor's expression change, or was it just the shadow playing across his face as the taper flickered in the draft?

"My father stayed too long and was killed. He wasn't the only one. If someone has been killing his murderers, then it's no crime in my opinion."

"One of those involved in your father's arrest was a private investigator by the name of Barysthenes. You arranged to meet him the day before he was killed."

Nikandor paused before replying.

Skaphis watched the shadows play games of light and dark across his face, without coming to any conclusions about the games being played inside his head.

"The night before my father was arrested, he came to me. He told me that things were getting dangerous for him inside the city, and he was going to have to leave for a while. He told me he had put some money in the safekeeping of this Barysthenes in the Piraeus. My father was trying to escape arrest. I had no idea Barysthenes was part of the plot."

Skaphis tried to decide whether he believed this disavowal. On balance, he didn't.

"The family's property was seized when my father was condemned, and we were disenfranchised. I left the city with my mother and sister. We stayed with a trader in Thebes who had once done substantial business with my father. The move was hard on the women though; my mother died that winter. I accompanied the trader on a buying trip up north and discovered I have a good eye for quality merchandise and a good head for business. Next trip, he sent me on my own, and let me keep a proportion of the profits.

"I was back in Athens in the autumn, and was able to locate this Barysthenes. I passed a message for him to meet me."

"But you didn't talk to him."

"I was distracted – a slave brought a message for me."

"It must have been an important message."

"I recognized the slave."

"The slave couldn't have waited till you'd conducted your business with Barysthenes?"

The youth brushed the curls temporarily from his brow. As he did so, the folds of his cloak fell away from the upper arm.

"By the time I'd finished reading the message, Barysthenes had left. I tried to catch up with him, but lost him in the streets. I didn't have time to arrange another meeting, as I was shipping out up the Chersonese coast the next day."

He paused. Had he come to the outer limits of a fabrication, or was he just collecting his thoughts?

"I fully intended to collect next time I was in town. I didn't kill Barysthenes, if that is what you are inferring. Why would I? He was holding my money."

"I don't suppose anyone can verify that you did indeed sail up the coast that evening?"

Nikandor thought for a moment.

"Zoster of the deme Gargettos: he was on the ship. He wrestles most mornings at the Academy."

"By the way, who was this important message from?"

"My sister"

As soon as it passed through the Dipylon Gate, the road to the Academy plunged into the middle of the city's main cemetery. Grave markers crowded to both edges of the road, ceding it grudgingly to the living, like civilians yielding priority to a military convoy. Skaphis hunched beside a large marble slab and let the early sun massage the stiffness out of his aching limbs. Rather than hike back and forth to the Piraeus, he'd spent the night curled up in a dark corner of the Kerameikos. The first half of the night he'd slept soundly, but a few hours before dawn, the temperature had dropped sufficiently to penetrate his cloak, and the unfamiliar night sounds of the metropolis had kept him on edge and able only to doze fitfully. He had risen stiff and sore as soon as he had perceived a lightening in the sky.

A group of mourners were chatting as they returned to the city: normal life resuming with the warmth of the new day. Skaphis examined the gravestone he was crouching beside. A group of alabaster girls were frozen onto its surface. One girl was having her hair combed, while another girl carried a garland. A third girl was preparing water for washing. Preparations for a wedding, Skaphis surmised, the defining event in a young girl's life. Beside the tomb was a tiny grave marker consisting of a simple stone block surmounted by a marble urn. The urn was delicately carved, but plain. There was no name engraved on the miniature stone. The memory of a half-forgotten grief welled up into Skaphis' throat. He stretched and rejoined the road, walking quickly to put his dead behind him.

A company of ephebes, military trainees, was drilling in the Academy. Their oiled bodies glistened in the sunshine as they marched and countermarched to the strains of a twin aulos pipe. They trained naked, but each trainee carried a ten-foot long spear, and three-foot diameter bronzed shield. Eventually they would need to be able to maneuver as a densely packed eight-deep line of men. Formidable though this overlapping shield wall could be in full frontal assault, it was hard to maneuver, and required lengthy training.

"Worrying, when you think our safety rests on boys like these."

The speaker was an older man who was watching the evolutions with a critical eye.

"Pretty enough, I daresay," he nodded in the direction of a small group of men who seemed to be closely following the youths' progress, "but just not the same caliber as they were in my day.

"These new shields are much smaller than the ones we used to carry. They say it makes the infantry more maneuverable, but I think the youth of today are just not strong enough to carry the proper weapons, too much soft living, not enough time spent out here in the gymnasium. Their spears are longer than ours used to be: 'better offensive weapons', they say, 'we need a modern, lighter, better-armed infantry'. Rubbish, I say, put this lot up against a Spartan spear line, and see how far they get."

The playing stopped, and the ephebes stacked their arms. They drew lots to pick wrestling partners.

"Do you know Zoster of the deme Gargettos?"

"That's him over there."

A pair of men stood locked in a wrestling embrace. Both were well muscled, but one had a significant weight advantage. The smaller man held the larger's left wrist with both his hands, while the larger man pushed with his right hand on the shoulder of the smaller. Beads of sweat mingled with the oil and dirt on the wrestlers' bodies. They twisted and turned; jostling for position, but always came back to this same equilibrium. Skaphis noticed, however, that the smaller man's back was beginning to arch. The larger man first pulled up with his left hand, momentarily putting his opponent off balance, then pulled it down sharply, thus maneuvering him into a position where he could bring all his weight to bear. As a sail caves in when a boat bears too close to the wind, the smaller man's legs buckled, and he was thrown by sheer brute force."

"He's the one still standing."

Skaphis walked up to the wrestlers. Zoster was lending a hand to lift his erstwhile opponent out of the dirt.

"Not exactly an equal match, was it."

"Melanippos fights well for a shrimp. How about yourself, do you wrestle?"

"I never learned the rules. I came here to talk, I have a couple of questions for you."

"This is a gymnasium, not a barber's shop. There's a law, you know, against folks loitering around here ogling the young boys."

Skaphis ran his fingers through his matted hair.

"I've been avoiding the barber, I'm going for the Spartan look."

"I told you: ogling boys is forbidden. A bout of pankration, then, there's only one rule to worry about."

"What's that?"

"No eye gouging."

"You'll talk with me after we fight?"

"Don't worry about your cloak, Melanippos will see nobody steals it."

"The only things hidden in the seams of that cloak bite back."

Skaphis stripped off his cloak, and took the proffered flask of oil. He rubbed the oil onto his skin, then picked a handful of dirt from the ground and sprinkled it over his back. Melanippos softened the wrestling ring with a spade. Zoster poured water over the newly turned earth, transforming it into mud.

At close quarters, Skaphis suspected his opponent's wrestling experience would work to his advantage. He circled, looking for an opening. Zoster moved forward to come to grips. Skaphis feinted to his left, then surged right. As his opponent adjusted his balance, Skaphis kicked hard at his ankles with a scythe like sweep of his left leg. Zoster fell, but on his way down managed to clutch at Skaphis' thigh. Still unbalanced by his kick, Skaphis went down too, and the pair were sprawling in the mud. Skaphis rolled away from his opponent, onto his knees, then onto his feet. Surprisingly, for such a big man, Zoster had already regained his feet and was again closing on Skaphis. He'd expect another feint, so Skaphis did the opposite, lunging ferociously at the wrestler. Zoster took the charge in his midriff, but stood his ground, bending over the top of Skaphis' back and wrapping his arms round his torso. Skaphis felt Zoster attempt to lift his legs off the ground, and resisted by straightening his back and pushing up for all he was worth, trying to lift the wrestler onto his own shoulders. It was as futile as trying single handedly to launch a beached warship.

All of a sudden it went dark. Zoster had worked his free hand over his eyes: not gouging, just covering them. Unable to see, Skaphis felt vulnerable, and shifted his grip to wrest the offending hand away from his face. Too late, he felt Zoster switch from lifting up to pushing down, and found himself flat on his face in the mud with the big wrestler on top of him. He still couldn't see, but now it was the mud, not his opponent's hand, which occluded his vision. He attempted to turn his head to the side so he could breathe, but something was preventing him.

The fleet sailed for the shore leaving the battle survivors in the water. The swell was beginning to pick up, and a storm was clearly brewing. Skaphis held onto the shaft of a broken oar and tried to raise himself above the surface, but something was pulling him down. The water was strewn with wreckage. The battle had been hard-fought, but had been a victory. Why had the fleet not stopped to rescue survivors? As he pulled himself to the surface, a huge wave broke over his head.

"You fight well for a Piraeus water rat."

Zoster was standing over Skaphis holding a pitcher.

"You know, they don't allow the Pankration in Sparta."

Skaphis staggered to his feet, smearing mud away from his mouth and nose.

"Too soft for them?"

"Too dangerous, a Spartan will never admit defeat. Come, friend, scrape off the mud and we'll take a bath."

The bath water was the same deep brown color as the gymnasium's mud. Whatever efforts its previous occupants had made to scrape off the grime acquired during their course of exercise, they had not been sufficient to the task, and a thick suspension of muck suffused the bath water. However, the water was hot, and Skaphis could see that he was contributing at least his fair share of dirt to the mixture. As the warmth surrounded his body, Skaphis started to feel somewhat better disposed towards the big wrestler, and asked him about Nikandor.

"Yes, I'm sure of the date, I was traveling north for a wrestling competition. On the night your partner was killed, Nikandor and I were half way up the Euboean coast."

"You wrestle in competition?"

"Not so much as I used to."

"Lose often?"

Zoster twitched his head skyward – no.

"But come, eat some bread with me – take the taste of the dirt out of your mouth."

Skaphis declined.

"I may have to go north myself tomorrow. I should start packing."

CHAPTER 25

A sickly dawn curdled into a new morning. Skaphis hunched his cloak closer round his shoulders to ward off the chill. With the new day's light, the jurors began to arrive: at first the eager outliers jostling purposefully into court, then clumps of men chatting noisily amongst themselves, then a continuous stream, filing into the vast jury enclosure. Five hundred in all, plus the magistrate, made five hundred and one. An odd number so there was no chance of a tied vote.

One of the jurors had been assigned the task of operating the water clock. As Orthagoras got to his feet to open the prosecution, the juror unstopped the outlet of the uppermost jar and an enthusiastic jet of liquid arched into the lower receptacle.

Orthagoras started his speech with a sanctimonious explanation of why, although not a close relative of he deceased, it was his duty as an Athenian, and member of the victim's phratry, to pursue the prosecution, distasteful as such a task may be. To do otherwise would be to expose his city to the unanswerable pollution of an unresolved homicide.

The Palladion court met in a grove outside the temple of Pallas, itself a little way from the city. A small crowd of onlookers had gathered beyond the rope which delineated the court proper. Skaphis looked for a friendly face in the crowd. He was sure he recognized the profile of Euboulos, in earnest conversation with someone Skaphis did not recognize.

Orthagoras launched into his theory of the case. He told a story of a guileless older man married to an attractive young wife who took a younger man into his business – a younger man he had met during the fight to restore the democracy. The younger man, and here Orthagoras paused and looked straight at Skaphis, leaving the jury with no doubt that he was talking about the defendant, the younger man ingratiated himself with his mentor to such an extent that he was persuaded to adopt him as his son.

"Not satisfied with making himself the heir to his partner's considerable means, this scoundrel," Orthagoras' voice lowered for effect, and oozed with contempt, "this utter scoundrel dared to start a liaison with his wife."

This piece of salaciousness played well with the jury. Their disapprobation was almost palpable. The juror's pay of three obols a day was barely enough to eke out a living. A few civic-minded souls felt it their duty to contribute their time to the state for this important duty: farmers mostly during the off-season. The bulk of the jury, however, were older men of the poorer class, for whom jury pay constituted a form of state pension. Problems of wayward wives were ones in which the jury would naturally side with the wronged husband.

Orthagoras went on to describe how on the night of the murder, Skaphis had gone up to Athens, while Barysthenes had arranged to stake out a nocturnal meeting. Skaphis had returned from Athens and taken the opportunity to surprise and kill his partner, leaving him to make free with his estate and his wife.

Skaphis identified Psamathe amongst the spectators. She caught his eye, and tilted her head slightly to the right, the direction of Euboulos. She raised her arms in an unconscious gesture to fix the comb that held her hair up at the back. As the last prosecution droplets trickled out of the clock, the familiarity of the gesture tugged at his reluctant mind.

Skaphis rose to take the oath before the Basileus, swearing to a somewhat hollow innocence. The jury chattered noisily through this formality, but a hush fell over them as the water clock was opened for his defense.

"Gentlemen of the jury, I'm inexperienced in court matters, having spent most of my years fighting for you at sea and on land, first against the Spartan enemy, then against the enemies within."

Lysias' defense speech stared with a sequence of contrasts. Skaphis' honorable service for his country was contrasted with Barysthenes' illegal impersonation of an Athenian citizen. Skaphis' straightforward and unflinching support of the democrats was contrasted with Barysthenes' ambiguous, if not downright treacherous role in the revolution. The problem was, Skaphis could see, the jury fully expected this sort of self-serving pleading, and he supposed they were discounting it heavily. In fact the jury didn't seem to be paying much attention to his speech at all. Several were chatting with their neighbors, and in the back of the jury enclosure, a full-blown argument was under way.

This brought home to Skaphis the fundamental asymmetry of their situation. For these jurymen, the proceedings, if sufficiently juicy, might at best offer a topic for conversation at the Agora tomorrow. At worst they represented a rather tedious, but reliable way of earning a couple of obols. For himself, it was the difference between Lusilla's snug upper room and the lonely road out of town.

Skaphis had faced worse situations before though, in the battle line and on the rowing bench. The key was to focus on the task at hand and not consider any longer term implications. He concentrated on his speech, aiming the delivery at the group in the top tier who were still absorbed in an intense discussion, though, as far as Skaphis could tell, not about the matter at hand.

He tried a rhetorical trick Lysias had taught him, gradually lowering his voice so the jurors had to strain to hear him. He noticed one of the jurors in the row in front of the argument turn round and gesture at the disputants to quiet them. Having got their attention through this device, he raised his voice and talked directly to them, maintaining eye contact, and willing them to stay focused on his case.

He wished the case he had focused them in on was a bit stronger. He was now at the part of the speech where he detailed his movements on the night of Barysthenes' death, and it rang hollow to him. His opponent had produced the magistrate to attest to Skaphis' discovery of the body. He in turn had not been able to produce as a witness the messenger who had summoned him to the scene.

Having protested his innocence, Lysias' speech had Skaphis build a list of people with grievances against Barysthenes. The list was long. Skaphis described Barysthenes' long standing relationship with Syracusan elements that exercised ruthless control over dockside labor. Such an allegiance would surely bring a man enemies. Specifically, he was involved with these types in a scheme to corner the market in grain, an enterprise fraught with risk and ripe with opportunity for mayhem.

Barysthenes' occupation as a private investigator was one that had a tendency to create many enemies and a few dangerous friends. In particular, Barysthenes had survived during the rule of the thirty by making himself useful to the regime, betraying and arresting prominent democrats. This could make him a target for revenge by families frustrated by the amnesty from pursuing him through the legal channels. Alternatively, his fellow miscreants, having blended successfully back into Athenian society, might have found it necessary to silence their former comrade to protect their own reputations.

On top of all this, Skaphis pointed out to the jury, Barysthenes was not in fact Barysthenes at all, but a foreign imposter, guilty for years of the crime of impersonating an Athenian citizen. An Athenian citizen whose death he was no doubt responsible for himself. Would it not be understandable for Barysthenes real family to take revenge on this criminal?

Lysias had timed his speech well, and Skaphis had delivered it without any serious lapses of memory. As he concluded with a final strong recapitulation of his innocence, the water in the clock sputtered to a stop and the Basileus put the court into recess before the prosecution's second speech.

This was the vestigial remnant of the recess that allowed homicide defendants who sensed the case was going against them to escape with their lives and go into voluntary exile; a nicety not afforded in lower courts.

Skaphis looked for Euboulos in the knot of spectators, but did not see him. Lysias was at the far side of the crowd, taking a detached interest in the proceedings. He had warned Skaphis against being seen to consult with him. Although the practice of hiring speechwriters was widespread, their use smacked of professionalism, which was an anathema to an Athenian jury.

Psamathe was still there, squinting in the sunlight, the way she had stood framed in the doorway and squinting into the gloom of the Piraeus tavern the afternoon before Barysthenes was killed. She had a patient beauty that always brought Penelope into Skaphis' mind. Penelope: unraveling the long nights till Odysseus' return. It suddenly occurred to him that perhaps he should be thinking of a different Achaean queen. Clytemnestra, Agamemnon's wife was killed by her son Orestes and daughter Electra, in revenge for their father's death. The Psamathe of his fantasy may be a Penelope surrounded by suitors awaiting the return of her true love, but the Psamathe of reality was an avenging Electra.

The first half of the prosecution's second speech dealt, rather too handily in Skaphis' opinion, with his own arguments.

"The defendant has given a long list of people who might have killed Barysthenes, but were any of them present, as he was, when the body was found? He gives a plethora of reasons why persons unknown might want to kill him, but did any of these persons unknown inherit the dead man's estate?"

He went on to recapitulate, in abbreviated form the theory of the case he had presented in the opening speech, and finished with an appeal to the jury,

"Gentleman of the jury, it is traditional in our city for a man to wait till he has achieved a level of maturity before marrying. The same goes for jury duty. Both, I think require a certain wisdom that is only acquired with experience. This is an excellent custom that has served our city well over the centuries. However, there is the problem that sometimes a wife, be she ever so virtuous, can be led astray by some younger man who inveigles himself into the family home. This is all this case is about: a younger man who won the affections of a wayward wife, and, not satisfied with the wife, took his benefactor's estate, and his life. For this, he should pay the penalty prescribed by law. You have made a solemn oath to listen to both sides equally and to give judgment in favor of the better case. To uphold this oath, you must vote in favor of the prosecution."

Again, Orthagoras finished as the last drops of water dribbled out of the water clock. A low murmur from the jury suggested to Skaphis that they agreed wholeheartedly with the prosecution. An experienced orator, according to Lysias, would pick up specific points from the prosecution's arguments and rebut them in his final address.   He strongly recommended Skaphis stick to the script.   The problem was, Skaphis didn't have much faith that the script was getting him anywhere with the jury.   He decided to improvise.

"In my first speech this morning, I contrasted the contributions to your city of Barysthenes and of myself.   I contrasted my military service with Barysthenes' shady dealing.   I compared my support of your democracy with his unprincipled opportunism.   I testified to my innocence in the crime.

"Now, I'd like to tell you a story.   Unlike the story told to you by the prosecution, however, this one happens to be true.

"After you had lost your ships, and the Spartans had surrounded your city, the gang of thirty seized control of your government and went about arresting and killing their enemies.

"Thersippos was a prominent democrat, a good man, who elected to stay in the city rather than flee into exile when the thirty took control.   Perhaps he did not want to uproot his family.   Perhaps he believed his friendly relations with members of the regime would protect him.   If he did believe this, he was mistaken.   In due course, his name made it to the top of an arrest list and a squad was detailed to detain him."

Skaphis could no longer see Psamathe amongst the spectators.   Euboulos also had disappeared.   However, at the other side of the spectators' area he recognized two figures.   Astra was there, with Barysthenes' aunt and a beardless man whom he had not seen before.

"Barysthenes was a private investigator.   How did he survive the purges in the rule of the thirty?   He made himself useful to the regime, as a functionary in their pogroms. And it was Barysthenes, who was assigned to bring in Thersippos."

Skaphis went on to tell the story of the arrest, and of Barysthenes' fraudulent banking scheme. He finished this part of his narrative as the water clock dribbled to a halt. He had much more to tell. This was the danger of an unrehearsed speech. He had no idea how long the telling would take. He paused as the juror plugged the hole in the top pot and reversed the two. The second half of his defense speech began to flow.

"Thersippos left a wife and two children: a teenage son and a daughter. With their estate confiscated, the family fled, destitute to Thebes. The widow never recovered from the change in her circumstances, and died that winter, leaving her son to fend for the family. Helped by a family friend, he went into business, trading throughout Greece.

"His sister was left in Thebes with no marriage prospects, and nothing to do but brood over the cruel fate which had stolen away her beloved father. Over time the brooding turned to hatred, hatred for the men who had betrayed her father.

"It was this woman who, three years later, hired Barysthenes to find Aristophon. She knew the alley he would be lurking in that night, because she assigned him the task. In the Piraeus, the night has many women and she would be an unremarkable figure. Except that the women of the Piraeus night are for sale, and on this night she was not. She found Barysthenes in the alleyway where she had stationed him. Did she approach him on the pretext of revising his instructions, or did she simply slip unseen through the shadows? I don't know, but in the dark entrance of a Piraeus warehouse, she silently slid her dagger under his ribs and killed the man who had led her father to his death.

"Before he died, however, he managed to crawl across the road and mutter the name 'Clytemnestra'. He was trying to give a clue to his murderer: Orestes and Electra killed Clytemnestra in revenge for the death of their father Agamemnon, just as this latter day Electra killed the man who betrayed her father to the Thirty."

The thin stream no longer issued horizontally from the water clock, indicating a reduction of pressure behind it. He segued into Lysias' ending.

"Gentlemen of the jury, I have taken an oath to present a truthful case, and you have taken an oath to adjudicate fairly and without bias. I have discharged my oath faithfully by presenting the true facts of the case as I have been able to determine them. I ask you to honor your oaths and to rule in my favor."

As soon as Skaphis had finished his speech, the herald stood and called on the jurymen to cast their votes. The jury filed out of the enclosure, and past the voting table. Each man was given a voting pebble and a token. The pebble he slotted through the lid of one of the two urns standing on the table: the first for acquittal, the second for conviction. The token he would exchange for pay at the end of the day.

The first juror put his pebble in the urn for conviction, then the second, then the third, and Skaphis thought that all was lost, but then a couple of jurors voted to acquit, and a glimmer of hope returned. The votes continued, roughly evenly divided, but with a small bias in favor of conviction. An argument between two jurors who were waiting in line to vote momentarily distracted Skaphis, and he lost track of the count. He was losing by 38 to 41.

When the last juryman had filed past, the vote counter poured the votes from the first urn into a wooden tray on the table, and started to place them into the round holes of a counting board. He then repeated the procedure with the second urn, using a second, identical, counting board. Under the eyes of the Basileus, the counter proceeded to tally the vote, counting each board row by row. The Basileus nodded his head, and the court herald proceeded to announce the result:

"Votes in favor of conviction: 234, in favor of acquittal: 267. The defendant is cleared of the charge."

With the trial over, the small crowd which had gathered to observe the determination of the will of the people dispersed. Lysias remained, staff in hand, standing a discreet distance away from the court proper.

"A narrow victory, Skaphis. But it's as my old boxing coach used to say."

"What's that?"

"A narrow win is better than a narrow loss. I'm not sure I approve of you throwing away the finely crafted symmetry of my summing up for the rather basic narrative structure of your second speech."

Only the very corner of Lysias' mouth betrayed the ironic nature of his remark.

"Still it had the desired effect, I suppose, and I can always re-use the words in a speech for a different trial. I give no refund, though, for unused material. Seriously, Skaphis, you should have told me you had solved the case, I could have written you a much more effective ending. We could have had those jurors spellbound by your story, and you could have won by a hundred votes, not just twenty."

"The thing is, I hadn't solved the case until I saw Psamathe in the spectators' enclosure. Something in the way she was standing, I suddenly saw the resemblance to Nikandor, and then everything made sense. She was his sister, and she has been a woman on a mission for the last three years in Athens, to track down and kill the men she feels were responsible for her father's death. There was only one role in society she could play that gave her the freedom of action and access to information she needed to pursue these men, and she played it with a vengeance."

Lysias smiled.

"Or should I say for a vengeance. Perhaps she knew Aristophon's identity before coming to Athens, or perhaps she learned it after she got here. However, she set up a liaison with him in order to discover the identities of the other conspirators. Was Nikandor involved? I suspect not, but my guess is that he ran into her in Athens and told her of Barysthenes' involvement in their father's arrest. Now, she had the names of all her victims, and was ready to move into the second phase of her revenge, but there was one problem: Aristophon had disappeared. So she came up with a beautifully symmetric scheme: hire one victim to find the other, then kill them both. Thus the blame for the first killing could reasonably fall on the second victim."

"I'm walking back to Piraeus, Skaphis, will you accompany me?"

"I was worried, back there I might have to walk further than the Piraeus."

"I have to admit, my friend, so was I. I'm not sure, for all its skillful construction, if my second speech would have carried that jury."

"So you admit that sometimes the truth is a viable legal strategy."

"I'll admit that a good story is sometimes a viable legal strategy."

"What will happen to Psamathe?"

"By rights, as Barysthenes' next of kin, it's your responsibility to prosecute her. However, killing

Aristophon is a much more serious crime than killing Barysthenes. Not only was he, indisputably, an Athenian citizen, but he was rich and well-connected. My guess is that if you wanted to prosecute, you'd have to get in line.

"However, I do know where you can get a good speech written, should you decide to go ahead."

Lusilla's was busy. A single gesture with her thumb cleared a table for Skaphis, sending a bevy of chattering girls into the dark nether regions of the tavern. She sent over a pitcher of wine, and joined him at the table, bringing a platter of fish and one of bread.

Skaphis had never been given this sort of treatment.

"I'm touched, a celebration of my legal victory?"

"I prepared this to celebrate your departure, but these fish don't keep, so we might as well celebrate your victory instead."

"Lusilla, there's something I've been meaning to ask you, but I thought I'd better get the trial out of the way first."

She leaned closer and combed her hair back with a coquettish gesture which brought a smile to Skaphis' lips.

"Go on, I'm all ears."

"I'd like to buy Thrassia's freedom. How much would it cost?"

"You silly boy, you don't need to buy her. I can make an exception to my house rule for a special occasion."

"Humor me, Lusilla, what is the going rate for a slave?"

"Three obols a time, you know that."

"The sale price, I mean."

"I paid ninety drachmas for her at the slave market, but she was a wild northerner with no culture at all. I've invested a considerable sum in her education. Besides, I've grown quite fond of the girl. However, if I were offered two fifty, I'd find that hard to turn down."

"This fish tastes fresh-caught, Lusilla, I didn't think you knew where the fresh fish stand was in the market."

"A special occasion, I thought I was going to get my upper room back. I might get it back yet mind you, here comes your relative."

Lusilla rose from the table as Astra entered the tavern, escorted by the man who had accompanied her to the trial.

"Skaphis, I'd like to introduce my kinsman Zenothemis. He would like to talk with you."

Skaphis gestured for them to sit at the table, and reluctantly offered some of his fish. It seemed whenever Lusilla was forthcoming with the better quality viands, basic hospitality forced him to share with some underfed guest or other. However, Zenothemis took only a polite portion and Astra none at all.

"I am, I believe, the closest male kinsman of the real Barysthenes, and should by law be the heir to his estate. However, I'd need to go to court to prove it and frankly, I have no great faith in the Athenian courts. Also, I have business interests abroad that I would rather not leave for the length of time which would be required to pursue the case. As the heir of the false Barysthenes, you have inherited certain assets, and certain liabilities. I have a proposal for you.

"I have built a prosperous business in the western colonies, and have spent most of my life traveling. The result is that I have never had time to find myself a wife. Now as Barybromos' and Barysthenes' kinsman, it is really my responsibility to look after Astra here. I propose that I take her off your hands, assuming we can come to reasonable terms on a dowry."

"Reasonable terms being all of Barysthenes' estate?"

253

"We will be returning to Italy, and have no need of his house."

Astra sat silent, her head bowed, a liability whose disposition was under discussion and who had no voice in the matter.

"Is this what you want, Astra?"

She looked up at him and met his gaze for a brief second, before nodding almost imperceptibly. In the second that their eyes met, he read something more than indifferent acceptance of her fate but what it was he couldn't tell: desire, hate, love?

"It is true that my partner was not the real Barysthenes, but Astra was his wife nevertheless, and I am his legal heir. So she is my responsibility. As for the estate, what you suggest is reasonable. I would, however like to retain a small amount to help me with some short term expenses related to my joint business with Barysthenes."

"How much?"

"Two hundred and fifty drachmas."

Skaphis awoke from sleep convinced he had heard his door creak. A small draft caressing his naked back confirmed that the door had opened. He groped under his pillow for the ornately handled dagger that slept there. With one hand stroking the handle and the other grasping the sheath, he risked opening an eye fractionally. In the feeble light through his casement from a city lit only by the stars, he became aware of a hooded figure standing over his bed.

With one motion, he span off the bed, unsheathing his knife and warding off a blow he felt sure was coming from above. The blow did not materialize, and Skaphis followed through by lunging horizontally at the hooded figure, catching it around the midriff with his shoulder and crashing to the floor, hopefully dislodging any weapon which the intruder was wielding. With his assailant pinned to the floor, and his own knife lodged in the floorboards by his side, Skaphis paused to catch his breath. The body he had pinned to the floor under him had a sinuous reptilian strength which was, however, no match for his sheer bulk. And it was a female body.

He sat up, dislodging his knife from the floor, and pulled the hood from the head of his nocturnal visitor.

"Psamathe, what are you doing here?"

"I didn't come here to hurt you. Although, now, I'm not so sure. Skaphis, you scared the hell out of me. Not to mention the mess you'll have made of my thighs. I bruise very easily you know."

"I would have thought you'd have been on your way out of town."

"I am, I'll be on a ship for the Hellespont by the morning. I wanted to see you before I left."

"You wanted revenge?"

"Revenge? No, I wanted to ask you to come with me. I have financial resources, and will make a good life for myself in the east. But a little protection would come in handy, and besides…"

She looked at him, but her image flickered in the grainy half-light and he was unable to see what was in her eyes.

"Besides, I like you. We'd make a good team."

"You mean, you kill them and I find the bodies."

"That's unfair. And besides you have it wrong."

"You didn't kill them?"

Skaphis raised himself from the floor and sat on his bed. He still held the dagger in his hand, but he gestured for Psamathe to sit beside him. The first second-hand shafts of dawn filtered through his window, and in its pale light he was able to make out her features. For the first time since he had met her she looked vulnerable, and he was tempted despite himself to take her up on her offer and fly with her to the Black Sea, or wherever else she should lead him. The vulnerability was probably a trick of the light, he decided.

"Men are used to considering women to be powerless, and so are not as guarded in their conversation as they might be with other men. And in certain circumstances, men can be quite reckless in their talk. They will divulge all sorts of sensitive information, just to make an impression. I had, as you correctly surmised, used my relationship with Aristophon to discover the identities of the men responsible for my father's arrest, and I did indeed plan to kill them. I had identified three of the culprits, but not the fourth. However, when I did discover their identities, I found I lacked the will to carry the act through to its conclusion, so I waited.

"Then Aristophon disappeared in the Piraeus, and my plan seemed to be unraveling. However, a friend of mine in the Piraeus assured me he could find Aristophon for me. He also told me a curious story about how he and a boyhood friend had come over illicitly to Athens, impersonating an Athenian soldier whom they had murdered in Syracuse. This friend was a private investigator by the name of Barysthenes, and was married to the murdered man's sister-in-law. He also talked about how this Barysthenes had worked with the cavalry, arresting enemies of the governing council. The description fit the man I was looking for. I decided to hire Barysthenes to find Aristophon for me. While he was investigating Aristophon, I could investigate him.

"I started, as soon as I left here that afternoon by going to his house and talking with his wife. At first, she wouldn't let me in, but I told her I had news of her previous husband. I traded the story of his death in Syracuse for information about Barysthenes' activities against enemies of the regime, although she didn't tell me anything conclusive one way or another. I eventually got a message from my brother, which implicated Barysthenes. However, by the time I got the message, he was already dead."

"So you turned to Aristophon."

"Aristophon was a troubled man. He had not been successful in business and presided over the ruin of his family's estate. Under circumstances such as those, a man might be forgiven for giving in to despair."

"And Kallictor?"

"Kallictor was a drunk. What *is* surprising is that he managed not to come to some harm before."

"And what of Euboulos, has some accident befallen him? I saw him in court this morning."

"I've heard talk around the Piraeus of a scheme to manipulate the grain market. Certain influential and well-connected figures lost a lot of money when the cartel collapsed. A rumor seems to have started that Euboulos was involved in exposing the scheme; I doubt that Athens will be a safe place for Euboulos for a long time to come.

"As for me, after your speech this morning, I find I have a strong desire to travel. Antigone accompanied her father into exile, and shared his sightless wanderings. I share only a blind memory of my father."

"Antigone returned home and ended up under ground."

"A mistake you can be sure I won't make."

Skaphis had fallen in behind a detachment of ephebes: military trainees marching, he supposed, to do their stint of frontier duty. They carried weapons, but Skaphis carried years. The ephebes came out ahead. It was worth eating their dust for the pace they set. A pace which Skaphis' aching legs would not have matched on their own.

Other travelers deferentially pulled to the side of the road to let the soldiers past, and so it was when he caught up with Zenothemis and Astra. Each held the halter of a laden donkey. A third donkey was led by a surly individual that Skaphis took to be a slave.

Astra spoke first,

"Skaphis, what on earth are you doing here."

"You didn't tell me you were leaving town, I wanted to wish you luck."

The hilt of a short sword nosed through the flap of Zenothemis' traveling cloak, which he folded back over his right shoulder with a sweep of his arm. The slave carried a very functional looking staff. The ephebes disappeared from sight over a low hill, leaving them alone on the road.

"I am needed back in Italy. I had already spent too long in Athens. We are on our way to pick up a ship of mine in Corinth, but that is no business of yours."

"You know, I wondered who was funding my prosecution. Not even the magistrate bought that nonsense about a member of the phratry prosecuting from sheer civic high mindedness. Somebody paid him. Zenothemis, you are not an Athenian citizen, and cannot represent yourself in court, so you hired an intermediary. If I was found guilty of his murder, it would be easy for you to make a case that the estate should go to you, along with the wife. And it seems a bit of a coincidence that you happen to show up in Athens after all these years."

Astra spoke, "Zenothemis is a merchant, he visits the Piraeus regularly."

"And doesn't pay his respects to his aunt in town? But then, under the circumstances, I don't suppose he would.

What I don't know, however, is if you were also involved in the murder, or if that was all Astra's work. My guess is the former. In fact, I believe it was you who sent the message that brought me to the scene. A fact that did not come out at the trial was that Barysthenes was killed with my knife. It didn't come out at trial because I removed the dagger from the scene of the crime. I felt it would be too difficult for me to explain how it got there. But I needed an explanation for myself. I left my knife on the table at Lusilla's tavern. I first assumed that the killer had to be present at the tavern and to have lifted the knife. But then I thought that Barysthenes may have taken the knife with the intention of returning it to me, and been killed by the knife he was carrying. The third possibility did not occur to me: Barysthenes took the knife from the tavern and left it at home.

"Astra, you used it to kill him, and left it at the scene to incriminate me. Psamathe told you that the Barysthenes you knew was not your first husband's brother, but his murderer. You followed him to his rendezvous, carrying with you my knife. Unluckily, you were accosted by a couple of drunks who took you for a prostitute and started bidding for your services. You were not for hire, but they mistook your reticence for a ploy to drive up the price, and sent for the magistrate. You slipped away, caught up with Barysthenes and left my knife between his ribs. But you hadn't killed him, not quite. He was able to crawl across the road and mutter your name. He called you Clytemnestra: the wife who with her lover killed her husband, home from war. He was an unlikely Agamemnon, but you made a perfect Clytemnestra."

"Skaphis, you have to understand, although I was young, I loved Barybromos. He was a fine man, strong and kind and gentle. I was almost mad with grief when the news came of the disaster in Sicily. Zenothemis here helped me at that difficult time. Then the man I thought was my husband's brother miraculously returned from the dead, and I thought, perhaps, I could be happy with him. But, my love, you know how Barysthenes was. He was a difficult man at the best and at worst an evil tyrant in his home. I grew to hate him, but for my ex-husband's sake I did my duty by his brother. When Psamathe told me who I was really living with, I killed him. I killed him for all the misplaced allowances I made for him over the wasted years on his brother's account."

"That's all very well, but I never did your late husband any harm, and you did your best to bury me."

"What do you mean?"

"All the 'Skaphis, my love,' played out in full view of the neighbors – you were building a wall of motive round me that came close to becoming my tomb. My only crime was to have inherited Barysthenes' estate – something I never asked for – and thus prevented it from going to Zenothemis as you had planned."

"I was in a corner, Skaphis, I had no choice."

"Only the dead have no choice."

"And you Skaphis, what do you choose?"

"Me, I'm going to walk back to Athens. The law puts the price of exile on Barysthenes' life. Exile is where this road leads. I'll leave you to it."

Thrassia sat on a three legged stool which had survived Astra's hurried estate sale, probably due to its antiquity and the impression that it was on the verge of becoming a two legged stool. Other survivors included the hoplite breastplate and, inexplicably, the loom. Skaphis supposed that Astra had simply asked too much for the loom and been unwilling to bring the price down enough for a quick sale.

"You say I am to be free – free to do what? I was well-fed at the mistress's and had friends. If I'm free, who will feed me and who will be my friend?"

Skaphis stared at her where she sat, a child, but not a child, a woman, but not a woman, a Greek, but not a Greek. He could not imagine any slave not wanting to be free. Himself for example…yet here she was debating the case. Still the 250 was spent, or at least 220 of it, he had bargained Lucilla down in price, and she had thrown in a spare set of clothes for good measure.

A knocking at the door, tentative at first then more insistent interrupted his reverie. Thrassia instinctively jumped to her feet and scrambled to answer it. She returned followed by the cat-like presence of Lysias. The lack of furniture afforded no couch and pillows for the speechwriter, instead he folded his lanky frame atop the stool while Thrassia shrank into the next room.

"I thought we had got rid of the Spartans," he said, "You seem to have adopted their living style."

"Temporarily only, Astra liquidated as much as she could before taking to the road. You wouldn't be interested in a fine bronze breastplate would you?"

Lysias laughed, "I have a warehouse full of those. Warfare is changing, infantrymen need to be able to move as well as to fight: the old armour and the old shields make good wall-hangings, for fighting you need smaller shields, longer spears and lighter body armour. I'm not surprised nobody bought that old clunker.

"Listen, I looked for you at Lucilla's, I have a task you could help me with, you might make enough money to buy a few sticks of furniture. She told me you had bought one of her slaves, the girl who answered the door?"

"Yes, but it turns out she doesn't want to be free, doesn't know how she'll make a living."

"There's only one way she could make a living, and she's much safer doing it at Lucilla's than in the streets of the Piraeus. Take my advice, don't free her, employ her. You have a loom here, put it to use; not for ornamental ware mind you, utilitarian: soldier's cloaks and tunics. There will be wars, but they won't be fought by static battle lines of armored infantry, they'll be fought by skirmishing parties foraging for food and by marines landed from ships. If you can find a slave with leather working experience, buy him. Leather is the bronze of the future: lower cost and lighter weight. Meanwhile, soldiers' cloaks, I say. And a slave, as you must have noticed, can pass unnoticed in the streets and will be very useful for the business I want to discuss with you.

"May I tell you a story?"